HOPE'S WAY

Copyright © 2020 by David Johnson
ISBN 9798663089692

All rights reserved. Except for use in any review, the reproduction or utilization of this work in whole or in part in any form by any electronic, mechanical or other means, now known or hereinafter invented, including xerography, photocopying and recording, or in any information storage or retrieval system, is forbidden without the written permission of the publisher.

This is a work of fiction. Names, characters, places and incidents are either the product of the author's imagination or are used fictitiously, and any resemblance toactual persons, living or dead, business establishments, events or locales is entirely coincidental.

Printed in the USA.

Interior Format

Hope's Way

DAVID JOHNSON

Other Titles by David Johnson

Ransom's Law
Ransom Lost
The Woodcutter's Wife
The Last Patient
Toby
The Tucker Series: *Tucker's Way (vol. 1)*
An Unexpected Frost (vol. 2)
April's Rain (vol. 3)
March On (vol. 4)
Who Will Hear Me When I Cry (vol. 5)

"Life never runs in a straight line."

CHAPTER ONE

INTENT ON WAKING HER SIXTEEN-YEAR-OLD daughter for school, thirty-six-year-old Hope Rodriguez puts her hand on the bedroom doorknob for the fourth time this morning. But, again, the feeling of someone squeezing her heart makes her let go, and fear and dread push her away from the door. She takes a couple of tiny steps backward while still listening for sounds of Lisa stirring inside.

Last night, they'd argued about Lisa wanting to quit school and get a job. "I'm sick of school!" Lisa said. "It's all about drama, who's screwing who, who's wearing what, who are we going to make fun of today. I want to get a job so I can save some money and get out of Bardwell. I don't know how you stand living here."

"I thought quitting school was the answer for me, too," Hope countered, her mouth full of the bitter bile of regret, "but now look at me. No education or training, working a job that barely pays the bills; I'll never get a better job that'll help me get ahead. You've got to stick it out, at least until you graduate, and then you can go to college or technical school somewhere."

"You don't have a decent job, because you don't ever keep a job, Mom. You have to actually show up for work to keep from getting fired."

The intended barb found its mark. Hope countered, "I can't help I get depressed. It's just so overwhelming at times; it feels like I'm living in quicksand. You don't know what it's like."

Lisa's eyes opened wide, and she raised her eyebrows. "I don't know what it's like? My god, Mom, you really don't know me, do you?"

Their argument ended when Lisa slammed her bedroom door shut, giving a loud exclamation point to her angst.

Hope tried to talk to her live-in boyfriend, Luther, about Lisa, but he said what he usually said, "She's your daughter; make her do what you want her to do. If she was mine, I'd..."

As soon as he said, "If she was mine," Hope tuned him out. In her opinion, the fact that he has three other children he never sees or pays child support for who live with their mothers gives him no room to dole out tips on parenting. She's asked herself many times why she's still with him but can never come up with a better answer than the fact that his job working on a barge keeps him away from home for twenty-eight days at a time. The downside is, he's then home for twenty-eight days.

Now, as the silence on the other side of Lisa's door screams at her, Hope feels like running and barricading herself in her own bedroom. Ever since she was sixteen years old, a closed bedroom door has terrified her.

Taking in a ragged breath, she steps forward and puts her ear to Lisa's door. Tapping, she says, "Lisa, it's Mom. Are you all right?" Still no sound. Gripping the doorknob, she turns it and opens the door.

CHAPTER TWO

September 11, 2001

FIFTEEN-YEAR-OLD HOPE RODRIGUEZ LEANED TOWARD her mirror, taking in her pouting lips, wide mouth, high forehead, and small eyes hiding behind glasses.

I hate my face. It's too round.

For the last several years, she'd worked hard not to smile, so she wouldn't reveal her missing eyetooth. She'd lost it when she fell on the sidewalk at age twelve, an event she told her parents was her fault, when in fact she was bullied and pushed to the ground by some neighborhood girls.

Through the thin walls of the apartment she and her parents lived in, she heard her father spewing a stream of Spanish either at the TV, which he argued with often, or toward her mother, who, though not Hispanic like her father, had become bilingual over the course of their marriage. Hope's own Spanish had developed by osmosis from living with him, and because a significant number of the students in her school were Hispanic.

Slowly, she backed away from her full-length mirror until she could see her bulging belly.

Seven months pregnant.

Even though she couldn't deny the obvious, it still felt unreal to her that she was going to have a baby. And while Hope wasn't happy about it, her mother was actually excited. Maybe that's because Hope's older sister had died of a drug overdose and her oldest sister in a drive-by shooting, leaving Hope as the only chance of making her mother a grandmother.

On the other hand, while her father was marginally happy about the pregnancy, he was quite upset that the father of the baby was black. Although he never said it, Hope was certain he preferred the father be Hispanic like him. "It will be too confusing for the child," he said to her. "Will she be white, black, or Hispanic? Which group will embrace the child?" The fact that Hope was half-white and half-Hispanic didn't seem to register with or bother him, probably because she looked Hispanic and had always fit in with that group of students.

Of course, how her parents thought or felt didn't matter to her. She just wished she wasn't pregnant and would probably have had an abortion if not for her Catholic upbringing. Although she didn't buy into everything the church taught, she for certain didn't want to take the chance of committing a mortal sin.

There was a knock on her door, and her mother stepped inside. Smiling, she said, "Good morning, my beautiful daughter. How are you feeling?"

"Pregnant."

"Of course you do. You're going to have a beautiful baby—a gift from God. Smile, be happy."

Her mother's bubbly nature and constant optimism had never rubbed off on Hope. Actually, it irritated her. "How can you always be so upbeat and positive about things? Don't you ever have days when you wished you weren't here anymore or you could run away? I'm going to be having a baby when I'm sixteen years old. My life is over."

Putting her arm around Hope's shoulder, her mother said, "My dear, sweet Hope, your life is over only if you let it be. I know you don't think you can get through this, but you can. Your father and I will help you raise your child. It'll be fun! We live in the most exciting place in the world. Do you know how many people would love to live in New York City?"

Hope rolled her eyes. "Mother, we live in public housing. I don't care what city you live in; public housing is public housing. There's nothing glamorous about it."

Suddenly, her father appeared in the doorway. "We need to leave for work," he said to her mother. Smiling at Hope, he said, "Good morning, daughter." Walking into her bedroom, he stood beside her mother.

Hope looked at them, dressed in their uniforms with the familiar logo of the Twin Towers.

Underneath her father's name was stitched "Maintenance," and underneath her mother's was "Housekeeping."

Her father gave a fake frown (because he could never make himself be angry with her) and shook his finger at her. "Don't be skipping school again."

"Yes," her mother chimed in, "you must keep up with your schooling and not fall behind."

To appease them, Hope gave them the answer they wanted to hear, though it was an untruthful one because she'd already made up her mind to stay home today. "I'm not going to miss school."

They beamed at her, and after simultaneously giving her a kiss on opposite cheeks, they headed out of the apartment.

At 8:46 a.m. that morning, Hope looked out of the apartment window facing the Twin Towers in the distance, trying to make sense out of what she was seeing. It looked like a plane flew into one of the towers, but that was impossible.

It must be some kind of optical illusion.

She blinked and rubbed her eyes to see if it would bring things into sharper focus.

As an inky black plume of smoke began rising above the tower, Hope felt like ice water replaced the fluid in her spinal column, causing her to shiver. As if in a trance, she continued to stare at the smoking image until fifteen minutes later another plane struck the second tower. Her body shook, and her baby pushed hard against her ribs.

Grabbing her belly, she fell to her knees and

cried out in pain. "What is happening?"

In a few minutes, scores of sirens began playing a symphony filled with dissonance, a concert so sharp and shrill, it pierced the windows and walls of the apartment. On the verge of hyperventilating, Hope reached for the windowsill and pulled herself up. Down below were dozens of firetrucks, police cars, and emergency vehicles careening through the streets, the fearless men and women who embraced their roles as first responders rushing toward unseen horrors. That day, they would face horrors no one had ever imagined.

Some people were standing like statues on sidewalks and street corners, their mouths open in shock and arms pointing toward the Twin Towers. Others were running toward the towers, crashing into people who were running from the towers.

———

For the next week, Hope never ventured out of the apartment. She kept the TV turned off because it frightened her even more than she already was. Each day, she kept expecting her parents to arrive home and tell a harrowing tale of how they'd escaped the horrors of the inferno that destroyed the towers. But after seven days, her optimism collapsed underneath the weight of what she suspected all along to be the truth.

The sadness that came on the heels of her acknowledging that her parents were never coming home made her feel like one of the collapsing towers. For one whole day, all she did was sit in the recliner and stare at the peeling paint on the wall.

When there was a knock on her door, she wasn't sure if it was real or imagined. Turning her head toward it, she heard it again, a little louder this time.

"If you're in there, open the door, kid." It was the raspy, no-nonsense voice of Mama T, her mother's mother, a woman whose personality was as prickly as a cactus. Hope had never liked her.

Though a part of her didn't want to open the door, Hope knew she was running out of food, and she thought maybe talking to anyone about what had happened was better than talking to no one. Hoisting herself out of the recliner, she unlocked the door and opened it.

Mama T stood barely five feet tall and weighed seventy-five pounds at the most. Her face was creased and fractured by the ravages of the sun ("Too many days on the beach at Coney Island, kid, but boy did I have me some fun," Mama T would explain). Her hair was dyed brown, but Hope had never seen her when there weren't gray roots where her hair parted.

She brushed past Hope without a word or glance. "What do you have to drink around here besides the nasty tequila your father keeps around? I swear, it seems like it's the only thing Mexicans like to drink." She disappeared into the kitchen, where Hope heard cabinet doors opening and closing.

"My father grew up in Honduras, not Mexico," Hope said as she made her way to the kitchen. This point had been made numerous times to Mama T, but it never deterred her from referring to him as a Mexican.

"Kid, all these cabinets are nearly empty, and so is the fridge. When's the last time you went out and bought some groceries?" She turned and fixed Hope with a stare, but before Hope answered, Mama T continued. "Don't tell me. You've been lying around here, feeling sorry for yourself because your parents got killed by some psycho, oil-rich Arab s.o.b.'s. Buck up, kid, life's not easy. Deal with it and move on. How's your baby?"

Hope found it impossible to latch onto any piece of the conversation and give a sensible response, because what she wanted was someone to hold her, console her, and tell her everything was going to be alright. Sadly, she knew Mama T wasn't the place she was going to get it.

Finally, she said, "My baby's fine."

"Good. Now go pack your bags, you're coming to live with me."

Hope had resigned herself to the reality that this was eventually going to happen. With no other family available to her, she had no other place else to go. She just hated it was her only option. Living with Mama T wasn't going to be easy.

Six months later, when Hope returned from

a doctor visit with her baby, Lisa, she walked into Mama T's small house and found it eerily quiet—the TV that normally ran continuously, even if no one was at home, sat silent on its stand; no sound of Mama T yacking on her phone or puttering around in the kitchen.

"Mama T?" Hope called out. "Are you here?"

As she stepped slowly through the living room, Hope felt rising tension in her chest and feared she was going to have another panic attack, the kind of torture she'd been experiencing ever since 9/11.

The pacifier tumbled out of Lisa's mouth and fell to the floor before Hope could catch it. Bending down to pick it up caused enough of a stir to wake Lisa, and a small cry of complaint came from her pursed lips. Hope pushed the pacifier back in her baby's mouth, quickly calming and quieting her.

"Shhh, you're okay," she reassured the child and gave her a kiss.

A little voice in the back of Hope's mind told her she needed to lay Lisa on the couch before going through the house, looking for Mama T. After wedging her between the back of the couch and a couch pillow, Hope moved more cautiously through the house.

"Mama T?" she called out again, but her question was met with silence.

In the kitchen, everything seemed in order—the smell of coffee permeated the room, breakfast dishes rested in the dish drainer (Mama T never trusted a dishwasher to get things as clean as she wanted them), an ashtray sat on the table, with several extinguished cigarette butts cradled by ashes.

Turning toward Mama T's bedroom, Hope stared at the closed door. *That* was unusual, because Mama T always kept her door open.

Hope's legs began shaking, but she forced them to take her to the door. With her mouth inches from it, she said loudly, "Mama T, open your door! Are you all right?"

When she stepped back, she looked down and saw the corner of a piece of paper sticking out from under the door. Before bending down to pick it up, she allowed herself to linger for a few seconds in the false hope her grandmother would open the door and everything would be fine. But neither false hope nor denial change the truth, so she pulled what turned out to be a piece of stationery from under the door. There, in Mama T's perfect penmanship, was the message:

Sorry, kid, life's too much for me. I'll see you on the other side.

Hope felt as if someone had turned a spigot somewhere in her body and everything inside slowly drained out. She stood there, empty and shaking, staring at the note. Sometimes people can have a knowing of what's about to happen, but they try to shove the thought under a rug and tell themselves they must be wrong.

Later, when trying to remember how long she stood in front of Mama T's door, Hope couldn't recollect. It was like she was there but she wasn't there. However, her next moment of awareness was a memory she spent the rest of her life trying to forget. She stood in the middle of her grandmother's bedroom and stared at the macabre site of Mama T lying on the white sheets of her bed with crimson splashed from a large hole on the side of her head. A pistol lay on the floor on the opposite side of the bed, where the recoil from a self-inflicted gunshot had flung it.

CHAPTER THREE

Keeping his hands firmly on the steering wheel of the large U-Haul truck, Michael Trent looks for a sign along Interstate 57 that'll tell him how far away he is from Paducah, Kentucky, which he's started referring to as 'the jumping off place,' the last city of any size he'll see before he heads toward his destination—Bardwell, Kentucky.

Gray, leafless trees border the highway and stand against the backdrop of the blue February sky as a flock of geese in V-formation fly parallel to the south-bound U-Haul. Michael's shoulders ache and his butt is numb from the long drive that began in the wee hours of the morning in Topeka, Kansas.

Lord, let this be the place my life will finally come together.

This prayer has practically become his mantra ever since he was fired from the church he pastored in Topeka and was then hired by the Grace Community Church in Bardwell. "It's my chance to start over and get it right this time" he'd told himself and his wife, Sarah.

As a car passes him, he looks down, hoping to catch sight of a woman in a short skirt or low-cut top, but his ogling is fruitless, as the passengers are two young males. As the car finishes passing and pulls into the lane in front of him, a sudden blast of cold air slams against him, and the roaring sound of the truck tires fills the cab.

"I'm jumping!" Sarah yells over the noise.

Michael jerks his head in her direction and sees her perched on the edge of the passenger seat, holding open the door. "Sarah, stop! What are you doing?" But the buzz of his tires running off the side of the highway force him to turn his attention quickly back to the road.

"I'm going to jump out of this truck. I saw you trying to look out the window, hoping to see a woman's boobs, and I saw the way you looked at the waitress back at the Cracker Barrel. You'd rather have her than me. You'd rather have anyone than me. I'm going to kill myself so you can do what you want to do and quit being miserable with me."

He sneaks a quick look at her and sees her inching closer to the open door. The wind smacks her short hair against her face as he grabs for her but is unable to reach her.

"Get back in here!"

"I know you hate me because I'm fat," Sarah cries.

Part of Michael wants to say, "Then go ahead and jump," because he's grown weary of her threats to harm herself, as well as her accusations thrown at him. Instead, he lets his foot off the gas and slowly comes to a stop on the shoulder of the highway.

Black streaks of mascara run from Sarah's eyes and over her round, blotchy cheeks. "Why did you stop? Is this where you play the sympathetic, understanding husband and tell me I'm imagining all this, that everything will be all right? How many times are you going to tell me that before you realize things are never going to be all right?"

Michael feels defeated before he tries to do or say anything. *If I try to empathize with her, she'll accuse me of being insincere. If I do nothing, she'll say I don't care and may very well find a way to kill herself, and that would for certain derail my efforts to pastor this new church before we even unload the U-Haul. Who's going to want a pastor whose wife just committed suicide?*

Breathing heavily, they stare at each other from opposite sides of the cab—five feet and a million miles apart.

The woman he's looking at bears little resemblance to the vibrant, vivacious woman he met four years ago when he saw her working in the library of the seminary school he was attending. Even though he knew he was supposed to be focused on the spiritual aspect of life and less upon the fleshly, an ideal he'd battled ever since he was a young teenager and had discovered a Playboy magazine in his father's dresser, he had to admit, it was her dazzling smile and cute figure that first drew him to her and gave him the courage to ask her out.

They'd only been out on a few dates when he began feeling like he was possessed. He couldn't quit thinking about her and fantasizing about her, and he couldn't keep his hands off her. Although she initially resisted his efforts to become intimate, once she let down her guard, it seemed as if she became possessed by the same spirit as he. They were together nearly every night and always ended up in bed, where their lovemaking left the sheets tangled and damp with perspiration.

They admitted to each other what they were doing was wrong and prayed for forgiveness, vowing never to do it again. But as soon as they were alone in his apartment, their resolve evaporated like a brief summer shower striking hot asphalt.

Two years later, after they married, she began to change. She quit fixing her hair and wearing makeup, and she gained a lot of weight. Her smile disappeared, and he often found her crying in the bathroom. When asked what was wrong, all she would say was, "I'm fat, and you hate me."

As he looks across the truck cab at her now, he softens his expression. "Sarah, please get back in the truck and shut the door."

"You're tired of me, aren't you? I can tell by the tone of your voice you don't want to be with me anymore. Marrying me was the biggest mistake of your life."

Michael fights the urge to agree with her, to be mean and hurtful for all the misery she's put him through. He's exhausted with trying to buoy her moods and keep her afloat in the sea of emotions she always seems to be on the verge of drowning in.

"I love you, Sarah. Please, we're both tired from this long trip. Let's get to Bardwell and get a good night's sleep before we begin unpacking."

"What was it you liked about her?" she asks.

Confused, he replies, "What are you talking about? Who?"

She narrows her eyes. "Don't treat me like I'm stupid. You know exactly who I'm talking about: that waitress at the Cracker Barrel. I watched her touch your shoulder when she poured your coffee. You looked like you wanted to take her right then and there and lay her across a pair of tables. You disgust me." The last three words come out of her mouth like darts.

He conjures up the image of the waitress—blonde hair, cobalt blue eyes, sparkling smile, and a really hot figure.

Yeah, I did think about screwing her, because I could tell she wanted me to.

Shaking his head, he lies, "I don't know what you're talking about, Sarah, I barely even noticed her. Quit acting so childish. We can't sit on the side of the road forever; a state trooper will give us a ticket."

Just then, they hear the brief chirp of a siren.

Michael looks at his side mirror and sees the flashing blue lights of a patrol car. Exasperated, he swears and says, "This is just great! Now look what you've done."

Sarah scrambles back inside the cab and shuts the door.

Like water seeping into a submerged car, silence fills the cab as they wait to see what happens.

He keeps his eyes glued to the mirror until he sees the door of the trooper car swing open and the officer steps out. When the officer stands and stretches to unkink, it's obvious to Michael it's a female officer—a shapely female officer. Excitement and dread swirl inside him. He can't wait to see what she looks like up close, but he knows in Sarah's twisted, paranoid mind she'll accuse him of setting up the whole thing. He can already hear and feel the barrage of thorny indictments she'll hurl his way.

As the trooper approaches with the heel of her hand resting on the handle of her holstered pistol, Michael rolls down his window and leans forward to pull his billfold out of his hip pocket. By the time she arrives at the window, he has his driver's license in hand.

He smiles nervously at her mirrored sunglasses and says, "Good day, Officer."

"You having trouble with your truck?" she asks.

Her voice has a bit of a twang, the sort of thing Michael was expecting to find when he moved here. But coming from her, it doesn't sound like she's a hick.

"Uh, no, Officer, my wife thought she was going to be sick and throw up, so I pulled over to the side. I probably shouldn't have, I know, but I didn't know what else to do."

The expression on the trooper's face shows no signs of empathy or understanding. A long pause passes while she stares at him. Finally, she says, "I'm guessing you've rented this truck."

"Yes, sir...I mean, ma'am." He feels himself getting flustered and unnerved by her unflinching demeanor.

"I need your license and your rental agreement."

After he hands them to her and she returns to her patrol car, he turns on Sarah. "See what you've done?! Christ, Sarah, you've got to get your act together, or things are never going to work out for us." She bursts into tears, and he immediately regrets speaking without thinking. "I'm sorry, I shouldn't have said that. Please, I really didn't mean it," though he knows he really did.

Dear God, I feel like I'm losing my mind at times. I hate who and how I am and that I can't control my tongue or my thoughts. Please, God, deliver me from—"

"Here's your license and papers." The trooper's voice interrupts his brief plea.

Taking them from her, he says, "Thank you."

"Where are you folks headed?"

"Bardwell, Kentucky."

"You got family there? Because that's about the only reason people move there."

Is she trying to flirt with me? "Actually, we don't know anyone there. I've been hired as the pastor for the Grace Community Church in Bardwell." A part of him is always reluctant to share his vocation with people, especially pretty women, because it puts a chill on any kind of conversation that might be flirtatious.

"I hope it works out for you," she says. "My brother goes to church there, so I know they've had a rocky start to things. Now, you need to get this truck off the shoulder of the highway."

"Yes, ma'am."

As he cranks the truck and rolls up his window, he watches her hips bounce and sway as she retreats to her car.

When he pulls back onto the interstate, Sarah asks, "What did she mean the church has had a rocky start? You didn't tell me anything about that."

"I really don't know. It caught me by surprise as well."

He squeezes the steering wheel as a queasy feeling twists his stomach.

CHAPTER FOUR

A FOG SO THICK SHE CAN barely see her hand in front of her face envelops Hope as she races through the woods behind her house. Small twigs and branches grab at her hands, face and hair, but she ignores the pain.

"Lisa!" she cries out. "Lisa, where are you?" But her voice is swallowed up by the wet blanket of fog.

She comes to a stop, gasping for breath and uncertain of her exact location. Hot tears sting her cheeks as panic runs up her throat and threatens to choke her.

Suddenly, up ahead, she sees a diffused yellow light. "Lisa, is it you?" she calls as she takes tentative steps in that direction. In spite of her eagerness to find her daughter, she's also afraid of finding her.

A shadowy figure passes between her and the yellow light, and she hears a voice but is uncertain from which direction it comes. Falling to her knees, sharp rocks and sticks stab them, but the pain is swallowed up by an overwhelming feeling of dismay and hopelessness.

It's pointless; she's gone.

Slowly, Hope pulls herself out of her dream and finds herself lying on her side on the floor of Lisa's bedroom. She sees several pairs of Lisa's shoes lying at odd angles under her bed, where they've been pitched or scooted. There also appears to be half of a sandwich on a paper plate resting there.

Without moving her body, she forces herself to look at Lisa's closet but immediately squeezes her eyes shut. Nonetheless, the image remains burned in her brain—Lisa hanging limply from the closet door, clothed only in a bra and panties, a belt around her neck, her eyes open and swollen, expressionless face an unnatural purple hue.

Not even the dams created by Hope's tightly shut eyelids can hold back the torrent of tears that pour from every corner of her shredded and broken heart. A primal scream erupts from the bowels of her being and echoes through the house as she writhes on the floor.

It can't be...it can't be... is the only thought looping through her mind, blocking out any rational thought.

Eventually, though, her body stills, and her tears subside. Grabbing the side of Lisa's unmade bed, she pulls herself to a wobbly standing position. As she looks around the room, she feels as if scales have fallen off her eyes, letting her see things she hasn't noticed before now.

Maybe it's because it's been so long since I've come in here and sat down...and talked.

She feels a fresh wave of tears approaching. That's what truth can do; a simple statement pulls the cork from a fermenting bottle of emotions, and they rush out like the spray from a bottle of champagne. But this champagne has the flat, metallic taste of blood.

Walking slowly around the perimeter of the bedroom, Hope stops at Lisa's dressing table and touches the scattered and overturned dozen or so bottles of nail polish.

When's the last time she wore nail polish? She used to always like to paint her nails. I used to paint them for—

She makes herself stop before finishing the thought, because she knows it, too, will trigger another wave of emotions, emotions she's not ready to deal with yet.

There are photographs stuck around the edge of Lisa's mirror—candid, happy shots of guys and girls Hope doesn't know or recognize.

Have I been so disconnected?

She moves to the desk, sits in the rolling chair, and visually sifts through the items resting there. A wide tooth comb still has some strands of Lisa's hair caught in it.

Her eyes are stopped by a lone razor blade that appears to have dried blood on it. Memories of her own struggle with self-mutilation years ago following the death of her parents and grandmother come hurtling forward and threaten to drag her back into the past. She shakes her head to clear it and feels the urge to inspect Lisa's body to see if she's been cutting, and where.

And why didn't I know it?

But instead of turning her head to look at the body, Lisa's closed laptop arrests her attention.

What is in there? What will I find? Are there any answers there? Will a finger of blame point in my direction?

The last question is useless, because she's already pointed a finger of blame at herself. Accusations line up in single file as far as her imagination can see.

If I'd been a better mother...if I'd done something different...if I hadn't chosen to move her out here in the middle of nowhere...if I'd cared more...loved her more... hadn't fussed at her...taken more time to talk to her... listened better...hadn't been so depressed myself.

Like a crochet hook pulling a thread of yarn, this last indictment is the thread most prominent in the afghan of blame her mind is weaving.

When she first started getting to know Luther, she'd warned him about her depression. "My depression makes me moody and hard to deal with. Most people describe their depression in terms of color, like a blackness, but mine feels like quicksand. I feel it sucking my body down, trying to swallow it. There are days I can't pull myself out of bed, go to work, or do any housework because I have absolutely no energy."

"How long have you been depressed?" he'd asked.

"Probably ever since I got pregnant with Lisa when I was in high school."

"Maybe you need to get some medication

from a doctor," was his reply.

She gave a derisive laugh. "Prozac, Paxil, Zoloft, Effexor, Xanax, Seroquel—and probably more I can't remember—none of them have given me relief."

"What about a counselor? You ever thought about that?"

"I talked to a social worker one time, but all she wanted to do was talk about her bad marriage and how depressed she was over it."

Now, even as she sits staring at Lisa's laptop, she can feel herself being pulled down. It is a feeling so familiar, it is almost comforting. To be drawn into a place of nothingness, where neither mind nor body responds—depression is the closest to death a person can get. And death is something Hope has contemplated many times, but she never found the energy to carry out the death wish.

But my baby did. Oh, Lisa ...

As she reaches for Lisa's laptop, her vision blurs. When she opens the lid of the computer, it immediately awakens, and the screen is filled with the credits from what Hope supposes is a movie Lisa had been watching.

Curious, she touches the mousepad to discover the name of the movie. Her search reveals a title only vaguely familiar to her: *13 Reasons Why*. But an hour later, after skipping through episodes of the Netflix series, she stares in stunned disbelief at what she just witnessed.

Slowly, she turns the chair toward Lisa and takes in her appearance one more time. Aloud, she says, "Is that what happened to you? Were you like Hannah Baker? Did people make fun of you? Did suicide feel like the only solution?"

Standing up, she moves toward her daughter and sees scars and scabs on the outside of Lisa's thigh, where she was cutting herself. Hope touches those signs of a tortured soul but quickly jerks away her hand, repulsed by the lack of warmth in the lifeless body. Another wave of nausea passes through her, but she forces it back down with a hard swallow.

"Why didn't you tell me? Did you try to tell me, and I didn't listen? Is that what last night was about? Did anyone else know you were planning this?"

A mixture of grief, anger, and regret moves through her, and she feels herself sinking deeper into the quicksand. Overwhelmed with the desire to hug her daughter, she ignores her repulsion toward the cold body and wraps her arms around her, resting her warm, damp cheek against Lisa's chilled abdomen.

What will I do now? How will I survive?

CHAPTER FIVE

EASING HIS WAY DOWN DOUGLAS Avenue, Michael reads the house numbers, searching for the church-owned house they'll be moving into. All the houses on the quiet, tree-lined street appear to be around thirty or more years old, but they all look well-maintained, with nicely kept yards, some with colorful pansies encircling the base of the mailbox, creating puddles of color in an otherwise drab landscape.

"I wonder if those are maple trees?" he comments on the leafless trees. "I'll bet they're beautiful during the fall." When Sarah doesn't respond, he takes a peek at her and sees she appears to be locked into finding the house. "What number is it?" he asks.

"Two zero four," she replies. "We're getting close, because we just passed one ninety-seven." She turns her head to look at the other side of the street. "It's going to be on your side."

About that time, Michael sees a cluster of cars and pickup trucks up ahead, some parked on the street, but others parked at odd angles in the front yard. Brightly colored helium balloons tied to the mailbox dance in the February breeze.

Smiling, he says, "There it is. Looks like we have a welcoming party."

"My hair looks awful," Sarah says. "And I'm sure my makeup is a mess. I hate for this to be their first impression of me." She flips down the sun visor, then slams it back up against the ceiling. "Of course there's no mirror in here."

Knowing her anxiety is rising, Michael worries how she'll behave when they get out of the truck. He himself has learned how to fake it ever since he was a child. Growing up as the son of an evangelist, it was drilled in him always to put on a positive front for people. "Or it'll reflect badly on your father," his mother would say. So now, no matter his mood, he can flash a relaxed, engaging smile.

He reaches over and pats Sarah's arm. "It's going to be fine. These are people, just like you and me. They know we've had a long trip. Just be yourself."

A faint smile tugs at the corner of her mouth. "I'll try."

"That-a girl. We can do this together. We're going to make it work, right?"

Covering his hand with hers, she replies, "Together."

He feels the distance between them shrink and his own hopes lifted by the positive turn in her demeanor. "I do love you, Sarah."

She lifts his hand to her lips and kisses it. "And I do love you, too. I'm sorry I'm such a—"

"Don't say it," he interrupts. "We've both

expressed enough apologies to fill the back end of this truck. Let's just focus on doing better in the future than we have in the past, okay?"

A larger smile spreads across her face, and her dimples appear.

"There's the smile that won my heart," he says.

Turning his attention back to the house, he brakes to a stop in the middle of the street because there's no room to pull in the driveway.

Immediately, a small clutch of smiling men and women approach the truck, while a few other men dash to the vehicles blocking the driveway and begin maneuvering them out of the way.

Michael rolls down his window and looks down at the welcoming faces. His heart is warmed by their willingness, perhaps eagerness, to meet him and Sarah, but he also feels the pressure of wondering if he can meet their expectations of him, knowing everyone probably has differing hopes.

It was weird to him that they hired him without ever meeting him or hearing him preach. In his phone conversations with the members of the hiring committee, they said they were confident he was the right man for the job because a few of them had heard his father hold a revival in Paducah several years ago. "And even if you're only a tenth of the preacher your father is," one man had told him, "you'll be better than the one we had." Michael still isn't sure if the comment was meant as a hyperbolic joke or the truth.

A man, youthful-looking despite the gray at his temples, dressed in light blue matching athletic pants and sweatshirt, jumps onto the running board of the U-Haul and thrusts his hand through the open window. "Brother Michael, I'm Jed Rochelle, chairman of the deacon committee. We spoke on the phone a few times. Welcome to Bardwell, Kentucky." An engaging smile crinkles the corners of his eyes. Looking past Michael, he looks at Sarah and adds, "And welcome to you, too, Sister Sarah. We're awfully glad to have you as well."

Michael is thankful Jed includes Sarah in his greeting. Too often it's been his experience that the wife of a pastor is shoved into the shadows and neglected by a church, which, over time, can crush her self-esteem. When he shakes Jed's hand, he immediately recognizes Jed wants to see how firm a handshake he can give. Each time he increases the pressure, Jed matches it and increases it even more, as if this is a game of poker, with the players trying to find out who's bluffing. Despite the fact that he feels like the bones in his hand are going to crack, Michael refuses to give in and let go of Jed's hand.

This one's a real competitor. A salesman of some kind, maybe?

Meanwhile, the women have moved over to the other side of the truck and are opening Sarah's door and casting bouquets of warm words of welcome to her. Michael is touched by their thoughtfulness and encouraged that this might be a place of healing for his marriage.

"Hey, Jed," a short, round man with a round, bald head to match, calls out, "get out of the way so we can get this truck backed in and start unloading. You can sell Brother Michael an insurance policy another day."

All the men laugh, and Michael smiles.

Winking at Michael, Jed says in a loud voice, "You have to overlook Bobby, he forgets he's retired from the army and not in charge of giving orders anymore."

Another chorus of laugher erupts from the men, including Bobby, and Michael makes a mental note. *A man who can laugh at himself and has a clear sense of who he is.*

A tall black man with broad shoulders puts one arm around Jed's waist, lifts him off the running board, and sets him on the ground.

"Thank you, Brother Lester," Bobby calls.

"If you weren't so big, you couldn't do that," Jed says to Lester.

In a voice reminiscent of James Earl Jones, Lester says, "But I am that big." Turning his attention to Michael, he offers him his hand and says, "If you want, I'll back the truck in there for you. I've been driving trucks my whole life. Hamilton will get your car off the dolly behind the truck. We'll just need your keys."

Michael puts his hand in Lester's grip, where it's swallowed up. He quickly decides against getting in a hand-squeezing contest with this man, lest his hand is truly crushed. Even though he's had experience driving trucks for his uncle during his summers in high school and college, Michael decides to accept Lester's offer, knowing it'll make Lester feel good about helping.

Switching off the truck engine, he says, "I'm more than willing to let you do it. I'd probably have run over two or three of the members' vehicles."

After handing his car keys to Lester, he turns to look at Sarah and sees she's exiting the truck into the friendly embraces of the women of the church. Even from the back, he can tell she's smiling.

Thank you, Lord.

He jumps down out of the truck and begins shaking hands as all the men begin introducing themselves, even as Jed gives good-hearted warnings and commentary on each one. Michael does his best to keep up with everyone's name and face, cataloging them in a way he'll remember by having them repeat their name and then spelling it back to them. "Nothing sounds as sweet in a person's ears as the sound of their own name," his father used to say.

The warning beep from the U-Haul backing up draws everyone's attention, and Michael sees Sarah and the other women walking toward the house. His eyes are immediately drawn to a tall, lithe, auburn-haired woman whose porcelain skin shines in contrast to the dark red lipstick she's wearing. Her face is symmetrical, with high cheek bones and dark eyes. When she notices he's looking at her, she smiles at him, showing off her bright, perfect teeth. He's not for certain, but he thinks she gives him the tiniest of winks, and he tries to imagine her without any clothes on.

Before he takes another step in that imaginary direction, Sarah steps between him and the auburn-haired woman. The stony look she gives him has the same effect as if he'd been thrown into a cold shower. He knows she knows what he's thinking, and sometime before this day is over he'll pay for his momentary lapse in moral resolve. He silently asks God's forgiveness.

Another round of introductions ensues, the men to Sarah, and the women to Michael. It turns out the auburn-haired woman, Liz, is married to Jed. Michael tries to focus on everyone equally, but he can't help returning his gaze at Liz, and every time he does, it seems she's looking at him.

Lester slams open the cargo door of the U-Haul and announces, "Brothers and sisters, let the games begin."

For the next few hours, the church members march in and out of the house like an army of ants, placing boxes and furniture in the rooms Sarah and Michael instruct them to. Each time he passes Sarah, he gives her a smile, and she returns it. But he recognizes it to be a forced smile, and behind it he sees the anger coupled with self-loathing, all of which fills him with dread because he knows they're the clouds that precede an emotional, sometimes violent storm.

When the winter sun begins its early descent, a fresh wave of men and women from church arrives, bearing food and drink for the fatigued workers. Cries of relief and appreciation erupt, and everyone does their best to crowd into the spacious kitchen.

Michael spots Sarah, moves beside her, and holds her hand, though hers is limp in his.

As if on cue, a hush descends on the room, and Jed maneuvers himself and Liz beside Michael. "Brother Michael, would you like to offer thanks for the food?"

Smiling, Michael replies, "Sure I would, but first Sarah and I want to thank you for this unbelievably warm and helpful welcome to Bardwell. I sense a wonderful spirit of love and cooperation among you, and we're blessed to have been asked to come and be a part of it. Let's pray."

Just before bowing his head and closing his eyes, he notices everyone is reaching for the hand of the person beside them. Liz is beside him, and she slips her hand into his. He feels his face flush in reaction to her soft, warm hand. With great effort, he shoves fleshly thoughts from his mind and leads a brief prayer, the words of which he'd be hard-pressed to recall.

As soon as he says, "Amen," Sarah jerks free of his grip.

"You two go first," Liz says to them, "but get all you want the first time through, because I assure you, nothing will be left after this bunch goes through the line."

Several "Amens" support her pronouncement.

After everyone begins eating, a different kind of silence fills the room; it's the silence borne of fatigue and appetites being satisfied.

Twenty minutes later, there's a knock on the

front door. All eyes turn to Michael.

Taking a risk, he decides to try a little humor. "Well, we know it's not Jed trying to sell me an insurance policy, because he's already here." His effort is rewarded with resounding applause and laughter.

Jed seems to take it well as he smiles and says, "Don't you worry, I know where you live. I'll be back."

Michael pushes himself off the floor where he's been sitting and makes his way to the door. Opening it, he sees an older man with a receding hairline and wire-rimmed glasses. His face is slack and solemn.

"Are you Michael Trent, the new pastor for the Grace Community Church?"

"Yes, sir, I am. How can I help you?"

"My name is Ezra Marshall, with Marshall's Funeral Home. First of all, let me welcome you to Bardwell."

"Why don't you come in?" Michael asks. "We've just paused to eat a meal, and there's a little left if you'd like."

Ezra's face brightens a little. "Well, I have been baching it this week, with my wife having gone to be with her sister who had surgery. Something other than restaurant food or fast food sounds pretty good."

Holding the door open and backing out of the way, Michael says, "Come right in."

As soon as Ezra steps inside, several people welcome him by name, and he reciprocates.

Although Michael is curious to know the

reason why he's come to his house, because it certainly isn't just to welcome him, he decides to let the man tell the reason when he's ready.

Bobby's wife, Lucy, takes Ezra by the hand and leads him toward the food. "Come on, Ezra. Let's see what kinds of scraps we can find for you."

Once he has his plate and perches himself on the arm of the couch, Ezra takes a few bites before saying, "This will be an unusual request, Pastor Trent, but I wasn't sure what else to do."

Michael's curiosity grows.

"We've had a horrible tragedy befall our community," Ezra begins. "It's the kind of tragedy people read about all the time but never expect to happen here."

The atmosphere in the room darkens, and everyone stops eating and looks blankly at their plates.

"One of the children in our school, Lisa Rodriquez, a sixteen-year-old girl, committed suicide by hanging herself."

Michael is taken aback at this news and can figure no reason why Ezra came to tell him this.

"The situation is," Ezra continues, "Lisa didn't attend church anywhere, nor does her mother, Hope, who's a single mother. So, I was wondering if you'd like to have the opportunity to conduct the funeral service. It would be a nice gesture on your part, and it would be well-received by the people in town. It would sort of help get your name out there."

Before Michael can process the unusual request

and formulate an answer, Jed speaks up. "It's an awesome opportunity, Michael. Thank you, Ezra, for thinking to ask."

CHAPTER SIX

ONLY IN THE PERIPHERY OF her senses is Hope aware of the sounds of Luther's Jeep and the sights of the passing gray, dreary landscape as he drives them back home from their visit to the funeral home. Mostly, she hears, sees, and feels nothing.

When he showed up at the house last night unannounced, she was surprised because he was in the midst of his twenty-eight days on the river, and she hadn't contacted him about Lisa, nor had she really wanted to. But somebody – probably somebody who knew somebody who knew somebody, which is the way of small towns – had gotten in touch with the captain of his tugboat, who then arranged to drop him off at a port. From there, the company driver had picked him up in a van and driven him home.

Even though her feelings for him have grown to be ambivalent, she is still closer to him than anyone else, and when he walked into the house and scooped her up into his arms like she was a child, she buried her face into his chest and wept uncontrollably.

"There, there, my sweet butterfly," he'd said in his thick voice, using his term of endearment for her. "Let it go, and cry it out."

She tried to "cry it out," but when her tears were exhausted and breathing returned to normal, the feeling that a knife was sticking in her heart remained. Oceans of tears can't heal the pain of such a loss.

He then took her to bed and made love to her, but not because she wanted to. However, she didn't stop him, because she knew it was his way of showing he cared, and he wanted to comfort her. As he held her tightly and breathed heavily, she tried to feel something, but there was an impenetrable wall of numbness blocking her, perhaps because if she felt anything, it would be the nauseating feeling of regret threaded through the fabric of her grief.

When he rolled off her, he turned her onto her side, spooned against her back and slipped his arm around her waist. Pulling her close to him, he said, "I'm really sorry about Lisa, Hope. And I'm sorry I didn't try harder to get close to her. Maybe if..." His voice trailed off, leaving another 'what if' hanging in the air.

"Thank you," was all Hope could think to say in response.

Not that it was the only thought in her head, because her head was full of self-condemnations and accusations in an attempt to find a place to lay the blame for why Lisa took her life. Was it her classmates? The school administration? A boyfriend? Luther? The fact that she never knew her real father? Or was it because her mother sucked at being a mother? Part of the persecution of grief is its relentless demands for answers when sudden loss occurs. Although scores of answers come together like a police lineup, knowing for certain who's guilty is impossible to determine.

Hope tried to stay awake all night, because every time she closed her eyes, she saw the image of Lisa hanging on her closet door. Occasionally, exhaustion would pull her into a brief sleep filled with nightmares from which she'd awake with a start and in a panic.

On the other hand, Luther slept like he usually did—heavily and snoring like a bear. This was just another reason she preferred him to be away working rather than at home. It's not that Luther was a bad man or mean to her, it was just she'd grown indifferent to him in the same way she had with every other man she'd been with since Lisa was born. She'd already been thinking about breaking up with him *because it's just what I do*. She had multiple variations of the line, "It's not you, it's me," she used each time she ended a relationship, because it was the truth. "There's something broken in me," she told one guy. "I'm just not made for long-term relationships."

When dawn finally arrived, she forced herself to get out of bed, leaving Luther sleeping, and made her way to the kitchen to put on some coffee. She felt as if she was moving like a sloth and wondered if that animal was aware how slowly it moved, or if it thought it was moving at the same pace as the other animals in the rainforest.

Or maybe sloths are just chronically depressed and have difficulty making themselves motivated to move.

Sitting at the kitchen table and staring into her cup of black coffee, she heard the floor creak. Her head snapped up. "Lisa?" But the hopeful thought was shattered as she saw the gaunt form of Luther walking toward her, and the truth suddenly slapped her in the face—she would never see Lisa walking toward her again.

Since Luther was wearing only sweatpants, every one of his ribs showed in spite of the tapestry of tattoos adorning his torso. His scraggly beard and moustache she once thought was cute now irritated her. It was as if his face couldn't make up its mind whether to grow a real beard or not. After getting himself a cup of coffee, he joined her at the table.

"Did you sleep any?"

"Not much."

"Me neither."

Hope knew this was a lie, but she let it stand unchallenged.

He put his hand on hers and said, "You know, we've got to go the funeral home today and make arrangements."

She lifted her head and looked at him. "I hadn't even thought about that." *A funeral home. A funeral.* There was such finality in the sound of it, as if they were nails being driven into her own coffin of hopefulness in which she'd awaken from this awful nightmare. Her voice trembled as she said, "She's really gone, isn't she? Lisa is dead." In desperation, she searched his face for any sign she was wrong, that she'd had some kind of psychotic break, that Lisa was sleeping in her bed.

He tried to return her stare, but he looked away. "I'm sorry," was all he said.

Now, as they ride back home from making funeral arrangements, Luther says, "I had no idea a funeral was so expensive."

"Me neither." She was actually shocked by the prices of each item and type of service the funeral home would provide.

"It was nice of Ezra to cut us a deal on the casket. I think it was because my grandpa used to work with his dad at the funeral home."

"Is there anybody in Bardwell you don't know?"

Her question is a rhetorical one because she knows the answer, and it irritates her. It's like someone generations ago built a wall around the town so no one moved away and few moved there. Sometimes she feels suffocated by the fact that everybody knows everybody's business and everybody knows her name but she doesn't know theirs. She doesn't like the feeling of being an outsider either, a feeling she's had ever since she got on a bus with her baby and left New York City.

Luther ignores her question or chooses not to answer it for the hundredth time. "Are you sure you're okay with having this new pastor preach Lisa's funeral? I'm sure my Grams could get her pastor to do it."

It had been an awkward moment when the funeral director asked them who would do the service. Luther didn't go to church anywhere, much to the dismay of his mother and grandmother, and Hope hadn't gone to church anywhere since landing in western Kentucky. One time she went with Luther to his Gram's church. She barely tolerated the loud shouting and dancing, but when they brought out rattlesnakes, she was done and hurried out the door.

"I'm an outsider, and Lisa was an outsider," Hope says. "I want an outsider to preach the funeral."

"Okay, whatever you say."

This is another irritation about Luther. He always defers to her and lets her have her way. She wishes the two of them could engage in the kind of loud, passionate arguing her parents used to do when she was growing up. It wasn't like they were angry with each other and there was a chance the arguing was going to get out of control, it was just their way. Hope actually found it entertaining and exciting. The room pulsed with the energy, and they usually ended the argument by laughing or kissing.

One time she thought she'd found a man she could have that kind of relationship with—James. The problem was, she miscalculated how angry he'd become if she kept coming back at him with her views and opinions. The first time he shoved her against a wall was enough of a warning sign to her. She moved out the next day, while he was at work.

"I sometimes have a hard time remembering what my parents looked like."

"Huh?" Luther sounds surprised. "What are you talking about?"

"I'm talking about my parents. I've got pictures they took of me and my sisters, but there aren't any photos of them. It's been so long since they died, I'm not sure my memory of what they looked like is accurate. Is that what's going to happen with Lisa? Will I forget what she looked like?"

She'll never know if Luther had any intention of trying to answer her, because as she finishes her question and he turns off the paved road and onto their gravel driveway, they both see five or six cars parked in front of their house.

"Who all is it?" Hope asks. "I don't want to talk to anybody."

"I recognize some of the cars as belonging to my cousins, but there's a couple of them I don't recognize. Do you?"

Hope slides down in the seat so she can't see over the dashboard. "Make them leave."

"They've probably brought some food to the house."

"Why?"

"It's just what people from around here do when somebody dies, they take food to the family."

"I don't want their food, and I'm not going to eat it. I don't eat other people's food, who knows what's in it or how clean their kitchen is."

"Hope, they're just trying to be nice. It'll hurt their feelings if we refuse to take their food."

"So, let me ask you this," she snaps. "Whose feelings are more important? Who had a daughter commit suicide? Who feels like there's no more reason for living?" Her voice rises in pitch and volume, but she doesn't care; she doesn't care about anything.

Luther pulls to a stop behind a white pickup truck. As soon as he does, doors start opening, and people emerge from the vehicles. All the women have bowls or casserole dishes or baskets, and everyone's expressions are somber. The men zip up their jackets and shove their hands in the pockets of their pants, looking uncertain of what to do next.

Sitting up, Hope looks at the faces and suddenly recognizes Justin Barkley from the casino. Without his customary security guard uniform, she almost didn't know him. *Crap, what's he doing here?* She feels herself blushing, and she gives Luther a quick glance, but he's busy getting out of the Jeep and hugging his cousins or shaking their hands, depending on their gender because "guys in my family don't hug."

Justin walks toward her side of the Jeep, followed by Carol Ann and Whitney, who work with her. She squirms in her seat as Justin reaches for the door handle.

Justin backs up and lets Carol Ann and Whitney step closer and lean in the open door.

Carol Ann's eyes are red, and her cheeks are blotchy. Her chin quivers as she hugs Hope's neck. In a choked voice, she says, "Oh my God, Hope, I am so, so sorry."

Carol Ann makes room for Whitney, who holds Hope's face in her hands and looks into her eyes. "Listen to me, girl," she says in a whisper only Hope can hear, "you are going to survive this. I don't know how, you don't know how, but you will. You will not give up. Do you hear me?"

Suddenly, Hope's strong facade breaks, and tears spring from her eyes. She pulls her friends closer and buries her face in her necks, washing them with her tears.

Eventually, she releases them, and they step back. Then Justin reaches for her. Putting his hands on her waist, he lifts her out of the car, stands her up in front of him, and engulfs her in a bear hug.

She whispers to him, "What are you doing here? Are you crazy? What about Luther?"

He whispers back, "Luther don't know anything about us. I couldn't stay away. I'm just so sorry for what happened to Lisa."

CHAPTER SEVEN

OBEYING THE VOICE'S INSTRUCTIONS FROM his GPS, Michael turns on his blinker and slows to turn onto what he assumes is the gravel driveway that will take him to Hope Rodriguez's house, but first he has to wait in the road until a string of vehicles exits.

Even though he has a couple of books on the topic of funeral sermons and has spoken at some funerals, he's never done a funeral for someone he has never met. "I don't even know where to start," he'd lamented to Sarah. "I mean, what can I say about the girl when I know nothing about her? What does her mother want me to say? Does she have favorite passages of scripture she wants me to quote?"

"Have you tried calling the mother?" Sarah asked.

"Yes. The funeral director gave me her number, but every time I call, it goes straight to voicemail, and she hasn't called me back."

"Why don't you go to her house and talk to her? She doesn't live alone, does she?"

He heard the wary tone in her second question,

no doubt born out of her paranoia and distrust of him, and he hated it—both for her and for him. Her constant questioning of him was wearing thin, yet he knew he was mostly to blame for her lack of trust.

How long, oh Lord, am I going to have to pay for my sin? Is she ever going to forgive me and let it go?

He knows he should have included in that oft-used prayer a request to take away his lustful eye. But he can't bring himself to do it, because it is the one thing in life that gives him the most pleasure. Nothing comes close to the thrill he gets from looking at porn and masturbating. Where he had messed up was when he had had sex with a woman in his church, a woman Sarah was friends with, and her husband found out about it, which led to him being fired.

"Are you ignoring me?" Sarah's question jarred him out of his musings.

"No, I'm sorry. You are correct, she doesn't live alone. She lives with a man named Lucifer."

"Lucifer? What kind of person would give their child one of Satan's names?"

"Did I say Lucifer? I meant Luther."

"They aren't married?"

"I guess not. Ezra Marshall emphasized the word 'boyfriend' when describing their relationship."

"Clearly, these people around here need a revival, a call to follow the Lord, and you can be the one to do it, if you can manage to walk the straight and narrow yourself. Michael, you are one of the most gifted evangelists I've ever heard."

He gave her a look of surprise.

"I mean it. You have a way with words and the ability to take heavenly truths and present them in a way even a child can understand them."

Michael hardly knew how to react to this morsel of rarely-given praise. He'd often thought of himself as "praise starved" because he didn't grow up in a home where those kinds of words were doled out. His father was a stern man who expected nothing less than perfection, and his mother was as stoic as a brick. Thus, when Michael began speaking in churches and hearing words of admiration and acclaim from audience members, it was nothing short of intoxicating. He *craved* it.

"That means a lot to me, Sarah. Your opinion really matters to me. So, you think I should just drive out to their place unannounced?"

"If they act put out about it, simply tell them you tried to call. You'll be able to smooth it over, I'm sure."

Now, as he turns into the driveway, he can't for the life of him remember the mother's name. *Luther's the boyfriend. Lisa was the daughter. What in the world is the mother's name?* Thankfully, just as he rolls to a stop in front of the trailer, her name pops into his head. *Of course, Hope, is her name. Perfect for a lot of reasons.*

When he steps out of his car, the gravel crunches underneath his dress shoes, the soles of which are so thin, he can feel some of the larger rocks pressing uncomfortably on the ball of his foot. A sudden blast of cold February air upends his thick hair, leaving it in complete disarray.

"First impressions, Michael," he hears his father's voice saying, "you cannot overstate the importance. Comb your hair, tuck your shirt in tightly, make sure your shoes are clean, and put on a relaxed smile."

Using his fingers, he rakes through his mass of hair in an attempt to restore order, but as he reaches for his head, he feels cold air on his stomach and realizes he's pulled his shirttail out of his pants. He's cramming it back in when he hears a man's voice.

"Can I help you?"

Michael looks up and sees a skinny, shirtless, tattooed man with a semblance of a beard and moustache, dressed in camo pants. "Are you Luther?"

"That's me." He reaches to shake hands as he walks out to meet Michael.

Taking the offered hand, Michael smiles and says, "I'm Michael Trent, the new pastor at Grace Community Church, in Bardwell. I'm supposed to do the funeral for Lisa Rodriguez."

"Oh, yeah, right. Nice to meet you, and thanks for doing this."

When Luther doesn't invite him in, he continues. "I was hoping I might could talk to the girl's mother, Hope, and get a better since of who Lisa was and maybe what Hope would like for me to say at the funeral."

"Well..." Luther looks over his shoulder toward the house. "Hope's not much on meeting people she doesn't know, and she's not doing very good right now."

"I'm sure she's not. It's a horrible thing that happened." Michael shifts nervously from one foot to the other, not sure how to proceed. "It's just sort of hard to talk about someone I've never met and know nothing about, you know what I mean?" Another shot of wind plays with the ends of his hair, trying to find a way to grab hold and create another tumult. Michael slaps his hand on his hair and with his other hand squeezes shut the front of his suit jacket as a cold shudder runs through him.

Luther gives him a once-over look that says, 'People around here don't wear dress shoes and suits, especially if it's this cold.' Instead, his face softens a bit, and he says, "Tell you what, why don't you get back in your car and warm up a bit, while I go talk to Hope and see if she's up to talking to you."

Michael readily agrees and quickly slides inside his car, cranks it, and turns the heat on high. *What have I gotten myself into? What if she won't talk to me, then what do I do?* Looking in his rearview mirror, he works some more on his hair.

After a few minutes, Luther reappears and walks to the driver's side door. After Michael rolls down his window, Luther says, "She says she'll talk to you."

As soon as he steps inside their home, Michael is struck by the spartan look of things. The only furniture in the living room are two recliners and a large flat-screen TV hanging on the wall. On the floor beside one of the recliners are two crumpled beer cans and one standing upright and unopened.

Pointing to one of the recliners, Luther says, "Have a seat." He sticks his head in a hallway and calls out, "Come on, Hope, he's here."

Michael stands when she enters the room and takes in her appearance. Dark circles rim her eyes, the symptom of grief no amount of makeup can cover. If Luther is skinny, then Hope is unhealthily thin. She doesn't *wear* her clothes; they seem to hang on her body. *Is she anorexic?* She has straight, shoulder-length brown hair with streaks of royal blue in it. Her eyebrows look like opposing apostrophes, and one is pierced. Colorful tattoos peek out of the neck and sleeves of her shirt, pleading to be seen.

She walks past him without saying anything or looking at him and sits in the other recliner.

Unsure of what he should do, he looks at Luther, who nods for him to take a seat.

When he sits down, Hope pulls her legs up underneath her and makes a motion like she's picking a piece of lint off the arm of her chair, but Michael is certain there is nothing there. Even though he's confident he appears calm on the outside, on the inside he feels like all the muscles in his body are pulled taut like the strings of a piano.

He decides he will make the first move and says, "Hope—", but his voice betrays his anxiety, and her name squeaks out of his throat. He clears his throat and tries again. "Hope, I'm so very, very sorry for the loss of your daughter. I know how you feel."

Like a snake uncoiling, her legs jerk out from under her, and she lunges toward him. Her eyes look like lasers as she says, "Have you ever lost a child?"

"Well...no...I haven't...but..."

"Then let's be very clear about this, you do *not* know how I feel. You cannot even imagine what it's like." Her words fall like hailstones on his head, and he feels like covering it with his arms.

"Now Hope, the pastor is just trying—" Luther tries to change the tenor of the interaction.

But Hope cuts him off by jabbing her arm and finger at him as if they were a javelin. "Don't you say a word."

The force of her action coupled with her words shove Luther backwards a step. He holds up his hands and looks down at the floor in defeat.

When she turns back to face Michael, he says, "You're right, I don't know how you feel, and I'm sorry I said I did."

His honesty appears to dampen her ire, and she folds back up in the chair.

An uncomfortable silence ensues as he tries to decide if he should say something or let her start the conversation.

He's just about to speak when she says, "Did she go to hell?"

Unprepared for such a question, he glances at Luther for help.

"She thinks suicide is a mortal sin."

Hope says, "I don't want you to preach her into hell, even if it's what you believe has happened. So, what do you intend to say?"

Although she's put him on the spot, he finds her directness and honesty refreshing. He gives her a small smile. "It's what we all want to know, isn't it? Heaven or hell? Where will we be? Where will our loved ones be?" He waits for a rejoinder from her while he tries to decide how to answer her. The question is one that was hotly debated in dorm rooms at seminary, with classmates giving all sorts of Bible-supported answers from every side of the argument.

"Well?" Hope asks. "What do you believe?"

If honesty worked once, maybe it'll work again.

"Here's the truth: I don't know what I believe about suicide, but I do know I believe God will always do the right thing—the just and merciful thing."

Instead of striking at him from her coiled position, this time she slowly shifts positions. "Hmm...a preacher who's honest about what he doesn't know. You'll not last long around here with that attitude."

CHAPTER EIGHT

SARAH STARES AT THE PILE of clothes she's tried on and quickly discarded while trying to decide what to wear to the funeral.

Why does everything make me look fat? People who see me will be disgusted before they even speak to or know me. Michael will be embarrassed to be seen with me, even though he'll deny it.

She hears the voice of her father as he used to introduce her and her two sisters to people when they were children. "Martha is my smart one, Tiffany is my athletic one, and little Sarah here is my chubby one." He always laughed at the end, as if he was joking and it would take away the sting of his words, but a large part of Sarah became permanently crushed—one introduction at a time.

It was not until her senior year in high school that she discovered she could make herself throw up to lose weight. Pounds fell off her like leaves off a tree in the fall. The change was so dramatic, it couldn't be missed by others, and people kept telling her how much better, prettier, and sexier she looked. While the attention she garnered from friends and family was initially both uncomfortable and embarrassing, she soon found it thrilling.

All her life, she'd been ignored by guys, but after the weight loss, they began flocking after her like hummingbirds to her mother's red impatiens. She began embracing the attention recklessly, and the physical release she achieved from having sex washed away all those old feelings of shame and self-doubt, even if it was only briefly.

What she was unprepared for were the unwanted advances by guys. She had never learned how to set boundaries with boys, because she'd never had to. And so, one night she found herself surrounded by a group of guys she barely knew. She thought it was all innocent flirting until two of them pinned her to the ground. No amount of her pleading and screaming for help prevented them from having their way with her.

Ashamed to tell anyone what happened, she kept it to herself and began making earnest plans to get away from town and start attending college, which was where she met Michael.

Glancing at their wedding picture lying in a half-opened box, she says aloud, "And I thought for sure a man in seminary would have his heart set on God, not on sex."

She shakes her head and pulls another dress out of her suitcase. Unzipping it, she steps in and pulls it up while pushing her arms through the armholes. With some effort, she zips it up and goes into the bathroom to assess the look.

Simple, black, and flowing, it hid the roll of her stomach and thick thighs.

It'll have to do.

Before giving her hair and makeup a final once over, she checks the time on her phone. "Oh my God, I'm running late!"

Hurrying outside, she's thankful for the cold air that helps dry the perspiration on her forehead and above her upper lip. She walks to the car one of the women from church loaned her and Michael until they decided whether to buy a second car. She tries to remember the woman's name.

Cindy? Cynthia? Cheryl? Something starting with a 'C.'

Her mind is quickly distracted from chasing the name because of the need to familiarize herself with how to operate the car. Getting in is the first challenge. To slide in behind the steering wheel, she has to maneuver the seat backwards, even though it makes it difficult for her feet to reach the pedals. It's a problem she's become accustomed to during this past year of gaining extra weight.

After she starts the car, she closes her eyes and takes a slow breath. "Dear God, please calm my anxiety, and help me not do or say anything that'll embarrass Michael or make him ashamed to be seen with me." As she backs out of the driveway, she grits her teeth and adds, "And if I had a dollar for every time I've said that prayer, I could make a down payment on gastric bypass surgery."

She's surprised at how quickly she arrives at the funeral home. *Adjusting to a small town is going to take some time.* Her second surprise, though, is how few cars are in the parking lot. She'd expected there to be a huge outpouring from the town at the death of a child, and she can't wondering what the lack of response means. *At least I won't have to feel like I'm parading in front of half the town when I walk in.*

Before she can reach to open the door to the funeral home, it opens slowly, and the funeral director who was at their house yesterday greets her with an appropriately somber yet detached mask of grief on his face.

He extends his hand to her and says, "Sister Trent, I'm so glad you came. Let me show you to the chapel where the service will take place."

Sarah searches frantically for his name. All she can remember is Ezekiel, so she replies, "Thank you, Ezekiel."

"Name's Ezra," he replies, with a slight look of annoyance.

"I'm sorry, Ezra. I'm horrible with names, but I do love your name. It's such a strong sounding..."

But Ezra walks away from her, evidently intending she follow him.

So, I've made my first enemy, or at least failed at my first chance to make a good impression on my own. She swears silently.

Organ music is playing through speakers in the ceiling of the chapel as Sarah enters. It only takes a few measures before she recognizes the song, *Nearer My God to Thee*. Mostly empty, unevenly spaced and unmatched church pews fill the room. Some have black scuff marks on the back from children's shoes, and others have darkened areas on the top, where the oil from people's hands gripped them tightly so they could resist the altar call.

Sarah easily counts seven people seated in the chapel, with only two of them sitting together; she assumes it's the mother and her boyfriend sitting on the front pew. The flat-gray open casket sits unadorned, without the typical spray of flowers resting on top, and only one flower arrangement is in the room.

As Ezra shows her to an empty pew, Sarah's heart fills with sadness. *This is the most pitiful sight I've ever seen at a funeral. The poor mother.* She wants to get up and go speak to her but expects Michael will be entering any moment to start the funeral. And she's correct, because at that moment the organ music stops, and Michael enters through a side door, walks to a thin metal lectern and sets his black Bible on it. The stand sways underneath the weight.

She wishes he'd let her give him a once over to be certain he looked his best before he left the house, because his sandy hair is sticking up in back, betraying his troublesome double crown. The deep furrow between his dark, deep-set eyes that peek out from underneath his heavy brow give him a perpetual look of concern suited to his vocation.

She pays little attention as he reads the obituary, having been distracted by the dimple in his chin. It's always been her favorite place on his body to touch and kiss. *When was the last time we kissed, other than a perfunctory hello or goodbye kiss?* She thumbs through a calendar in her mind and decides it's been four months. Even then, it didn't go well. She was convinced he was thinking about someone else while he was making love to her and challenged him about it right in the middle of their lovemaking.

"Who are you thinking about?" she'd asked.

Resting on his knees while he was inside her, Michael's face morphed from one of pleasure to one of frustration, and she felt him begin to shrink. "Damn it, Sarah!" It was the only cuss word she ever heard him say, perhaps because it was a Bible word and somehow that made it okay to use. He moved to the side of the bed and sat down. "Why do you have to screw up the one thing we used to be so good at? You—I was thinking about you, okay? But it doesn't matter now. You've ruined the moment."

Like a carpenter hammering a nail, each of his accusations drove her self-esteem a notch lower, and she began to cry. "I just can't stand to have sex with you when you're thinking about another woman, and I know you are. You can't possibly be turned on by me. I'm fat and look disgusting, so I understand the fact that you have to fantasize about someone else to get aroused. I understand it; but I can't stand it. It's like you're not even here in the bed with me. You just use my body parts to satisfy yourself."

He turned and gave her a look she'd never

seen from him, a look of malevolence. Without a word, he grabbed his clothes off the chair, tossed them on and left the house, slamming the door behind him.

The sound of the door made her flinch. A feeling of desperation seized her, and she hurried after him as she dragged the bedsheet off the bed and wrapped it around herself. "Michael," she cried into the night air as she saw him getting into their car. By the time she reached the driveway, he'd started backing into the street and then sped away.

Stunned, she let go of her grip on the sheet, and it fell away, leaving her standing there, naked and alone.

The sound of organ music brings her back to the funeral chapel. She looks at Michael, who's taken a seat in a folding chair behind the lectern. One last, damning thought from that night torments her.

That's the night you had sex with my best friend, Toni, for the first and only time. At least you say it was the only time.

CHAPTER NINE

STANDING BESIDE THE GRAVE, HOPE stares at Lisa's coffin and waits for someone to tell her it's time to leave, because it'll give her an excuse to rip open and unleash the bag of emotions she's been holding inside. She wants to break something, smash something, hurt someone . . . hurt herself. *Curse God and die!* The words from the Old Testament story of Job keep ringing in her ears because they're the only words that make sense to her. *What's the point in living? Lisa was the only thing that gave my life meaning, and now she's gone.*

Around her, she hears the clicking sound of the naked branches of dogwood trees as a frosty wind blows across the cemetery. Lost snowflakes feather sideways in search of a cold place to land. The end of her nose itches, and she knows it's about to drip, but she ignores the impulse to wipe or rub it.

The words of a song she sang in middle school choir come to her:

Earth stood hard as iron, water like a stone.
A perfect description of how my heart feels. There

will never be anything that can warm me; I won't let it happen. Cold is safe.

Luther holds a handkerchief in front of her face and says quietly, "Let me wipe your nose for you."

She slaps away his hand, sending the handkerchief sailing through the air, where it lands on top of the casket—a cotton/polyester flower of sadness on the cold, gray metallic resting place of her beloved daughter. "Leave me alone," she yells. "I'll leave when I'm ready, and I may never be ready. So, go whenever you want to."

Retreating a couple steps, Luther murmurs, "I'm sorry. I was just trying to help."

It's obvious she's hurt his feelings, and she feels good about it. She wants her grief to suck the life out of everyone just like it is her.

No one has the right to be happy.

"Excuse me."

It's the voice of the pastor. She looks toward him and sees the cemetery workers, who helped take the casket from the hearse and place it over the grave, standing in the distance, dressed in coveralls and gloves, poised with their shovels.

Then a thought occurs to her. Looking directly at Michael, she says, "I want to bury my daughter."

He steps closer to her and gives her a look of confusion. "That's why we're here, to bury Lisa. But the service is over, and it's time to leave. You can come back later, after they're finished." He nods toward the two cemetery workers.

It's the same even, caring tone of voice he used at the funeral home. She felt his sense of caring more than she remembered what he actually said. She can't bring herself to strike out at him like she did Luther.

"I don't want them to do it," she says. "I want to do it myself. They didn't know Lisa and don't deserve to cover her up. It's my last chance to do something for her." Emotions swell in her chest, and she's afraid they may swallow her like a sinkhole.

Michael looks uncertainly toward Luther, then at the workers, and finally at Ezra. "She wants to shovel the dirt into the grave herself."

Ezra moves forward, and the three of them form a small triangle. "Miss Rodriguez, burying is a task best suited for strong men. It's much more difficult than perhaps it looks."

Hope narrows her eyes. "Are you telling me I'm not allowed to do it because I'm a woman?"

From the edge of the triangle, Luther says, "Ezra, Hope might look skinny, but she's wiry, like Barney Fife. She can do more than some men." He gives a nervous laugh.

While she appreciates him speaking up for her, it grates on her that he tried to lighten the mood with a little humor. Without looking at him, she says, "Just shut up, Luther. Will you?" She watches Michael and Ezra exchange a look but is uncertain what's meant by it. "Listen to me, I'm not leaving until I do this. Tell your man to lower the casket, then pull the grass carpet off the dirt. All I want is a shovel."

Michael starts taking off his jacket and asks Hope, "Can I help you do it?"

It's now her turn to be caught off guard. In her experience, limited though it is, men of the cloth aren't men who know how to do manual labor. She quickly decides he's just trying to be nice and doesn't expect her to accept his offer, so she elects to call his bluff.

"Sure, I'll let you."

Without hesitation, he lays his jacket on the ground and says to Ezra, "Get us some shovels."

Ezra shrugs and waves over the workers. "Go ahead and lower the casket, Joe. Then the mother and the preacher are going to shovel the dirt in. You all stick around in case they need some help."

The two men look at each other, then at Ezra. "Whatever you say."

Hope takes the handle of the offered shovel and watches as Lisa's casket slowly disappears into the blackness below. It takes a few seconds before she realizes she isn't breathing, so she takes in a sharp breath of air.

Touching her arm, Michael asks, "Are you okay?"

She flinches at the touch and pulls away. "I'm fine." Thrusting the shovel into the pile of soft dirt, she lifts a shovelful over the grave and lets it trickle down.

"Here," Luther says as he steps forward. "Let me do it, Hope."

Swearing at him, she says, "You get away. Go home or go back on the river, I don't care. I'll find a way home."

The sound of a heavy thud turns her attention back to the grave, and she sees Michael has thrown in a shovelful of dirt and is in the process of throwing in another. For the second time, he's surprised her.

Maybe he's different from all the others.

She takes a moment to watch Luther walk away and notices a sheriff's car pulling into the cemetery. It pulls alongside Luther and stops. The window rolls down, and Luther and the driver engage in conversation for several moments, then the patrol car leaves. Hope is slightly curious what it's about, but not enough to call Luther back over to learn. She turns her attention back to the grave and joins Michael in burying her daughter.

It isn't long before she begins to sweat and peels off her jacket. She notices Michael has shucked his necktie and rolled up his sleeves. A sheen of sweat is on his face, and his hair has fallen into his eyes, but he hasn't said a word since they began shoveling in earnest.

Pausing to catch her breath, she says, "You're awfully quiet for a preacher, aren't you?"

Continuing to shovel, he says, "It's not my place to talk right now. It's my place to help you do this. Words sometimes get in the way of helping." He stops and looks at her. "You know the story of Job, I suppose."

She nods.

"Remember what Job's three friends did when they came to comfort him after all the tragedies that befell him?"

She thinks for a moment, but it's a part of the story she's unfamiliar with. "No, I don't remember."

"They sat down beside him and for seven days and nights didn't say a word. They were just there. Where they messed up was when they started talking after those seven days." Turning away from her, he returns to shoveling.

Hope watches him as she thinks about what he said.

As time passes, their pace slows, blisters form and tear open, but they continue until the top of the grave is a rounded mound.

A feeling of satisfaction enters Hope, but it lasts only briefly as she realizes there's nothing else she can do for Lisa. *Now what do I do?* She looks at Michael, hoping he'll read her mind and she won't have to say it out loud. The setting sun gives his face a golden hue, and there are dirt smudges on his face and white shirt.

He returns her gaze and asks, "Are we done?"

"Yes."

He takes her shovel from her and hands his and hers to the cemetery workers, who pitch them clanging into the back of their truck and quickly leave. Turning his attention back to her, he says, "What's your plan now?"

Fatigue has begun to settle in every corner of her body, and she feels it pulling her downward to the familiar place of despair. Without pausing to think first, she utters the thought on her mind.

"I want to lie down on top of the grave and go

to sleep and never wake up."

Michael shakes his head. "Well, I'm not going to let you."

The long shadows cast by the setting sun have disappeared, replaced by a dusky dark, making it harder for her to see his expression.

She begins, "You can't—"

But he cuts her off by saying, "I'm taking you home. Rest is what you need now. Eating and sleeping are the first things to fall by the wayside when people are grieving. You need both right now."

Her mind wants her to mount a protest, but she's too tired to muster the energy to do so.

"You stay right here," he says. "I'll pull my car up here so you won't have to walk to it. You look like you're about ready to collapse."

As if they'd been waiting for a cue from someone, her knees buckle, and she crumples to the ground.

Michael catches her head just before it lands. He unfolds her legs and lays her on her back. "Don't worry, I'm calling an ambulance, and they'll be here in a sec."

She manages to knock the phone from his hand. "No hospital, no ambulance."

"But Hope, you need medical attention."

"I'll be fine in a second. I just had a dizzy spell. I'm already feeling better. Help me up and take me home, please."

He presses down on the front of her shoulder. "Really, Hope, you need to let me—"

"No," she says more forcefully as she finds an

extra ounce of energy. "Quit talking and do what I asked."

On the drive to her house, Hope drifts in and out of sleep. Normally cautious to the point of paranoia toward other people, she can't believe how readily she got into the car with a man she doesn't know. Her only explanation is, there's something intangible about Michael that makes her feel like she can trust him, something beyond his title of "pastor." Or maybe it's just the fact that she's so exhausted, she doesn't have the power to resist his suggestions.

She's vaguely aware the car has stopped, and she squints at the sudden brightness of the interior lights coming on as he exits the car. When her passenger door opens, she gives no protest when he slips one of his arms under her legs and the other one around her shoulders and lifts her out of the car. Somewhere in the deep recesses of her mind, a warning bell rings, but she intentionally ignores it, which is a bad habit that's caused her plenty of heartache in the past.

She rests her head on his shoulder and says to herself, *I'm tired of thinking.*

Once they reach her front door, Michael says, "You think you can stand up now?"

She forces herself to come fully awake and realizes she hasn't given him one word of thanks for all he's done. "Yes, set me down; I'll be okay." In the past, she's always shown her gratitude to men by letting them have sex with her, and she barely stops herself from giving him a kiss and inviting him inside. "Uh...thank you...for everything. I couldn't have done all this without you." She's glad it's dark and he can't see her blushing.

"It was my honor to have had a small role in this most painful drama of your life. I cannot imagine what all this is like for you."

His answer deepens her blush. She gets the sense he's wanting to come in, *but that can't be.* She wriggles out of his arms and takes a step back while working hard to clear her head.

"I really appreciate you bringing me home. I'm okay now."

"I want you to promise you'll both eat and sleep now."

"I promise." Her feeling of uneasiness grows, and she quickly goes inside and locks the door behind her. *What was that all about?*

She starts walking toward her bedroom, stripping off her dirty, sweaty clothes as she goes. Lying on her pillow is a folded piece of notebook paper torn from a spiral notebook; its ragged edges are a mirror of her own state of being. Opening it, she immediately recognizes Luther's uneven handwriting:

I DID WHAT YOU TOLD ME TO. A VAN FROM WORK IS COMING TO PICK ME UP IN A FEW MINUTES, AND I'M HEADED BACK ON THE RIVER. I'LL SEE YOU NEXT MONTH, BUT CALL ME IF YOU NEED ANYTHING.

ONE MORE THING, THE SHERIFF CAME TO THE CEMETERY AND SAID THEY FOUND SOMETHING IN LISA'S

AUTOPSY YOU OUGHT TO KNOW. IT WOULD BE BETTER IF I TOLD YOU THIS FACE TO FACE, BUT ANYWAY, HERE IT IS – LISA WAS PREGNANT.
—LUTHER

CHAPTER TEN

"WHERE IN THE HELL HAVE you been?!" Sarah throws her question at Michael like a whaler's harpoon as she charges toward him.

Thoroughly spent from the day's activities (preparing a presentation for the funeral, the funeral itself, shoveling the dirt into the grave, and then carrying Hope home), all Michael wants to do is take a hot shower and go to bed. The last thing he wants to do is deal with Sarah raging at him.

"Look at yourself!" she continues as she points at him. "You look like you've been rolling on the ground. Didn't you at least have the decency to take the woman to a motel to have sex with her? You know, you really are an animal. You disgust me. We've been here for less than a week, and you've already found a whore. How do you do it? Is it some sort of built-in radar you have? Or do they even have a radar for your type?"

When she finally pauses, he says, "All I really want to do is go to bed. Can we talk about this in the morning?"

"Sure! Fine! Let's pretend everything's good and nothing happened. That's what I did last time, and I promised myself I wouldn't do it anymore. You're killing me, that's what you're doing, you're killing me."

In a flat voice devoid of emotion, he says, "I promise you, I have not been whoring around."

"Show me your phone. I want to see if you have any messages you're trying to hide."

Reaching in the pocket of his jacket, Michael pulls out his iPhone and hands it to her.

She jerks it out of his hand. "Is the password still the same?"

"Yes, it was our agreement after what happened in Kansas. You can look at my phone any time you want to."

She opens the phone and starts scrolling through it. Eventually, she hands it back to him and says, "This is the scariest part of you, you can lie with such ease, and I would never know it. You've probably found a way to delete things or hide things so I can't find them."

Reaching for her, he says, "Sarah, please..."

She slaps his hand away from her. "Don't touch me! You don't deserve to touch me, much less be in the same room with me. If you haven't been with a woman, then explain to me why you look the way you do." She curls back her lip in disgust.

"Can we at least sit down to talk about it?" he asks.

"Sure we can. It'll give you more time to make up your story."

They walk to the kitchen, move some boxes out of two chairs, then sit down at the dining table.

Michael begins, "I'm going to tell you exactly what happened, word for word, as best as I can. And I swear to you it'll be the truth."

She gives a derisive laugh. "You wouldn't know the truth if you poured it in a cup and drank it. But go ahead, this should be good."

As he begins telling her what happened at the cemetery, he's also thinking ahead and trying to decide if he should include the detail about Hope fainting and him taking her to her house, because he knows it'll infuriate Sarah and bring on a fresh batch of accusations.

So, when he gets to the spot in the story where they finish shoveling all the dirt, he decides to stop the story there and says, "And that's exactly what happened. I swear it."

She stares at him, unblinking, for several seconds, then says, "You know, I believe that's the most original story you've ever come up with. It was actually entertaining. As a matter of fact, it was so fantastic a tale, I don't believe you could have made it up."

A feeling of relief moves through Michael, and he says, "If somebody told me the story, I probably wouldn't believe it. I mean, I've never heard of someone wanting to fill in a loved one's grave. It was probably foolish of me to offer to help, but I felt like I should do something. What I did wrong was not calling or texting you and letting you know where I was and what was going on. For that, I am truly sorry, please forgive me." Finally, he sees Sarah's face relax and tears pool in her eyes.

"I'm sorry for being so angry and attacking you," she replies. "I just get things in my head, and it spins out of control."

"Don't apologize, Sarah. Whatever fears you have about me are my fault. It's going to take you time to see I'm a changed man. Just hang in there with me, and I'll prove it to you."

She reaches across the table, and he takes her hand. "I do love you. I just want you to be the kind of man I know you can be."

"And I love you, too. All I can tell you is, I'm trying."

"Why don't you go take a shower, and I'll fix you something to eat."

"That sounds great."

While in the shower, Michael prays, *"Please forgive me, Lord, for not being completely honest with Sarah. I just didn't think it was the wise thing to do, and I knew it would upset her even more. Thank You for guiding my mouth and hands today during all the things that happened. I pray You were glorified in all of it."*

Once finished with showering, he towels himself dry and thinks again about what happened at Hope's front door. *It seemed like she wanted to kiss me or take me inside for something more. But she also seemed nervous about it.* He began to fantasize about what it would be like to make love to a woman as slim as her. His fantasies and sexual acts have always been about women with lots of curves, but Hope is anything but that. He smiles at some of the images he conjures up and feels himself getting aroused.

Suddenly, he hears a knock on the bathroom door.

"You about done, honey?" Sarah asks. "I've got you something to eat."

He quickly busies himself with getting dressed. "Yes, I'll be right out."

During the middle of the night, Michael awakens and lies still to be certain Sarah is sound asleep. When he's certain she is, he slips quietly out of bed and tiptoes to what will eventually be his study. The ambient light is barely enough for him to make out shapes. Squinting, he moves slowly around the room, touching unopened boxes. Finally, he finds what he's looking for and takes a box off a stack and sets it in the floor. Using his thumbnail, he slices through the masking tape and pulls open the flaps.

Lying on top is a copy of Strong's *Exhaustive Concordance of the Bible*, a massive hardback book he bought while in seminary. Lifting it out, he opens it to reveal a hollowed out cavity where pages have been trimmed, and inside the hollowed-out area is an android cell phone. He takes it out, powers it on, and sits down on the floor.

Because the room is so dark, the glow from the phone's screen shines brightly. He quickly adjusts the brightness to a soft glow. He sees where he's received several text messages, all from the same number. He opens the app and reads:

BRITTANY: I REALLY MISS YOU. HOPE YOU'RE DOING OK. TEXT WHEN YOU CAN.

BRITTANY: I HAVEN'T HEARD FROM YOU IN NEARLY TWO DAYS. ARE YOU OKAY?

The last message was only a few hours ago: PLEASE TALK TO ME.

He types: HEY, I'M SORRY. IT'S BEEN CRAZY AROUND HERE TRYING TO GET SETTLED IN AND EVERYTHING. I'M HERE NOW, IF YOU CAN TALK.

Five minutes pass before he gets a reply.

BRITTANY: I'M SO RELIEVED TO HEAR FROM YOU. I FELT LIKE I WAS GOING TO HAVE A PANIC ATTACK. HOW ARE THINGS?

MICHAEL: NOTHING'S CHANGED. SARAH IS STILL PARANOID AND WATCHING ME LIKE A HAWK. SHE CAN BE BRUTAL.

BRITTANY: I'M SORRY. I WISH I COULD MAKE IT ALL BETTER FOR YOU.

MICHAEL: AND I WISH I WAS THERE WITH YOU RIGHT NOW BECAUSE THAT WOULD MAKE IT ALL BETTER.

BRITTANY: AND I WISH YOU WERE HERE, TOO, IN BED WITH ME.

Immediately, Michael's heart rate kicks up a notch, and he feels himself getting aroused.

MICHAEL: IF I WAS THERE, WHAT WOULD YOU DO TO MAKE IT BETTER?

BRITTANY: I WOULD DO THAT SPECIAL THING FOR YOU. THE THING YOU LOVE.

MICHAEL: SEND ME A PIC.

Her response takes a bit longer, but soon he receives a photo of her from the waist up, with her breasts exposed.

BRITTANY: HOW'S THAT?

MICHAEL: OMG! YOU ARE SO BEAUTIFUL AND SEXY.

BRITTANY: IS THAT A BANANA IN YOUR POCKET, OR ARE YOU JUST HAPPY TO SEE ME? LOL!! SEND ME A PIC OF YOU.

He pulls down his underwear, takes a picture, and sends it to her.

MICHAEL: THIS IS WHAT YOU DO TO ME.

For the next thirty minutes, they sext back and forth.

BRITTANY: I HATE TO SAY IT, BUT I'VE GOT TO GO TO WORK IN A FEW HOURS AND NEED TO GET A LITTLE SLEEP.

MICHAEL: I KNOW. I JUST HATE WE ARE SO FAR APART.

BRITTANY: MAYBE A CHURCH CLOSE BY WILL ASK YOU TO HOLD A REVIVAL, AND YOU CAN RETURN TO KANSAS.

MICHAEL: MAYBE, BUT I'M AFRAID

MY REPUTATION AROUND THERE IS RUINED.

BRITTANY: THEN MAYBE I'LL FIND AN EXCUSE TO COME THERE.

MICHAEL: THAT WOULD BE A LITTLE TRICKY, BUT I'D LOVE FOR YOU TO TRY AND MAKE IT WORK.

BRITTANY: UNTIL THEN, WE'VE STILL GOT THIS. IT'S NOT THE SAME AS THE REAL THING, BUT IT'S BETTER THAN NOTHING.

MICHAEL: YES, I AGREE. UNTIL THE NEXT TIME...

BRITTANY: UNTIL THE NEXT TIME...

He hangs up the phone and returns it to the secret compartment in the book.

Getting up, he heads to the bathroom to shower himself off. As the water cascades over him, feelings of guilt and shame begin washing over him.

What is wrong with me? I'm worse than a fool; I'm nothing but scum, a slave to lust. Why, why, why do I keep doing this to myself?

In anguish, he grits his teeth and repeatedly bangs his forehead against the shower wall as tears of regret mingle with the warm shower spray. He wants to pray and ask forgiveness, *but how many times can a man ask for forgiveness for the same thing?*

All of a sudden, he hears a tapping on the bathroom door as it opens.

"Michael, are you all right?" Sarah asks. "Why are you taking a shower in the middle of the night?"

He quickly finds a lie he can tell. "I couldn't sleep and thought maybe a warm shower would help me relax. I'm sorry I woke you."

One end of the shower curtain opens, and Sarah steps inside. It's then he sees she's naked. "I know you've had a hard day," she says. "Why don't you let me wash you? Just try to forget about today." She picks up a bar of soap and begins rubbing it over his chest, down his stomach, and then his groin.

The combination of emotions proves to be too much for him, and he begins to sob.

Sarah drops the bar of soap and hugs him tightly. "Oh, Michael, everything's going to be all right. Just cry it out; I'm here for you."

CHAPTER ELEVEN

THE LIGHT FROM HOPE'S TELEVISION flickers against the walls and ceiling of the darkened living room, but she has no interest in the images on the screen. She sits staring at Luther's note, lying on her lap. It's as if the word "pregnant" is written in overly large all caps and with a red marker. She cannot take her eyes off it.

Shock, that cushion for the mind in response to trauma, is wearing off since she read the note a couple hours ago, and now her mind is ramping up, firing questions in rapid succession: *Why didn't I know? Why didn't she tell me? Who's the father? How could I have not known she had a boyfriend? Did he say or do something to her that made her want to kill herself? Did anyone else know about the pregnancy? Did the boy know? How far along was she?*

On the heels of those questions, her mind shifts gears and begins throwing accusations her way. "I failed her. The one thing I thought I was doing right in my life obviously wasn't true. No wonder she hated me; I wasn't there for her. There has to be a curse on me, because I've lost everyone I've ever been close to. Maybe all of it's my punishment for getting pregnant as a teen and not being a good Catholic."

She feels the quicksand of her depression pulling her down and squeezing the life out of her, so much so, she feels like she's choking. She stands up, trying to get her breath, but a shallow wisp of air is all she can pull in. Staggering to the front door, she pulls it open and gasps against the cold, sharp night air. The fresh intake of oxygen calms her, and she notices headlights coming up the driveway.

It's the middle of the night, who in the world is coming out here?

For a moment, she thinks about retreating inside and locking the door in case it's someone bent on mischief. But a part of her wants a good fight—an excuse to unleash the white-hot anger lurking inside her because her daughter is dead and she wants to take it out on somebody. So, she steps to the edge of her porch and clenches her fists.

When the vehicle comes to a stop and its headlights are extinguished, she recognizes the truck.

The door opens, and Justin Barkley steps out into the moonlight, which reflects off his high forehead. He hitches up his jeans, a habit Hope has noticed and commented on to him. "None of us Barkleys have a butt," was his explanation. "If I don't keep them pulled up, they'll fall off." Hope countered that his lack of a butt was amply made up for by the rest of his anatomy.

"Hey, there," he says as he walks toward her.

"What are you doing here?" she asks.

Stopping at the bottom of the porch steps, he answers, "I just got to thinking about you and wanted to come here and see how you're doing. If you'd ever answer your phone, I might not have had to come out here."

"I hate phones. That's why I always keep mine on silent." This is a repartee she's had with many people since the dawn of cell phones, but no one's yet convinced her that being at the beck and call of another person is a good thing. "It just puts people on edge when they can't get hold of you immediately."

Justin holds up a hand. "I know, you've told me that before."

"You took a big chance coming out here like this. What if Luther had been home?"

"I checked with a buddy of mine who works for the same barge line as Luther and found out he'd shipped out." He shifts his weight. "Are we going to have this conversation out here, or are you going to let me come in?"

Hope hesitates, figuring he's going to want to have sex with her, but she's not sure she can get in the mood for sex, not tonight. Having sex with him is fun, and he's much better at it than Luther, but she's still reeling from Lisa's death, as well as from learning she was pregnant.

As if he's reading her mind, he says, "I ain't here for sex, if that's what you're thinking. I just wanted to check on you."

Even though she believes this is only a half-truth, she says, "Come on in."

As soon as he walks inside, he takes a seat in one of the recliners and kicks up the foot. Stretching his arms up and putting his hands behind his head, he says, "You got cable out here?"

This isn't a complete surprise to her, because one time she caught him looking with one eye at the TV in a motel room while he was making love to her, but still it makes her mad.

Putting her hands on her hips, she asks, "When's the last time somebody slapped you?"

"Huh?" He gives her a confused look. "What do you mean?"

"I mean slapped you hard enough to make your eyes rattle. You say you're here to check on me, but the first thing you do when you get inside is ask if I have cable. What does that sound like to you?"

Justin kicks down the footrest with a bang and springs to his feet, a shocking move because of how swiftly he does it. Looking at the floor, he says, "You're right, makes me sound like a selfish asshole. I'm sorry, it was stupid of me. If it'll make you feel better, go ahead and slap me."

This makes her even madder. She doesn't want to be in a forgiving mood. The momentary anger she felt a moment ago felt good, really good. She wants to feed it and make it grow. Without thinking, she swings as hard as she can and slaps him on the face. The resulting sting in her hand shoves every other feeling and thought out of her head.

Relief, finally!

In spite of the pain, she swings at him again, but this time he catches her small hand in his baseball glove-sized hand. She tries to jerk away from him, but he holds her fast. So, she punches him in the stomach with her other hand. The blow has no effect on him.

Rather than reacting defensively or angrily toward her, he looks at her calmly as he continues to hold her hand.

"Let me go!" she yells.

He lets her hand go, and with his arms hanging at his side, he says, "If it'll make you feel better, go ahead and hit me again."

She balls her hands into fists and grits her teeth. She tries to maintain control, fearing what might happen if she lets herself go.

He puts his hand on her chest and shoves her back. "Hit me."

"Don't touch me!"

He shoves her again. "Hit me!"

Everything turns red for her, and she swings wildly at him, striking his face, arms, and chest. She has no conscious thought but feels like a wild animal, wanting to rip and tear him to shreds. At some point, she becomes aware of hot tears coursing down her face, which makes her even madder, and an unearthly cry erupts from her mouth.

Several minutes later (a passing of time she's unaware of), Hope finds herself curled up in Justin's lap, with his arms folded around her. She stirs and tries to sit up but finds herself too weak to do so.

"So, you're back?" he asks.

"What do you mean, 'back?'"

"Well, you sort of disappeared for a while, kind of like you were somebody else and then passed out. Do you remember what happened?"

Hope closes her eyes and tries to find the memory. "It's weird, I remember you coming in the house and sitting down, but nothing afterward. How long have we been sitting like this?"

"We've been here for a bit, I guess, not sure how long." He helps her sit up, and she faces him.

"What do you mean I was somebody else?" She then sees a scratch and small trickle of blood above his eyebrow. Frowning, she touches it gently and asks, "How did this happen?"

He gives her a small smile. "I cut myself shaving."

His effort to lift the tone of their conversation falls flat when Hope says, "Quit! You're always trying to make a joke out of everything. Be serious, and tell me what happened. The last thing I remember is you coming in the house because you wanted to see how I was doing."

A wary look comes over him. "Well, I kind of messed up when I came in, because I sat down in the recliner and asked if you had cable, which was a stupid thing to do."

"Now I remember, and it made me mad." She tries to let the memory play out, but it dissolves into blackness. "I can't remember anything after that. What happened?"

Justin pauses, then takes a breath and relates to her how she attacked him. At the end of the story, he says, "You just sort of ran out of steam and slid to the floor like you were a helium balloon out of gas. So, I picked you up and sat with you here in the chair."

She has a difficult time imagining the scene as Justin described it and slowly shakes her head. "I assaulted you, and that's how you got that cut over your eye. Justin, I'm so sorry. I don't know what came over me, or why I did what I did."

"You don't have to apologize. It wasn't no big thing. I mean, you didn't hurt me. What I'm wondering is if you're okay now." He holds her chin between his finger and thumb. "How do you feel right now?"

"I'm upset over what I did. I've never done anything like it in my life. Oh sure, I've felt like doing it a hundred different times, but I've never actually gone through with it."

"Yeah, but you ain't never lost a daughter before either. That and the way she died..." His voice trails off.

Hope remembers the note from Luther, looks around, and spots it lying on the floor. Pointing, she says, "Luther left me a note before he went on the boat. It says the sheriff told him Lisa was pregnant when she died."

"You didn't know?"

"No, I had no idea."

This time, it's Justin who frowns. "And you don't know who the father is?"

She shakes her head.

"Do you think it had anything to do with why she...you know..."

"Hung herself?"

"Yes."

"I don't know."

"Maybe he was a jerk and told her he wasn't going to have anything do to with her, or maybe he said he'd deny the baby was his. He could have started bad rumors about her. What was her boyfriend's name? I can talk to my friend, Ron, who's the resource officer at the high school, maybe he saw or heard something, or maybe I'll just go find the kid and beat the crap out of him."

"You're right. We need to find out who the father of the baby is."

Justin looks confused. "Don't you think it's her boyfriend?"

She feels her face turning red with embarrassment. "I didn't know she even had a boyfriend."

"Well, her girlfriends will know. You can ask them."

Hope's embarrassment deepens. "I don't know the names of any of her friends, or even if she had friends." In a voice barely above a whisper, she adds, "We never talked about stuff like that."

CHAPTER TWELVE

SLIPPING OFF HIS NECKTIE AND loosening his collar, Jed Rochelle says loudly, "Hey Liz, have you heard from anyone who went to the Rodriguez girl's funeral? I wonder what kind of job Brother Michael did."

She steps out of her walk-in closet while tugging on a T-shirt.

Jed can't help admiring how trim she is and how dedicated she is to being healthy.

Pulling her long hair out from the collar of her shirt, she says, "I haven't heard, but I'm sure Clara Hindsver went, and she'd be more than happy to give you a critique." She smiles, and he returns the smile.

"The woman is a professional funeralgoer, if there ever was one. I wanted to go myself, but I wanted to go see Mark work out with the new baseball coach."

She walks to him and drapes her arms on the top of his shoulders. "Please remember, just because he's our son, doesn't mean he enjoys playing sports. You push him too hard sometimes."

"The boy has the potential to make it in the

big leagues if he'd just work at it. I don't know where he gets his lazy streak from. He sure didn't get it from either of us. I just hate to see people waste their potential."

She moves closer and presses up against him. "What's more important, to be successful or to be happy?"

It's a question she's posed to him before, especially when he'd spent seventy to eighty hours a week working on a proposal for a client and became cross and snappy with her and Mark. "Why can't a person be both?" he counters. "I'm successful, and I'm happy, aren't I?"

Giving him a light kiss on the cheek, she turns around and heads out of the bedroom. "Aren't you what?" she asks as she passes through the doorway. From the hallway, her voice echoes, "A person can be both, I'm just not sure that describes you."

He cringes. One of things about Liz he both appreciates and hates sometimes is, she doesn't tell people what they want to hear just for the sake of being nice to them. Unlike him, she doesn't B.S. people. All their friends say, "If you don't want to know what Liz thinks, then don't ask her."

She could never make a living in my line of work.

As for her line of work as a hairdresser, he tries not to show how strongly she feels she's wasting her talents. The closest he's come is telling her she could do so much more with herself. Her reply of "I'm happy doing what I'm doing, and I make other people happy. Why should I do something that might mess it up?" was maddening to him and made him wonder if it was her example that was blocking Mark from reaching his full potential, though he'd never say so to Liz.

Jed follows Liz into the kitchen, where she's pouring Ragu spaghetti sauce into a pan on the stove. Though some of his buddies might complain about eating sauce from a jar, he's simply thankful she's willing to come home from a long day at work and fix anything.

He takes three plates out of a cabinet and sets them on the counter. Trying to sound nonchalant, he asks, "Do you think I'm successful?"

A momentary pause passes before she answers, "Depends on how you define success, and what area of life you want to assess—your work? Or as a husband? Or as a father? Or your walk with Christ?"

Feeling frustrated with her, he answers, "You and your multi-point questions. Does it have to be complicated? I feel like I'm a defendant on the witness stand." But as is usually the case, her pointed question makes him look more closely at himself.

The longer he doesn't answer her, the louder the silence in the kitchen grows. He finally blurts out, "Anybody who can pull in a six-figure income in this small town would have to be considered successful. There are lots of guys in Paducah who are in the insurance business like me who don't make near as much money. I'm proud of what I've been able to do, aren't you? I mean, you like this new house and your new BMW, don't you?"

She takes a pot and begins filling it with water. "I'm not trying to make you feel defensive, Jed. I just think you sometimes get carried away with yourself and lose touch with your feelings."

"And that sounds like some Dr. Phil or Oprah crap. Everything is not about feelings. It's about performing well, meeting goals and challenges, being the best. It's what I want Mark to learn and do." He feels his face getting red and knows his blood pressure is probably going up.

I hate how she stays so cool about everything and I end up being on the verge of a coronary.

He watches her set the pot on the stove and drop some pasta into it. Turning to face him, she leans her elbows on the island between them and fixes him with her eyes. Her silence squeezes more words out of him.

"I think I'm a good husband. I don't talk down to you, I let you buy just about whatever you want, and I certainly have never hit you, like some men do their wives. I would never do anything to hurt you."

The whites of Liz's eyes begin turning red, and he knows he went too far. A feeling like he's being stabbed in the chest brings tears to his eyes, and he drops his head.

In a quiet voice, he says, "I know you'll never get over what I did, but like I've told you ever since, I've never done anything like it again, and I don't intend to. I would say I'll never do it, but one thing I remember from the marriage counseling we went to is, no one knows what they'll do given the right set of circumstances. The best we can do is say what we never want to do."

Her warm hand tugs on his, and he looks up at her.

She says, "And what I remember from our counseling is, you had the affair because you weren't happy, and you thought she'd make a difference. Ever since then, I've tried to pay attention to your happiness and for signs you aren't. I also learned I can't make you happy, no matter how hard I try, and that's a very helpless feeling for me." Tears pool in her lower eyelids until she blinks and sends them running down her cheeks. Letting go of his hand, she straightens up and swipes at her cheeks. "And I don't know why I'm getting so emotional." She turns to the stove and stirs the steaming pasta.

Jed's mood plummets like a skydiver whose parachute won't open. He knows the landing that awaits him is the familiar bog of guilt and self-recrimination. He presses his hands against his temples.

How in the world did we go from my question about Brother Michael and the funeral, to Mark, to me and Liz?

He shakes his head in an attempt to find a way to move the conversation away from such treacherous shoals, but nothing comes to him that won't sound like an obvious attempt to take the spotlight off himself.

Just then, they hear the sound of the front door opening and closing. The footsteps tell

Jedd Mark is home. Thankful for the diversion, he calls out, "Hey Mark, we're in the kitchen, come on in here."

Mark enters the kitchen and immediately goes to Liz at the stove and gives her a hug. "Gosh, that smells good. I'm starving."

Mark is the perfect blend of his parents' physical features, with Jed's athletic build and smile and Liz's height, fair skin, and eyes.

Jed says, "I thought you had a good workout with coach Skiles today. What did you think?"

In a disinterested tone, he answers, "I guess it was okay." He quickly follows with a question to Liz. "How was your day at work?"

She smiles at him. "It was really nice. Thanks for asking."

Jed notices how quickly and easily Mark and Liz engage with each other, so he tries again. "Did the coach have any comments about your workout or offer you any tips you've never been given before?"

"He told me I need to focus less on speed and more on location."

"How stupid! If you'll develop a hundred-mile-an-hour fastball, colleges will be lining up at the front door to sign you. Why, some teams in the majors might go ahead and sign you now."

Mark shrugs his shoulders, opens the refrigerator, and takes out a pitcher of tea. "You want some, Mom?"

"Sure," she answers.

"What about you, Dad?"

"Fine, me, too." He tried to keep from

sounding short but is certain he wasn't successful. *Why has it become so difficult to talk to my son?*

"What about school?" Liz asks. "Anything going on there today?"

While pouring the tea, he says, "School is just one boring day after another."

"What's the talk around school about Lisa Rodriguez?" she asks.

"Who?"

"Lisa Rodriguez, the young girl who committed suicide."

"Oh, yeah, I really didn't know her. I mean, in a school our size, everybody knows who everybody is, but it doesn't mean they really know them. Anyway, best I could tell, she didn't fit in with anybody at school. You know, her race and everything." Liz shoots him a look, and he quickly adds, "I'm not saying it's right, but there are still people who are racist about certain things. I mean, she was Hispanic, but she wasn't; she was black, but she wasn't; but she definitely wasn't white. So how was she going to fit in with a predominantly white student body?"

Jed knows he should feel uncomfortable about the tone in Mark's comments, but he can't find any reason to object to what he's saying.

Liz says, "And the Jews killed Jesus because He was, what? A Jew who didn't think like the rest of them? A Jew who treated Gentiles and Samaritans as if they were equal to Jews? If Jesus was a student in your school, how do you think He would have treated Lisa Rodriguez? And do you think if you or your friends had treated her like He would have, would she have killed herself?"

Even though Jed wants to jump in and protect Mark from this stinging cross-examination by his mother, he holds his tongue because he knows she's right, and there's wisdom in her words. He marvels again at how wise his wife is and readily acknowledges she's the better parent because of it. He watches as Mark appears to deflate.

But Liz isn't finished. "I don't know what I'd do with myself if anything like that ever happened to you." At her confession of fear, she breaks down and begins sobbing.

Mark touches her on her shoulder. "Mom?"

She turns around, throws her arms around him, and buries her face into his neck.

Jed rushes to them and wraps his arms around them both, hugging as tightly as he can.

CHAPTER THIRTEEN

ADJUSTING MICHAEL'S NECKTIE, SARAH SMILES and says, "Are you ready for your first day at the office?"

He returns her smile. "I think I am. A new place, a new work, a fresh new start—I feel good about everything. I'm curious to see what kind of secretary I'll inherit. My dad used to say a church secretary can make or break a pastor; they're more like an institution than a hired employee."

"I bet she's really nice. Everybody I've met so far has been friendly, especially the members of our church family. The only thing bothering me is how few people attended that girl's funeral."

"I'll have to agree with you. I want to be subtle and ask around about it. Our church needs to be known as the church with a heart, a church always responsive when there's a need in the community. Maybe my first sermons need to focus on, you know, setting a vision and an identity for the church."

Sarah's eyes sparkle. "Sounds like the Spirit is already planting seeds in your heart. You know what we always say, 'If the Spirit is knocking on the door, you better not ignore it.'"

He chuckles and nods. "Very true." He gives her a quick kiss and heads out the door.

In his car, the smell of his stacks of books in the back seat greets him. Many of them were used by his dad when he was a young preacher. "I don't use them much anymore," his dad told him. "I think you'll get more use out of them than me. Just don't get enamored with books written by men. There's only one book that matters, and that's The Book."

Glancing in the passenger's seat, he sees the Strong's concordance he placed there early this morning. He immediately thinks of the phone, then of Brittany. Deep in his gut, he feels torn between what he wants to do and what he ought to do.

Don't be a fool! Just don't open the book, and you won't risk the chance of calling or texting her. Leave it be!

He quickly puts the car in reverse, backs out of the driveway, and heads to the church building.

Once he arrives there, he parks, gathers an armload of books, and heads toward what he assumes is the main entrance, where the offices are located. He's pleased to find they have a security system involving a camera and speaker. He presses a button and waits.

A screechy voice, sounding like someone learning to play a violin, says, "State your name and why you're here."

"I'm Michael Trent, the new pastor." He tries

to smile, but keeping his grip on the books requires all his attention.

"State your birth date, please," the voice says.

What the—?!

He starts to snap an answer but manages to control his tongue. He states his birth date matter-of-factly.

"Just a moment," the voice replies.

A few moments pass before he spots a white-haired woman using a walker, heading toward the door.

Oh my Lord, please do not let this octogenarian be the church secretary.

She adjusts her glasses, which are secured around her neck by a decorative chain, and peers at him through the glass door, then unlocks the door and slowly backs out of the way. Pushing the door open with his hip, Michael eases inside and gives the woman a plaintive smile.

"Good morning, I'm Pastor Trent. I'm looking for Sister Vincent and the offices. If you could just point me in the right direction–"

"Well, you've already met her, because I am she." She slowly turns herself around while saying, "Once I get this ship turned around, you can follow me. I'm recovering from hip replacement surgery. I know what you're thinking, 'Why in the world does this church with a new building have such an old secretary?' That's because nobody's got the brass to fire me. Besides, I'm good at what I do. I actually know how to use a computer and put together PowerPoint presentations for Sunday and Excel spreadsheets for the treasurer. I even do most of my shopping online, so I don't have the hassle of dealing with poor customer service. I used to be a school teacher, in the days of the three Rs, and was a principal for twenty years. Once I retired, I was approached about taking on the secretary's job here."

Michael tries his best to keep up with all the details she's throwing his way, because he gets the feeling she's going to give him a test on it somewhere down the line. The muscles in his arms and shoulders are burning and begging him to find a place to set down the books. Unfortunately, he can't find a polite way to tell her to hurry along. So, he shuffles along behind her, even as he feels drops of sweat running down from his temples.

Eventually, she ushers him into an office he supposes is hers. Three closed doors are to the left of her desk: one's labeled CONFERENCE ROOM, another has the name PASTOR RANDOLPH on it, and the third door has no identifiers attached to it.

She stops in front of the door with the PASTOR RANDOLPH sign. "This is your office. I know, I know, the sign needs to be changed. Pastor Randolph was our former pastor. One of the deacons was supposed to have changed out the sign and put yours on the door, but one thing you'll learn is, if you want to get something done, do it yourself. Church members are eager to get things done in a hurry, except when it comes to church business. I'd have changed it myself if not for this blasted hip surgery." She grips her walker with her right hand and pushes open the door with her left. "Welcome to your new home."

Michael steps past her, spots an empty desk, and quickly unburdens himself from his load of books. He then takes a moment to give an appraising view of his office. He's pleasantly surprised by what his nose tells him is a fresh coat of paint on the walls. A red-leather loveseat and two matching armchairs form a sitting area on one side of the office, while a similar desk chair sits behind a large mahogany desk. Two walls are lined with empty bookshelves.

"Wow, this is nice, Sister Vincent."

"Don't call me Sister Vincent. Everybody calls me Helen. I'm the only Helen I know of in these parts, so if anyone ever mentions my name, you'll know it's me. And another thing, I'll call you Brother Michael. I'm not crazy about the title 'pastor.' Makes it sound too much like he's the one in charge, and if there's another thing I've learned, it's one man should never be put in charge of a church." Giving a wave of her hand, she adds, "But that's just my opinion, and who am I? I'm just the church secretary, and a woman. I'll leave you to getting yourself settled in. If you want some coffee, there's a coffeemaker in my office. I don't drink coffee, so you'll have to make it for yourself; I don't make coffee for you."

Michael watches her turn herself around and head to her desk. Part of him wants to burst out laughing at this odd, plain-spoken woman, but something tells him Helen isn't the kind of person you laugh at without consequences.

When he goes to his car to get another armload of books, he forgets about the church door closing and locking behind him. Again, he has to press the button to get Helen to open it for him.

Her unmistakable voice comes through the tiny speaker. "State your name, and why you're here."

Leaning down, he puts his face a few inches from the camera. "It's me, Helen. Michael Trent."

"Please state your Social Security Number."

This time, exasperation gets the best of him, and he says her name sharply. He then stops himself, apologizes to her, and says, "My Social Security Number is four, two, two—"

Helen's cackling laugh interrupts him. "Got you on that one, didn't I? I'll be there in a minute."

Feeling foolish and embarrassed, Michael waits patiently, with an extra apology on the tip of his tongue.

After she unlocks the door and he pushes through it, he says, "I am so sorry. I shouldn't have spoken so sharply to you. I think I'm still fatigued from all the changes of the past few days."

"Apology accepted," she answers matter-of-factly, "though none was needed, because you can't hurt my feelings. I don't care enough about you to let you do that to me. Besides, I was just funnin' with you."

While he rarely, if ever, finds himself at a loss for words, Michael doesn't know what to say. The fact that the church secretary just told him she doesn't care about him seems preposterous. Apparently, his plan to create a caring church is going to have to start twenty feet from his own desk.

For the next couple hours, Michael finishes unloading his car and arranging his books on the shelves by organizing them according to subject matter: commentaries, sermons, devotional, apologetics, funerals, counseling. This last section is the one area he feels the least prepared for. He took a class on counseling, but the teacher focused mainly on the moral pitfalls pastors must avoid, specifically becoming overly involved with someone of the opposite sex. Unfortunately, this is the very boundary Michael had crossed at his previous church. And while he'd promised Sarah he wouldn't counsel church members anymore, he knows it'll be expected of him to perform the service. His trepidation about counseling isn't about fearing he'll cross a line with a counselee again, it's how can he counsel an individual or couple when his own life and marriage are in tatters.

He finally sits down in his office chair and holds the last unshelved book in his lap—Strong's concordance. Opening the book, he stares at the phone, then runs his index finger over the smooth edges.

Oh Brittany, how much easier it would be if we just ran away together. I don't know if I'm cut out to do this kind of work.

He decides he'll send her a brief text, without the intention of going any further, maybe a quick "thinking of you" text.

Just as he lifts the phone out of the book, the phone on his desk rings. He jumps, drops the phone back into its hiding place, and slams the book shut. Like a frantic child trying to hide a cookie he secreted from the kitchen, his eyes cast about, looking for a place to hide the book.

The phone rings again, and Helen calls to him through the open door of the office. "You're supposed to pick it up and answer it."

He feels his face burning and is glad she can't see it. Picking up the receiver, he says, "This is Michael."

Helen answers, "Your wife is on the line for you. Do you want to take the call?"

Simultaneously, he answers yes and drops the book in the bottom drawer of his desk, shoves it as far to the back as he can, and slams the drawer shut. He cringes at the loud report of the drawer and knows Helen has to have heard it and wonder what's going on.

While trying to formulate an explanation if she asks him about it, he speaks into the phone, "Hi, sweetheart. Is anything wrong?"

Sarah replies in an icy tone, "Why do you always have to think something's wrong? I'm just calling to see how things are going and to ask you about your new secretary."

Yeah, right. You just want to know how old the secretary is and how attractive she is.

He lets out a sigh.

"And don't give me a sigh like I'm the worst person in the world or something. What's wrong with a wife calling her husband? Is it your guilty conscience making you so defensive? I swear, Michael, if you mess up again, I'm done with you."

He shifts into damage control by saying, "I'm sorry, Sarah; I shouldn't have reacted the way I did. I'm happy you cared enough to check in with me." *Even though it's a lie.* "I've just finished getting all my books on the shelves. It's a really nice office—roomy, with expensive furniture, and a fresh coat of paint on the walls." In a passive-aggressive move, he intentionally leaves off describing Helen just to see if Sarah will bring it up, because he's certain she will.

"That sounds nice," she says. She then pauses before asking, "And what do you think about the secretary?"

Again, he knows what she really wants to know, but he wants her to say it. "I think I'll be able to work with her. She seems pretty informed on the workings of the church and probably knows everyone's backstory, so that'll make her an important resource for me."

A longer pause passes as he waits for what he knows is coming.

"Sounds...like she...can be helpful," Sarah stammers. "I'm just curious..."

Here it comes.

"What does she look like?"

"Does it really matter? I mean, she's the secretary, no matter what she looks like. It's not like I can do something about it. At some point, you're going to have to get over not trusting me and always thinking the worst about me. I made one mistake, and you're making it seem like that's the kind of person I am twenty-four-seven. You've got to let things go and move on." It's much more than he intended to say, and his heart is pounding as he finishes.

I'm getting sick and tired of being quizzed about every step I take.

He waits for what he expects will be a furious and defensive response from Sarah. Instead, though, he hears her crying.

"I know you hate me, Michael, and I don't blame you. You'd be better off without me. I try not to make you miserable, but it seems like every word out of my mouth ends up having a sharp barb on it." Her next words are swallowed up by her sobbing.

A wave of guilt strikes Michael, and he says in a low voice, "Sarah, please don't cry. I'm sorry I spoke in a mean way to you. I guess I'm just overwhelmed by all these changes. Trust me, when you meet this secretary, you'll realize you have nothing to worry about."

When he finishes, he looks toward his office door and sees Helen standing there with her walker.

CHAPTER FOURTEEN

THE ALARM ON HOPE'S PHONE chirps to wake her up, but it could have saved its energy, because the solace of restorative sleep has eluded her ever since Lisa's death. She listens to the rhythm of the alarm and discovers it matches her heart rate. Just as she starts to get up, her depression wraps its arms around her, pinning her in the bed. Anxiety pounces on her chest and demands she take a deep breath, but she can't. Tears leak out of the corners of her eyes as she braces herself for an approaching panic attack.

"Will you please turn that damn alarm off?" Justin growls at her.

His voice startles her, and it takes her a second to remember she's in a motel bed with him. Thankfully, though, this brief mental diversion is enough to short circuit her rising panic. She turns her head and looks at Justin's hairy, hulking back. Sneaking around behind Luther's back to be with Justin used to be exciting, just like sneaking around with Luther behind her former boyfriend's back was fun for a time.

More than once, Justin's asked her to leave

Luther and move in with him. This time, however, she promised herself she isn't going to walk away from a man just because she's bored with him. Carol Ann and Whitney have accused her of being a serial monogamist, but only because they see her with one man at a time without knowing she's already established a relationship with a new man before she dumps the old one.

I'm good at starting, just not finishing.

Justin rolls over, faces her, and lets out a big sigh filled with the odor of stale beer, Doritos, and onion dip. "Are you still going to the school today?"

She squeezes her eyes shut at the stench, but it's her nose she wishes she could have pinched shut before being engulfed in the odor. "Go brush your teeth," she says and pushes herself to a sitting position on the side of the bed.

"Oh, yeah. Sorry."

As he walks into the bathroom, Hope runs her fingers through her hair and thinks about his question. She has only one more day of her three-day-bereavement leave from work—*three days. What a joke! As if anyone recovers from a death in three days, especially the death of a child. I won't be recovered in three* thousand *days.* But if she wants to go to the school to get some answers, then today's the day.

The bathroom door opens, and Justin walks out in his favorite outfit—nothing. Hope has had some boyfriends she thought looked sexy naked, but Justin is definitely not one of them.

"Have we got time for a quickie?" he asks.

Her desire to avoid just such a thing is enough to push her into action. She brushes past him on her way into the bathroom. "I've got to get a shower and head on over to the school."

Through the door, he asks, "Are you mad about something?"

"Just because I don't want to have sex with you, doesn't mean I'm mad."

Pulling off her T-shirt and panties, she turns on the shower and steps in. The cold water shocks her awake, and she forces herself to stand there until it warms, then she relaxes in the spray.

"Hey, you want me to go with you to the school?"

She starts to tell him to leave her alone, but then she thinks about how having a man with her might make the school officials take her more seriously. She hates the scornful, dismissive way she's looked upon sometimes either, because she looks too young to have a daughter Lisa's age, or because of how unhealthily thin she is and they assume the worst, or because she's a single mom.

"Sure," she answers as she begins soaping up. "I'd appreciate it."

Hope and Justin sit on one side of a large table in the school's conference room. A rather faded picture of Washington crossing the Delaware is on one wall, while on another wall is a picture of wild ducks cupping their wings to land on water as two hunters crouch inside a duck blind, ready to shoot.

On the other side of the table, Heather Brown, the guidance counselor, sifts through a sheaf of papers on her lap. She glances at a small watch pinned to her dress and says, "I'm sure Mr. Biddle will be here any moment. He was on the phone with the superintendent."

Hope's mouth is so dry, she can't swallow, and she can't stop her right leg from trembling. She crosses her legs and sticks her hands between them to warm them up.

She's surprised when Luther speaks up. "Looks to me like talking to a woman whose daughter committed suicide would be more important than anything else. Maybe he's trying to hide something and that's what he and the superintendent are talking about."

Hope can't help smiling inside at how astonished the guidance counselor looks.

Good for you, Justin.

Just then, the door to the conference room opens, and a man in a white dress shirt and bolo tie, khaki pants, and tennis shoes enters. His close-cropped red hair gives him the look of being ex-military. Hope can't make out the design on his tie clasp until he reaches across the table to shake her hand, then she recognizes it as a silver eagle inlaid in turquoise.

"Ms. Rodriquez, I'm Lloyd Biddle, the principal. I just want you to know how sorry everybody here is about what happened to Lisa. Such a sad, sad thing."

Hope manages to extricate one of her hands

from between her legs and offers it to him without enthusiasm or warmth.

He looks at Justin. "You must be Lisa's father. I'm so sorry for your loss."

Justin replies, "Whether I'm her father or not is none of your business. I'm here to help Hope find out what was going on with Lisa that made her take her life."

The principal takes a seat and looks from Hope to Justin with raised eyebrows. "I'm sorry, is there a problem here I'm unaware of? I sense some hostility or something."

Hope immediately dislikes him for trying to put her on the defensive. "The problem is, my daughter is dead, and I'm wondering if there were signs people here noticed but didn't do anything about." She hopes her voice doesn't sound as shaky as she feels inside.

Ms. Brown's eyes dart to Mr. Biddle, then return to her lap.

The principal leans forward, rests his forearms on the table, and focuses on his hands as he laces his fingers together.

Hope notices his fingernails are chewed to the quick, giving the ends of his fingers a stubby look.

"When things like this happen," he says, "everybody tries to figure out the why of it and ask themselves if there was something they could have done to prevent such a tragedy. I know I've asked myself this." He pauses, then lifts his head. "I imagine you've asked yourself if you could have done anything to have stopped her."

Hope feels gut punched. To question and accuse yourself in silence is one thing, but when someone who doesn't know you throws the accusation at you, it reinforces the judgment that you're to blame.

Yes, it's my fault, she wants to scream but can't find her voice.

Ms. Brown speaks up. "I think what Mr. Biddle is trying to say is, there's never just one reason why suicide happens." Her voice is tentative, and it's obvious she's purposefully trying not to look at the principal.

The tops of his cheeks turn pink, but he keeps looking at Hope.

Hope senses friction between the two of them and wonders what it's about.

In an irritated tone, Biddle says, "I said what I meant to say."

Justin slams his palm on the table, causing everyone to jump. "If you two want to have a pissing contest, how about doing it some other time? Hope here wants answers to some questions."

The principal's face turns crimson. "Do I need to call my school resource officer down here?"

Justin laughs. "Seriously? He and I are buddies. You think he can do anything? I work security and know exactly what he's equipped to do and what's he's not allowed to do. If he shows up in here—"

Hope interrupts him by placing her hand on his arm. "Calm down, Justin."

He rubs his hand across his face and sits back in

his chair. "I'm sorry for getting loud. I just don't want a bunch of B.S. being thrown around and us end up leaving here and knowing nothing more than we did when we came in. Hope deserves more than that."

Mr. Biddle imitates Justin's move and sits back. "I suppose we're all feeling rather emotional. This is the first time I've had a student commit suicide." His face softens, and he looks at Hope. "How is it we can help you?"

Hope remembers going to the Macy's Thanksgiving Day Parade with her family and a marching band passing by them. As the bass drum approached, she could feel her body vibrate with each strike of the mallet. It's how she feels now, with her heart beating so hard, she feels it throughout her body. Out of her mental list of questions, she draws out one.

"Ms. Brown, did Lisa ever come talk to you about problems she might be having?"

"Lisa was never a problem student for us. I don't recall any teacher ever talking about a problem they had with her. She seemed to be a quiet girl who mostly kept to herself."

"That's what I'm talking about right there," Justin says. "This is B.S. You must not have listened to Hope's question, because your answer had nothing do with what she asked. She asked you if Hope ever came to talk to you about problems."

Setting her papers on the table and sliding them away from her, she says, "Ms. Rodriguez, students come to my office all day long to talk about a wide variety of things, some of which may seem trivial at the time, but other issues that are life and death sorts of things. I often go home at the end of the day with a very heavy heart. The thing is, my conversations are confidential, to the point of being protected by law; it's why they feel free to come talk. So, I can't tell you if Lisa came to see me or not. I know it's not what you want to hear, but that's just the way it is."

The slender thread of chance Hope's holding on to to find an explanation for Lisa's suicide begins slipping from her grasp. Anxiety pours into her throat as silence fills the room. She feels tears coming but doesn't want to cry because she's afraid she won't be able to stop.

Justin speaks up. "Isn't there some kind of loophole to the confidentiality thing, like if someone's going to kill themselves, don't you have to report those things?"

"Yes. If I believe someone is going to kill themselves, harm someone else, or if I learn about child abuse, I have to report that to the authorities." She looks steadily at Hope as she says this.

Hope senses she's trying to tell her something without saying it out loud. She sits up, runs the guidance counselor's words through her head again, and something clicks.

"So, that means Lisa didn't talk to you about wanting to commit suicide. Is that what you're saying?"

Ms. Brown's eyes briefly dart toward Mr. Biddle before she says, "What I've said is really all I can say." She pauses, then says, "I was going to clean out Lisa's school locker today, but perhaps you'd like to do it yourself."

A mixture of excitement and dread creeps into Hope's chest, and she nods her head. "Thank you...and I was wondering if I could talk to some of Lisa's friends?"

Mr. Biddle cuts in, "If you'd give me a list of their names, I'll see if I can get the parents' permission for you to talk to them."

This is one of the parts of this visit to the school Hope was dreading most. Sitting back in her chair, she says quietly, "I was hoping...you all could tell me...who her friends were. Lisa and I have been...sort of...you know, distant lately."

A bell in the hallway rings, and Mr. Biddle says, "I'm sorry, but we're going to have to cut this short. If you'll wait in the office lobby, Ms. Brown will get you a box where you can put Lisa's things, and she and I will see if we can put together a list of her friends for you."

Justin reaches for her arm and helps her to her feet.

Once they exit and the conference room door shuts behind them, Ms. Brown says to Mr. Biddle, "She deserves to know the truth."

He tips his chair sideways toward her so his face is inches from hers. "And I told you, if you value your job, you'll keep your mouth shut."

CHAPTER FIFTEEN

HOPE SITS IN SILENCE IN the front passenger seat of Justin's truck, holding a box in her lap loaded with the items from Lisa's school locker. He's trying to engage her in light banter as he drives, but it's like when she's at home with the TV playing, just to have some noise going in the house—she's paying no attention to it.

When she stood in front of Lisa's locker, she wasn't sure she was going to have the courage to open it, fearing disturbing secrets were held inside the metal crypt. The inside of the locker was a small mirror image of the way Lisa kept her room—cluttered, with no apparent system of organization. She heard Lisa's voice in her head, "But I know where everything is. Don't bother it!" It was a battle Hope had finally given up on. Experience had taught her she was no match for Lisa's strong will, so much so that Lisa had basically been making her own decisions for herself since she was a pre-teen. Hope's rationalization for abdicating her parenting role was that her depression siphoned away most of her energy, leaving her just enough to help her work a job.

Emptying Lisa's locker one item at a time was like performing an autopsy, because each thing she touched seemed to pulsate with the spirit and energy of Lisa. Halfway through the procedure, her eyes were so blurred, she started grabbing and dropping items into the box. Once, when Justin tried to step in and finish it for her, she whirled on him and slapped him across the face. What she was unaware of was, a bell had rung, and the hallway was full of kids changing classes. The sudden silence of the crowd brought her to her senses, and she saw shocked faces standing in a half-circle around her and Justin. It was all she could do not to attack them, too, and tell them to leave her alone. What she really wanted to cry out was, "Do you know why my daughter took her life?" But instead, she turned back to harvesting the vestiges of her daughter's life out of the locker, while Justin shooed away everyone.

Justin touches her arm, and she jumps. "What?" she cries out.

"Are you even listening to me?" he asks.

"Leave me alone."

"I was just asking you where you wanted to go? The motel? Your place? My place?"

"Take me home." *That's a laugh. I haven't had a home since I left New York.*

After Mama T's suicide, Hope and Lisa were placed together in a foster home, but Hope didn't trust the system not to take Lisa from her eventually, so she took the paltry sum of money left to her and got on a bus, with the intent of traveling as far west as she could go. Her money ran out when she got to Paducah, Kentucky, a city she couldn't even pronounce correctly. As soon as she could, she got a boyfriend, who was actually a man twice her age, but she didn't care, because all she was looking for from him was a safe place to live. A couple years later, when a younger man started showing her attention, she left the older man and started living with him.

And that's the way it's been ever since. The serial monogamist. She laughed aloud at the misnomer.

"What's so funny?" Justin asks.

"Nothing."

When they arrive at Luther's place, Justin shuts off his engine and starts to get out.

"Don't get out," Hope says.

He gives her a surprised look.

"I don't want you to come in. I just want to be alone for a while."

"Are you sure?"

"Yes, I'm sure." She opens her door, but he holds her by her arm.

"You're not thinking about...I mean...you're not going to..."

She gives him a curious look, then it dawns on her. "No, I'm not going to kill myself, if that's what you're thinking. I just want to be alone with Lisa's things, and alone with myself."

"You promise?"

"Yes, I promise. Now let me get out."

He releases his hold on her. "Will I see you at work tomorrow?"

"Probably. My three days are up, aren't they?"

She doesn't wait for a reply to her rhetorical question and pushes the car door shut with her foot.

When she enters the house and shoves the door shut with her hip, a wave of emotion hits her so strong, it causes her to stumble. She falls to her knees, sets the box on the floor, and curls into a ball on her side. She feels as if someone is rubbing her heart against a coarse grater and all its pieces are falling into her bowels. Squeezing her eyes shut, she holds fast against the tide until she gives out and gives in. Tears and wails gush from her.

She's uncertain how long the episode lasts, but when she opens her eyes, she sees by way of the windows evening is well on its way. Sitting up on the floor, she discovers some of her hair is wet—*tears, saliva, sweat, all the above?*—she's uncertain, but it wouldn't surprise her if it was her blood, reminiscent of a story she remembers from church about how Jesus was so overwhelmed with grief, He sweated blood, a claim so fanciful at the time, she believed the priest made it up. But that was before she'd been to grief's basement.

What was it the priest quoted Jesus as saying? "'If it be possible, let this cup pass from me?'" Yes, that was it.

And if I was a praying person, it would be my request, too.

A silent witness to what's transpired, the box holding the contents of Lisa's locker sits on the floor, staring at Hope, its top yawning open, inviting her to peer inside.

Hope returns the stare. Finding the courage to empty the locker was one thing, but now to dissect each and every item? How bad can it be?

Very bad!

Can it hurt worse than losing Lisa?

I don't know. Maybe.

What are you afraid of?

Finding a truth I didn't know.

Her mind plays tug-of-war with her until she hears the voice of Mama T. "Buck up, kid, get on with it."

At this urging from the past, she walks on her knees to the box and peers down into it. Multi-colored spiral notebooks lie at odd angles and look up at her, tempting her to search their content for clues. Hope reaches in, pulls them out, and lines them up on the floor. The covers reveal only the class subject they were dedicated to, written with a bold marker in Lisa's unmistakable curlicue handwriting, and her name is printed on the upper right-hand corner.

For several moments, she flips through the pages of each notebook, but all she finds are class notes adorned with doodles in the side margins. One recurring doodle is of a magnifying glass sometimes projecting a beam of light onto an insect and burning it up, and other times the glass is filled with large, magnified letters that never seem to spell anything.

The next items out of the box are the heavy textbooks, which Hope holds upside down by the front and back cover, shaking them from side to side to see if any hidden pieces of paper will fall out. Other than a few candy wrappers, the books hold no secrets.

At the bottom of the box lies a rumpled shirt that, when Hope pulls it out, reveals itself to be a pale blue, long-sleeve denim shirt she doesn't remember ever seeing. She looks at the tag and learns it's for a large male. The collar is frayed, and so are the cuffs at the ends of the sleeves. She frowns at the shirt.

Whose is this or was this?

Pressing it against her face, she sniffs it and learns three things: the shirt was worn outdoors a lot, the man or boy it belonged to wore a fragrant cologne, and there was the faint scent of Lisa. The surprise of it pushes Hope back, and new tears spring up. She quickly wipes her eyes with the shirt and lays it aside.

It's then a tiny corner of a piece of paper peeks out at her from the pocket on the front of the shirt. She lifts the folded piece of paper from its hiding place and opens it.

This is for the times we can't be together. Think of me when you wear it.

The printed message has no signature but looks to be a male's handwriting. Questions start lining up like Christmas shoppers at the Wal-Mart check-out lines.

She had a boyfriend? Why didn't she tell me? Is this a recent gift from the boy? Does he know something he's not telling anyone?

She pushes the pause button on the questions and thinks for a moment.

Or is this from a long-lost boyfriend she couldn't let go of?

"Oh, Lisa," she says out loud, "I wish I'd been a better mother to you."

When she returns to explore the contents of the box, her eyes alight on a business card of some kind. She inspects it and finds it's for a tattoo parlor located in Bardwell. On the back of it is the now familiar doodle of the magnifying glass burning an insect.

What does it mean? What was she trying to say?

Hiding in one corner of the box is a tiny plastic bag, which, when Hope inspects it, she finds contains a white powder of some kind.

Drugs?!?

This one shocks her, because she thought her own past dalliances with drugs prepared her to be alert to any signs Lisa might be getting involved. But then her damning conscience speaks up.

Why should you be surprised? It's just one more thing you didn't know about your own daughter.

All that's left in the box are three blank, sealed envelopes. For reasons unclear to her, these frighten her more than anything else she's found, and her hand trembles as she takes them out. She decides to open the less bulky one of the three and finds a single sheet of paper folded in half. Unfolding it, she recognizes Lisa's handwriting:

I walked along the edges of darkness until I fell in
I sipped the poison for years until I gulped it down
It let me pretend for a while until it took my mask

away

I thought I could keep on living until I decided I couldn't

If it had been a pulsating neon sign, Lisa's message of "depression" couldn't be any clearer to Hope. But over the past twenty-four hours, she's been wondering if depression was the only thing that drove Lisa to take her life.

Her depression couldn't possibly be as bad as mine. She didn't suffer the kind of losses I have.

Perhaps one of the two remaining envelopes will finally shine some light on what was really going on.

She opens the thicker of the two envelopes and sees several small, folded pieces of notebook paper. Holding the envelope upside down, she shakes it, and they float down onto her lap. The first piece of paper she opens has one word written in a bright red marker—*Cunt!* The next one says *Loser!* The next one—*You don't belong here!* By the time Hope gets to the last of the dozen or so messages, all in the same vein, she feels both nauseas and furious. *Bullying!* She'd known in her heart this had to be part of what had been going on with Lisa; she just wasn't prepared for how vicious it was.

These people need to be held accountable!

She stuffs all the messages back into the envelope and then opens the final one. It appears empty until she sees lying in the bottom what looks like pieces of confetti. After pouring the pieces onto the floor beside her, she picks up one of the pieces and sees three or four handwritten letters on one side. On another piece she reads, *I was*. On every piece are letters, some spell words, but most are only partial words. Hope wonders if it's a letter Lisa was going to send but tore it up instead, and if so, who was it to? Or is it a letter she received? But if she tore it up, why didn't she throw it away? But mainly, *what does it say?*

CHAPTER SIXTEEN

WITH HIS ELBOWS PERCHED ON his desk and face resting on his hands, Michael reads from the open Bible in front of him, trying to find the perfect text for his very first sermon at his new church.

Help me see it, Lord.

He's reading from the book of John, having started in the first chapter and now finishing up the third. As he turns the page and begins the fourth chapter, his eyes light up at the familiar story of Jesus's encounter with the woman at the well.

"That's it!" he says excitedly.

"Sounds like you've found something." The unexpected male voice from the doorway of his office startles Michael. "Sorry," the man says as he approaches him, "I didn't mean to scare you. I guess you didn't hear me knock."

Michael stands up to meet the man who has a face of an aging bulldog and the body to match.

"I'm Price Jenkins," he says as they shake hands. "I'm the treasurer of the church. Yes, the treasurer's name is Price. Kind of ironic, isn't it?"

"He holds the purse strings," Helen calls through the open door, "but he's no Judas."

"Thank you for the ringing endorsement," Price calls back. To Michael he says, "You'll get used to her. She's as independent as a goat on a concrete pasture, but she has a good heart, and she can be trusted, which is perhaps the most important trait a church secretary can have."

"My father says they can either make or break a church," Michael replies.

"I never thought about it that way, but I suppose there's some truth to it, especially if your dad said it. I've heard him preach before. What a powerful man he is."

"Thank you." Waving toward the sitting area of his office, Michael says, "Want to sit and visit for a minute?"

"Sure. Does your office suit you?"

"Oh yes, very nice. I appreciate the new coat of paint and the nice furniture."

"Good. We want you to feel welcome and needed. I understand there was a good number of our members who helped you move into your house. I would have come to help, but my wife, Toni, is not well."

"I'm sorry to hear that. Is it serious?"

"She suffers from fibromyalgia; don't know if you've ever heard of it."

"I've heard of it but don't know much about it."

"For her, it's a debilitating pain that comes on without warning and can last for days or weeks, keeping her confined to bed. But then she can have good days and function normally. One of the frustrating things for her is, to look at her, you'd think there's nothing wrong with her. People just don't understand." He shakes his head, and his eyes look a little sadder.

"I hate it for her," Michael comments. "As far as getting moved into my house, you're right, there was a host of people. It really meant a lot to me and Sarah to be welcomed in such a warm way."

"That's good," Price says. "We have a lot of really good people in this church. We've all come from other churches around here, where we became disillusioned with how things were being done and have become a real community. I've never been happier at a church."

"I'm pleased to hear it. My hope is, I can become a part of you and encourage you to continue what you're doing."

Price's face contorts a bit, and Michael decides it's his best effort at a smile. "We're hoping for the same thing." He reaches inside his sport coat, withdraws an envelope, and hands it to Michael. "I'll be needing your tax information so I can pay you. We pay every two weeks. Also, inside the envelope is a gas card you and Sarah can use whenever you want to."

"Wow, how nice; I didn't expect that."

Price's face takes on an even more somber expression. In a quieter voice, he says, "We really want your relationship with us to work. I don't know if you know what happened with our previous pastor, but it nearly destroyed us."

"Actually, I don't know."

"He was an amazing, dynamic, charismatic man. He had a heart for our Lord, and for serving others. And he got involved in the community—president of the Lion's Club, substitute teacher at the schools, board member on the chamber of commerce—he was everywhere, and everybody liked him."

Wow—a hard act to follow. Instead of sharing his thoughts, Michael waits to hear the rest of the story, because clearly something happened. When Price doesn't proceed, he says, "But—"

"Yes, 'but,'" Price resumes. "What we didn't know is, he suffered from a bipolar disorder, and he wasn't following his doctor's advice on taking his medication. He became more and more manic and at times looked and sounded like a mad man. We tried talking to him, but he wouldn't listen. It was like he became enthralled with himself and believed he was above being accountable." He pauses again. "But his glass house came crashing down when women started coming forward telling of affairs he was having with them, two of whom were members here."

At the mention of an affair, Michael feels his face growing warm and fears Price will notice him blushing.

God, I hope Sarah doesn't hear this story. She'll beat me over the head with it.

He manages to say, "What a horrible thing for a church to go through." He also remembers the comment by the state trooper the other day.

"Like I said, it nearly broke our church to

pieces. We need you to help us heal from the hurt."

Michael thinks about his original idea to preach lessons on being compassionate servants to others. "I wonder if the way to healing could be by focusing less on the hurt and more on being Jesus's hands and feet in serving others. When I look at His walk on Earth, that's what I see Him doing—ministering to the sick and those who'd lost hope."

Price holds up both hands. "You're the pastor and know best. I'm not at all trying to tell you how to do your job. If God's hand is on you, then you'll do exactly what we need. I'll trust Him on that one." He stands up. "It's good to meet you, and I look forward to hearing your lesson on Sunday."

Michael wonders if he shouldn't have spoken so quickly about what he thought was important but rather should have listened more to Price's thoughts. He hears his father intoning, "Nothing takes the place of a good listening ear."

As Michael turns to walk Price out of his office, Jed strides through the door, flashing a smile, with another man trailing him. "Good morning, Brothers." Speaking over his shoulder, he says loudly, "I somehow snuck past the sergeant-at-arms out there."

"My advice, Bother Michael," Helen calls back, "is to always keep a pair of wading boots in your office, because when Jedediah Rochelle comes to see you, you're going to need them to keep from being taken under by the hubris."

Even Price finds this funny and joins in laughing with Jed and Michael.

"I still love you, Helen," Jed says.

"But do you love me more than yourself?" she answers.

Michael marvels at Helen's candor, because he's already come to suspect Jed thinks a lot of himself. But he's also wondering what's prompted Jed to stop by his office.

Jed winces. "There's no way to get ahead of that woman. I couldn't do it when I was in school, and I can't do it now." He laughs again. When he stops, he motions at the man with him;. "Michael, I'd like you to meet Lloyd Biddle, the principal of our high school. Lloyd is also one of our charter members here at the church and donated the land to build the church on."

Shaking his hand, Michael says, "Nice to meet you."

"Welcome to Bardwell," Biddle replies.

Jed looks from Michael to Price and says, "I guess you two have gotten acquainted?"

"Yes," Price says. "I gave him the gas card and some tax things to fill out for me."

Michael waits to see if Price will tell Jed about filling him in on what happened with the last pastor, and when he doesn't, he puzzles over why.

"Good," Jed says. "We want to get everything started on the right foot, don't we?"

Michael isn't sure if the question is meant for him or the other two men, and when neither of them says anything, he comments, "Absolutely.

Everyone wants the first bite of a meal to be a good one."

Biddle, who Michael assesses to be a no-nonsense kind of person, says, "Never heard such an expression before, but it's a true one." He nudges Jed. "We've got to get to that meeting."

"Sure thing." He offers his hand to Michael, "I just wanted to swing by and see how things were going, and to let you meet Lloyd here. I'll leave you in the good hands of Price."

"I was just leaving," Price says as he moves toward the door.

Michael shakes their hands and watches from his doorway as they leave. He's about to return to his desk when Helen says, "Get used to it."

"Used to what?"

"To people dropping by."

"I don't mind. I want people to feel like they can call on me anytime."

Helen purses her lips. "Mmm-hmm. It's what you say now because it's all new and fresh and exciting, but if you don't learn to say no and shut your door, you'll never last."

"You're actually the second person who's told me that since I've been here."

"Told you what?"

"That I won't last."

"I didn't say you won't. I said you won't if you don't take measures to protect your time. If you want me to be your gatekeeper, you just let me know. We can work out a system where I can defer people to come back at another time."

Michael treads carefully, not wanting to hurt

her feelings. "I really appreciate your advice and willingness to help, but I think for right now we'll just keep an open door policy."

She shrugs. "Up to you."

Sitting down at his desk, he thinks again about Price not letting Jed know he told him about the previous pastor. *Was it because Biddle was with him? Is there something Price doesn't want Jed to know?* Then a new thought pops in his head. *Did Jed stop by because he saw Price's car and wanted to know what we were talking about?*

His eyes fall back on his open Bible. *I've got to get some studying done.* But a light knock on his door pulls away his attention.

Standing there is Liz Rochelle, with her hair pulled back in a French braid, sunglasses resting on top of her head. She's wearing a turtleneck sweater, which makes her neck look impossibly long.

Flashing a smile, she says, "You busy?"

Michael is thankful his first thought didn't jump out of his mouth, because it definitely would have been inappropriate.

She's so beautiful, it hurts!

He motions her in while standing up. "Sure...I mean...no, I'm not busy. Come right in. How are you, Liz?"

"I'm doing well, thank you. I just thought we should put our heads together and talk some about what your plans are for this Sunday."

"Plans?"

"Yeah, like, what is your lesson going to be about?"

Still trying to catch up to the meaning behind her question, he stammers, "Well, I'm still sort of working on making up my mind." He gives her a puzzled look.

She laughs. "Oh my, you don't know, do you? I'm in charge of the music at our church."

The picture quickly becomes clear for Michael. "I had no idea, and strangely enough, I hadn't even thought about it, though I certainly should have. You put the music together for the service?"

"Yes, I direct the choir and praise band." She gives him a warm smile. "You and I are going to be spending a lot of time together."

CHAPTER SEVENTEEN

MICHAEL WIPES THE EVIDENCE OF his pleasure off the rim of the commode in his office bathroom, tosses in the toilet paper, and flushes. Riding high from the euphoria of his self-made orgasm, his mind continues to be filled with fantasies of Liz.

When she'd shown up at his office a couple hours ago and told him about her role with the church, he'd almost swallowed his tongue. And during their meeting, it took every bit of his self-control to rein in his impulses. Experience had taught him the importance of going slow with someone he saw as a potential for hooking up with. He paid attention to personal space and never initiated a movement toward her unless she made the first move to show him something, like she did when she leaned toward him, pointing to a piece of music in her hand. When he mirrored the degree of her posture, he came close enough to smell her hair.

Is that jasmine?

Whatever it was, he'd never smelled anything so alluring—unless it was the whisper of perfume she was wearing.

He lifts his arm to his nose and sniffs his sleeve. His eyes slowly close, and he smiles at the now familiar fragrance of Liz.

Stepping to the sink, he begins washing his hands and splashes some cool water on his face. When he straightens back up and sees his reflection in the mirror, all his pleasurable fantasies and feelings evaporate, replaced by a harsh, damning voice and wave of guilt.

What is wrong with you? You're a servant of God, chosen by Him to lead others to Him. Hell—that's what you deserve—hell fire and brimstone.

It's an emotional roller coaster he's all too familiar with: temptation, the excitement of chasing it, the thrill of embracing it, followed by a choking volume of guilt and shame, a volume so great, the only way he can pull out of it is by looking for another temptation.

He begins to weep and sinks to his knees. Clasping his hands in front of his face, he whispers, "Holy Father, You know my struggle, and I know I don't even deserve to call You Father. I am the vilest of sinners and deserve whatever punishment You choose to inflict upon me. But I'm begging you." His voice catches in his throat, and he waits until it clears. "I'm begging you as sincerely as I know how, please forgive me for what I've just done, and for the thoughts of what I wanted to do. Deliver me from this affliction Satan has cursed me with. I want to do right; I promise I do. I want to be the kind of child You can be proud of."

He falls silent, hoping to feel something—anything—that will let him know God is listening and has touched him with a measure of healing. But as with every other time he's uttered various versions of this same prayer through the years, he feels nothing, except lost.

Gathering the tattered pieces of his soul, he stands up, runs his fingers through his hair, and heads back to his desk. Not until he leans back in his chair does he see Helen in the doorway of his office.

"I'm heading home," she says. "Is there anything you need from me before I leave?"

"Uh...no...no, thank you. I'll see you tomorrow."

She turns and shuffles away without replying.

Not even a goodbye?

Suddenly, he feels very tired. *Dad always said emotional fatigue is much worse than physical fatigue.* So, he decides to head home.

Before leaving his office, he puts his Bible in his leather shoulder bag and adds a couple sermon outline books. His eyes are drawn to the bottom drawer of his desk, and he thinks of his secret phone. "No!" he says emphatically. "I'm not going to do it. Get thee behind me, Satan!" And he walks quickly out of his office.

When he enters his house, he hears a loud clang coming from the kitchen. Making his way there, he says, "Sarah, are you okay?"

In the kitchen, he smells chili cooking, and

he finds Sarah picking up the lid of a pot off the ceramic tile floor.

She smiles up at him. "I love this tile floor, but my goodness, it makes everything so loud." She straightens up, and he gives her a kiss. "Well, how was your first day at your office?"

On the drive home, he'd already decided he wasn't going to tell her about Liz coming by, because he didn't want to have to deal with Sarah's reaction. "Let's see, it was great, challenging, and interesting, and it was embarrassing."

"Sounds like you've got some stories to tell. Chili's just about ready. Why don't you change into more relaxing clothes while I put it on the table, and we can talk about it while we eat."

"Good idea."

He gives her a peck on the cheek and heads to their bedroom. When he enters, he stops short.

What the—?

Hardly any of the boxes have been emptied or their contents put away like he expected them to be. A smattering of clothes lie scattered on the floor, and the open doors of the closet show him their empty rods. Checking the labels on the boxes, he finds the one he's looking for, tears it open, and fishes out a pair of sweat pants and University of Kansas T-shirt. Next, he finds the box with his shoes in it and takes out a pair of tennis shoes.

As he changes clothes, his frustration rises. *What's she been doing all day? Watching TV? Playing games on her tablet?* But his mental tirade against Sarah is interrupted by the ever-present, ever-accusing voice in his head. *And what have you been doing all day? Fantasizing about another woman and masturbating?*

As he stomps out of the bedroom, he kicks a box, knocking it over on its side and causing it to spill its contents of Sarah's shoes.

And she spends too much money on shoes!

In the short distance between the bedroom and kitchen, he decides he's not up to having a row with Sarah, so he decides not to mention her lack of effort around the house today.

But as soon as he walks into the kitchen, Sarah says, "What's wrong?"

The question irritates him, because he doesn't like her being able to read him so easily. "Why do you always ask what's wrong? There's nothing wrong." His sharp rebuke shuts her off like he hoped it would.

Taking a seat at the table, he picks up a piece of cornbread, butters it, and takes a bite as he waits for her to place his bowl of chili in front of him. The combination of the warmth of the bread and mixture of its sweetness and the butter's saltiness relaxes him.

"Mmm...I love eating warm bread. This is delicious."

Sarah sets the chili in front of him and sits down across the table from him with her own bowl. Smiling, she says, "I'm glad you like it."

He offers a brief prayer of thanks for their food, and they both eat in silence for a few moments.

She breaks the silence. "So, tell me about your interesting day."

He relates to her in detail all that happened, except for Liz's visit.

"You are going to have to work at winning Helen over," she comments. "Even though she didn't say anything about it, I'm sure she didn't like your comment about her that she overheard."

"I agree with you, but I don't think she's the kind of person who's easily won over."

"Maybe you should take her some flowers tomorrow. Women like flowers."

He tries to remember the last time he bought flowers for Sarah, but he can't recall. He makes a quick mental note to do so tomorrow.

"That sounds like a good idea. And should I even make a reference to my comment and make some kind of apology for it?"

"You might make it worse if you do that. If she wants to bring it up, then let her. But I think you should just move forward." She pauses. "And I'll try to drop in and meet her. It might help."

He smiles. "Another good idea." Without thinking, he asks, "How was your day?"

Her crest-fallen look tells him the question was a mistake. "I tried to get some things done around here, but I just couldn't make myself. Every time I'd walk into a room to unbox and organize it, it just felt overwhelming, like I couldn't even find a place to start."

Outwardly, Michael expresses sympathy. "I'm sorry you had a bad day." But inwardly he's tired of this oft-used excuse. "Have you been taking your Prozac?"

With an edge in her voice, she answers,

"Why do you want to blame everything on my depression?"

"Because when you're depressed, it's hard for you to get going and get things done."

"It makes me gain weight."

"But it helps your depression." He wonders how many times they've uttered that couplet since they've been married. *Countless times.* "Look, church members are going to be dropping by to welcome you, and they're going to want to see the house. You know how important first impressions are. I just don't want them thinking badly of you."

She gives him a hard look. "Why can't you just be honest? You don't want them to think badly of *you*. If I'm not the perfect homemaker, then they'll wonder what's wrong with you that you're married to someone like me."

"That's not true."

Waving her hand and rising from the table, she says, "Whatever." She dumps her chili into the trash and heads toward their bedroom. "I'm going to put our bedroom in order so you'll be happy."

The sarcasm in her voice is impossible to ignore. With rising anger, he lies, "Don't do it for me. I don't care what this place looks like." He eats a couple more bites of chili, but it sticks in his throat, so he throws away the rest of it. As he's putting his bowl in the sink, he hears her heavy footsteps coming hurriedly down the hallway.

She enters the kitchen carrying the shirt he

wore to the office. Her eyes are wide, and her face is red. Waving the shirt in the air, she screams, "What is this?"

Even for Sarah, this behavior seems bizarre. "I have no idea what you're talking about. You know it's my shirt."

"I'm talking about the perfume it reeks of. Where have you been today, and who have you been with? I told you I wasn't going to put up with you if this happened again."

He takes the shirt from her and sniffs. Visions of Liz instantly appear, as well as thoughts of how badly he wanted to touch her hair. "I don't know what you're talking about. I don't smell a thing." He sniffs it again to reinforce the lie. "You're imagining things again, Sarah."

"I'm the crazy one again, is that it? If there's ever anything you don't like about what I think, do, or say, it's either I'm depressed or I'm crazy. Well, I know good and well what I smell, and it's a woman's perfume, expensive perfume." She slaps him hard across the face, then slaps him again.

He grits his teeth and tightens his fists until he can feel his fingernails digging into his palms. He considers how good it would feel to punch her in the face, to slam her against a wall, to choke her—to be rid of her.

"Go ahead," she taunts him and turns the side of her face toward him. "I know you want to; I can feel it, so go ahead and do it. Make yourself feel better."

Go ahead, go ahead, go ahead, and be done with it.

He starts to cock his arm but instead pushes his way past her, retrieves his car keys, and heads out the door. "I'll be back later," he says as the door slams shut behind him.

CHAPTER EIGHTEEN

TAKING ONE LAST LOOK IN the mirror before heading to work, Hope uses the tip of her index finger to massage the puffy bags that hang underneath her eyes. She's managed to cover up the dark circles by using extra concealer, but nothing has helped camouflage the bags. They were already bad enough from her ceaseless crying, but then she stayed up last night, trying to put the puzzle pieces together from the confetti-like letter she'd found in Lisa's things. It's proving more difficult to solve than a Rubik's cube. At two o'clock this morning, she finally gave in to sleep.

She dreads facing her co-workers and their perfunctory expressions of sympathy. How are you supposed to respond to people who say, "I'm here for you," or "Call me if there's anything I can do," or "It must have been her time," or "It's just God's plan," or the countless other useless things people say to someone who's grieving?

How about replying: *No, you're not; There's nothing you can do; How do you know?; I want nothing to do with that kind of God.*

The only person she feels like has been honest with her about their own feelings and hers is that preacher who did the funeral, and she can't even remember his name.

Walking out of the house to get in her vehicle, she's unprepared for the thick fog that greets her.

How perfect! The weather gods just couldn't resist sticking it to me, could they? Giving me a little sunshine was too much to ask.

At Three-Rivers Casino, she pauses before going inside and watches the flat, gray Ohio River as it moves silently past. Ever since she moved to Paducah, she's been drawn to it. No matter if the water level is high or low, it silently and relentlessly heads toward the end of its life by emptying itself into something bigger and stronger—the mighty Mississippi. She finds it difficult to comprehend how the Mississippi can swallow all that water without creating a flood.

I wish I could do that with Lisa's death—swallow it and act like nothing ever happened.

Taking a deep breath, she opens the employee's only door and steps inside. She doesn't want to make eye contact with any co-workers, so she keeps her head down and eyes focused on the floor. In spite of that, several speak to her, offering those generic terms of sympathy she hates. Instead of challenging their sincerity, she mumbles a thank you and moves quickly toward her office.

Just when she thinks she's made it, the familiar voice of Cara Hernandez, the casino's human resource director, says, "Hope, I'm so glad to see you."

Hope looks up at Cara. Not just looks up from the floor, but really looks up, because Cara is easily over six feet tall, with blonde hair in a French braid that always looks perfect, and wearing her ever-present casino wardrobe of navy skirt, white blouse, and Navy blazer with the casino's insignia embroidered on the front pocket. A deep furrow appears between her eyes as she places a hand on Hope's shoulder.

"We've all been so worried about you. I cannot imagine what this has been like for you."

But not worried enough to come to the funeral home. At least she didn't say she understood how I felt.

"Thank you." Hope starts to step toward her office door, thinking this brief conversation is over, but Cara's hand stays on her shoulder.

"Are you sure you're ready to come back to work? I mean, I know we have a three-day grief exception in our employee handbook, but this isn't a typical grief situation. If you need more time, I can make it okay."

Hope thinks it would have been nice to know that before she got dressed and came in to work, but, as is her pattern, she says nothing about the thought.

"I'm fine," she says as she shrugs Cara's hand off her shoulder and moves away.

As she steps through the office door, Cara says, "I'm here for you, Hope. If there's anything I can do, just let me know."

Hope rolls her eyes and closes the door behind her. Carol Ann and Whitney look up from their computer screens. They glance at her, then at each other, then back at her.

"Girl, what in the hell are you doing here?" Whitney asks. "No way you've had time to recover from what's happened. Did Her Majesty, Cara Hernandez, make you come back?"

Hope feels a small smile in her heart at Whitney's derisive comment about Cara, but the smile can't find its way to her face.

Carol Ann walks up to her and gives her a long hug that makes Hope feel suffocated. Seconds feel like minutes as she holds her breath until Carol Ann releases her. When she does, she steps back and takes a deep breath, hoping it'll slow down her heart.

Carol Ann frowns at her. "Are you okay?"

They are the closest thing to real friends she's ever had, which gives Hope permission to be honest with them. "Am I okay? Have I *recovered* from what happened? The truth is, I don't think I'll ever recover, and I'm never going to be *okay* again. So, there's that. I just want to work and get a paycheck. Don't take it personally. I've just got to do this my way, even if it looks wrong to everybody else." She pulls out her chair, sits down, and turns on her computer.

"Go ahead and let it out," Whitney encourages her. "You're not going to hurt my feelings. Of course, Carol Ann, Miss Sensitivity, might get a little weepy, but she'll get over it. I'm right here, no matter what you do and say."

Finally, a smile creases Hope's features as she watches the two of them make faces at each other.

Whitney chirps, "See? I know just what to say to make her smile."

Carol Ann moves back to her desk and sits down with an audible "Oomph." "I may be Miss Sensitivity, but I'm not someone who's been married three times."

Standing up, Whitney says, "Oh no, you're not going to play that card with me." She snatches a piece of paper off her desk, wads it up, and throws it.

The wad bounces off Carol Ann's head, who immediately picks up the phone receiver but keeps her finger on the button and says, "Help! Workplace violence! We need a S.W.A.T. team in the finance department."

Hope can't help laughing—a morsel of light for her darkened soul—and for an instant she forgets about all the sadness and confusion that surrounds her. It's nice to have friends who'll go out of their way to pick you up and carry you through stormy seas.

Carol Ann and Whitney break away from their banter and look at Hope. "It's good to hear you laugh," Whitney says.

"We're going to get you through this," Carol Ann adds, "whatever that means, no matter what it looks like."

"I really appreciate you guys," Hope says. Turning toward her computer screen, she says, "Let's get some work done."

For the next hour, the only sound in their office is the clicking of their keyboards.

It wasn't until Hope started this job that she discovered how much she enjoyed working with numbers. They were predictable and honest, sometimes brutally so, but you couldn't blame the numbers themselves for that. She also came to the realization that if her parents hadn't been killed and she hadn't gotten pregnant and fled New York, she probably could have gone to college and gotten a degree in business or something and had a very different kind of life, a successful life.

She quickly became astounded at how much money people spent at the casino, and even more surprised that the vast majority of patrons are senior citizens. "Granny's got money to burn," is Whitney's explanation.

For the most part, Hope keeps the events of the past days at bay as she focuses on her job. It's when she glances over at a photo on her desk of Lisa that it all tumbles down like a game of Jenga.

"She was pregnant, you know."

Her friends' fingers halt their frenzied pecking, and for a second nothing happens. Then Carol Ann asks, "Who, Hope?"

Still focusing on the photo, Hope answers, "Lisa."

Whitney swears in disbelief.

The two of them get up and walk over to Hope's desk, and Hope spins her chair around to face them. "They did an autopsy and discovered it. I had no idea."

Carol Ann kneels down beside her and takes

hold of her hands as Whitney pushes aside some papers and sits on Hope's desk. "Talk to us," Carol Ann says.

"I don't know what to say about it," Hope replies. "I didn't even know she was dating someone. What kind of mother doesn't know these things about her daughter?"

"My daughter is the same age as Lisa," Whitney answers, "and I'm telling you, it's like she became a different person overnight. With these cell phones nowadays, they can develop their own private world, like a shadow world. I threaten her all the time to throw hers away."

"It doesn't mean you were a bad mom, Hope," Carol Ann adds. "Do you think this had anything to do with her suicide?"

"How could it not? I went to the school to see if they could give me any clues about friends she had or boys she was hanging around. Don't judge me, but I took Justin with me. I thought having a man there might help."

"You just can't stop yourself, can you?" Carol Ann cuts in. "I love you, Hope, but isn't your life complicated enough?"

"Leave her alone," Whitney interjects. "If she wants to have three or four men on the side, that's her business. It's her way of being in control of her life, dangling them like puppets on a string. It gives her power, and I say good for her."

Rather than have a debate, Carol Ann turns the conversation back to the topic of Lisa. "What did they tell you at Lisa's school?"

"They weren't helpful at all. I got the feeling

the guidance counselor wanted to tell me something, but that principal, Mr. Biddle, practically put a gag order on her."

"Biddle?" Carol Ann whispers as her face turns pale.

"Yes."

"What's wrong with you? You look like you've seen a ghost," Whitney says. "You know him or something?"

"Lloyd Biddle?" Carol Ann asks.

"Yes, that's his name. Short-cropped hair, military style."

"Did he have on a bolo tie?"

"Yeah, but how did you know?"

Carol Ann sinks to the floor and has a distant look on her face. "I knew him. He was my high school basketball coach, a really good coach. We won the state championship my senior year, but..."

"But what?" Whitney questions her. "What are you not saying about him?"

CHAPTER NINETEEN

CAROL ANN PULLS HER KNEES to her chin and folds her arms around her legs. "He was a real hands-on coach, lots of hugs, pats on the back, and sometimes on the butt. I really liked him and admired him, maybe I thought I loved him, too."

The room becomes so quiet, the low hum of the heating/cooling unit can be heard as Whitney and Hope wait for her to continue.

She takes a deep breath and says, "My parents found a note he'd given me, and everything blew up after that."

"You mean, you two were having sex?" Whitney asks the unspoken question.

Carol Ann nods. "I thought I was the only one. Turns out I wasn't. My father wanted to kill him, but he and my mom went to the superintendent instead. Coach Biddle was let go at the end of that school year."

Hope's heart hammers against her chest as she tries to take in Carol Ann's story. "But didn't the police get involved, or Children's Services, or something? Wasn't he charged with a crime?"

"It wasn't like it is today, where people are quick to speak up and address those kinds of things. My mother told me they didn't want me to have to go through the public humiliation of a trial, so they agreed not to press charges if the school let him go."

"Holy shit," Whitney exclaims. "That's messed up six different ways. Somebody should have castrated him."

"Oh my God," Carol Ann whispers. "Could he have been the father of Lisa's baby?"

Suddenly, the panic attack Hope's been desperately holding at arm's length overpowers her. She grabs her chest and tries to catch her breath, but her lungs refuse to fill. It feels like an elephant has its foot on her chest and is slowly trying to crush her. She breaks out in a cold sweat and sees stars twinkling at the periphery of her vision.

This is it, this one's going to kill me.

Seizing Carol Ann's arm, she gasps, "I can't breathe!"

"Should we call an ambulance?" Carol Ann asks Whitney. "Is she having a heart attack?"

"No, she's having one of those panic attacks she's told us about. My sister has them. It'll eventually pass, but it would help if we had something, like a paper bag, she could breathe into to keep from hyperventilating."

Carol Ann dashes over to her desk and scrounges around in one of its drawers. In a second, she comes back to Hope with a Victoria's Secret sack.

"Will this work?"

"Yes," Whitney answers as she takes it and holds it up to Hope's mouth. "Just breathe in here. It'll help." Looking at Carol Ann, she says, "Try to find a cool, damp cloth we can wipe her face with."

The paper bag rustles as it inflates and deflates with each of Hope's breaths, while Carol Ann rushes out of the room. Hope's eyes are closed, and she tries to focus on Whitney's voice as she attempts to calm her.

"In...out...in...out...nice, steady breaths. You're going to be okay; it's not going to kill you."

Hope looks up at her and nods.

With a steady voice, Whitney says, "Good girl. Just focus on me, and not what's going on with your body."

In a moment, Carol Ann returns with a handful of wet paper towels, dripping water on the floor. Thrusting them at Whitney, she says, "This is the best I could come up with."

Whitney takes them but shakes her head. "Really?" She squeezes the excess water into a nearby trash can, then gently wipes Hope's forehead and cheeks.

Finally, Hope is able to take in an unlabored breath. Three more similar breaths, and she feels secure enough to remove the sack from her mouth. She gives her friends a weak smile.

"Thank you." A wave of nausea hits her. "I think I'm going to throw up."

Whitney holds the trash can underneath her face. "Let it fly, girl, that's from all that adrenalin that's been surging through your body."

Hope leans forward and wretches, but nothing comes up. Again, she wretches, with the same result. She rests back in her chair.

"You done?" Whitney asks.

Hope nods.

"Look here," Carol Ann says, "you have got to take care of yourself—eating, drinking, sleeping, that's what important right now. I'm going to ask you about it every time I see you, so get prepared."

The door to their office suddenly opens, and Justin sticks his head inside. "Just checking to see how..." Concern flashes across his face when he sees Carol Ann and Whitney hovering over Hope. Stepping inside, he asks, "What's going on? Are you okay, Hope?" He hitches up his pants and joins them.

"Everything is just fine, Cowboy," Whitney answers. "Nobody needs rescuing by you. We're handling it."

Ignoring her, he looks at Hope. "Can I do anything for you?"

Hope runs her fingers through her hair, pushing it back out of her face. "No, thanks, Justin. I'm all right."

"If you say so. But you all better start looking busy, because the big boss is in the building and making his rounds. I hear he's in a sour mood."

"Then get out of here," Carol Ann says, "or you'll be the one in trouble. You've got no business in the finance department." She pushes him toward the door.

As he leaves, he says, "You know how to get ahold of me if you need me."

Hope turns her chair toward her computer screen. "You two, get back to your desks. Maybe we'll talk some more later."

"Don't you worry about that," Whitney says emphatically. "We are definitely going to talk some more about *all* of this."

The rest of the day passes uneventfully, with each of them focusing on their jobs of "making the numbers work," as their supervisor, Faye Harris, is fond of saying. Hope is afraid her friends will try to drag her off somewhere at lunchtime and pry her with questions, but Mr. Horner, "the big boss," ends up treating them to the lunch buffet at the casino. Carol Ann all but force feeds her—"You've got to eat," she keeps whispering.

When 5 o'clock arrives, they simultaneously begin shutting down their programs and computers. As soon as her screen goes dark, Hope's thoughts turn to her empty house and Lisa's bedroom. Today had felt good, having her mind occupied on something else, but the thought of stepping into that house feels like she'll be sliding back into a pit of quicksand.

I just don't think I can do it.

She's certain Justin would gladly let her stay with him in a motel; a motel because Justin still lives with his mother. But Carol Ann's admonition about her duplicitous ways with men had stung, despite Whitney's opposing view.

Still uncertain about what she's going to do,

Hope stands up and finds her friends standing shoulder-to-shoulder and staring at her with resolute expressions.

"You're going with us," Whitney says.

Carol Ann continues the directive. "The three of us are going to go eat at Fast Eddie's, probably drink too much, and we're going to talk."

"Not necessarily in that order," Whitney concludes, with a smile.

The only part of that three-piece-menu of activities that sounds remotely interesting to Hope is the "drinking too much." It might feel good to get really drunk. She surprises them when she agrees without putting up a fight.

"That was too easy," Whitney says. "I was all set to do an MMA move on you and force you into submission." She holds her fists in front of her face, dances on her toes, and fakes a punch. "I could do it."

Carol Ann hooks her arm in Hope's elbow and begins walking toward the door. "Let's me and you get out of here before she makes a fool of herself. Oh, wait—she already has." She laughs as she opens the door and half-drags Hope with her, and they break into a brisk walk.

Whitney calls after them, "You can run, but you can't hide from Whit the Great. The Cinnamon Assassin is on your heels."

◆

Tears run down Carol Ann's cheeks as she says, "I don't know why it happened. I've never talked about it with anyone. He made me feel so special and good about myself. Then, when he got fired, I heard whisperings about other girls he'd done the same thing to. That's when I felt ashamed and dirty."

A waiter sets three drinks on their table and removes the three empty ones. "Are you all wanting to order something to eat?"

None of them looks at him. "Just bring us tonight's special," Whitney says.

Once he leaves, Whitney says, "I'll tell you why it happened. It was because he was a lecherous pedophile, a predator who groomed you. He knew exactly what he was doing. You were just a girl. You have nothing to be ashamed of."

"But if the school system knew about it, how can he still be teaching?" Hope asks.

They all take a sip of their drinks and silently consider Hope's question.

"Yes," Carol Ann speaks up, "shouldn't he at least have had his teaching license revoked?"

"Look, we all know how this works with white men of privilege," Whitney begins. "It's 'one hand washes another,' 'I won't tell if you won't tell,' 'the good-ol'-boys network.' The school system you attended got rid of him, that's all they cared about—'Get rid of him before we get sued.' They weren't concerned about you or any of the other girls."

In a small voice, Carol Ann asks, "Do you think he's still doing it?"

Hope feels the weight in the room tilt in her direction. When she learned Lisa was pregnant, her only thought was that the father had to be a student. But a grown man? A teacher? The principal?! She turns up her drink and drains it before setting it back down.

"Do you all really think it could be? My Lisa and Mr. Biddle?"

"Is there any way to know for certain?" Carol Ann asks.

Hope remembers the torn-up letter but is uncertain she's ready to reveal that detail with her friends. She's finding this all too much to take in.

CHAPTER TWENTY

WIPING SWEAT OFF HIS FACE with a handkerchief, Michael braces himself to greet his church members as they exit the building. In his opinion, his first sermon here couldn't have gone better. It was like God had placed each word on his tongue, like He did the prophets of old. And then when twelve people responded to the altar call at the end of his lesson, he knew he'd hit a home run. He'd never felt so alive, so powerful.

Jed approaches him, beaming. Michael sticks out his hand, but Jed ignores it and gives him a bear hug. "If I had even a tiny doubt you were the right man for our church, you easily erased it today. What an awesome sermon!"

"Thank you," Michael says.

A host of smiling faces line up behind Jed, eager to shake his hand and congratulate him. He expects Jed to ease out the door, but instead he anchors himself beside him and acts more or less like a chief of staff, introducing every person to Michael, telling some anecdote about them. He also manages to mention to several people how he was chairman of the pastor search committee that found Michael, which always prompts a word of praise in his direction. It agitates Michael more than a little, sharing the spotlight as it were, but he keeps a pleasant expression on his face.

One of the last persons to exit is Helen. For some reason, Michael is most eager to hear her appraisal of his sermon, knowing she'll be completely honest.

She doesn't offer to shake his hand. Instead, she keeps both hands on her walker and looks him directly in the eye. "You certainly have captured your father's delivery style, which appeared to be quite effective on the audience. Your content was quite heavy on emotion and a little light on use of scripture, which isn't my cup of tea, but it appeals to the masses nowadays, it seems, which makes it excusable, I guess. We'll see how long you last."

As usual, Michael is at a loss regarding how to respond to her. He hopes Jed will rescue him. But even if he was going to, Helen silences him, too, by saying, "Of course, you want to claim as much credit for yourself as you can, don't you, Jedidiah? Just be careful. If things don't go well in the long run with Michael, you'll find your fortunes sinking, too. Good day to you both."

Michael looks at Jed, whose face is crimson, but whether with anger or embarrassment, it's impossible to tell. For sure, though, he's had enough, as he says to Michael, "I'll see you tonight," and he heads to the parking lot.

Michael takes a deep breath and relaxes, thinking everyone has left, but when he turns around, Liz is standing there. She looks radiant. Her hair flows over her shoulders, and the tops of her cheeks are pink with emotion. Michael's heart quickens.

"You did a masterful job with the music, Liz," he says. "It was inspiring."

Her eyes sparkle as she replies, "You were the one who was inspiring. I've never heard such a moving sermon."

He starts to shake her hand, but she steps close, hugs him, and kisses him on the cheek. "You're going to be a blessing to us all," she says.

Before he can recover and offer a response, she exits the building, calling out to Jed, "Hey, Jed, wait for me."

Michael's imagination is about to take wing until he sees Sarah standing in the doorway between the vestibule and sanctuary. Her face is a mask of disgust. He knows what she's thinking, and he hates her for it, hates her because she's probably right. Ordinarily in these kinds of situations, she would accuse him of lustful thoughts, and he would vehemently deny them—their personal "dance of deception." But now, he knows she knows the truth, and she knows he knows she knows the truth. Even if per chance he wasn't having untoward thoughts, his denials mean nothing to her, so what's the point of trying.

They drive home in chilly silence, until halfway there she says, "You really outdid yourself with this morning's lesson."

It's the last thing he expects her to say. He hopes it's her attempt to get past their problems and focus on making things better. "Thank you, Sarah. That means more to me than the praise of anyone else."

But just as he's enjoying this relaxed moment between them, she adds, "It just shows that God can still use evil people for His Will, just as he used unbelieving King Nebuchadnezzar to punish the disobedient Jews in the Old Testament."

The sting is too much for him. He snaps, "How can you blame me for Liz kissing me on the cheek?! I didn't know she was going to do that. I was as shocked as you were by it."

Sarah retorts, "Why would she be comfortable enough to kiss you in the church building unless she'd kissed you before now? You definitely didn't push her away or tell her not to do it again, and we both know why."

Michael feels like he's losing his mind. This is just another version of the same conversation they've had scores of times. Running his hand through his hair, he says, "Maybe she's just that kind of person, really demonstrative, and she does that with everyone. I don't know. I do know you're going to believe whatever you choose to believe, and there's nothing I can do to change it."

"You have no idea how badly I want to believe you, how often I pray God will help me believe you. Living in my tortured mind is sometimes more than I can bear—it's hell. I wouldn't wish it on my worst enemy, but I wouldn't mind you living it for just one day, so you can experience my level of despair and hopelessness."

Her words and tone trigger alarm bells in Michael. He pulls into their driveway and shuts off the engine. Turning to her, he says, "You're not thinking of hurting yourself, are you?" *That would be just my luck. After having the best start possible to my new ministry, she kills herself, and the church lets me go.*

As if she's reading his mind, she says, "Worried about your job, aren't you?"

He starts to protest, but she stops him by holding up her hand.

"I won't say I haven't thought about it," she says. "But don't worry, I'm not that desperate—yet." She gets out of the car, slams the door shut and goes in the house.

MICHAEL: I JUST DON'T KNOW HOW MUCH MORE OF HER I CAN TAKE.

He's gone back to his office a couple of hours before the evening service, explaining to Sarah he needed to brush up on his notes for the evening lesson, which was true, but he knew what he really wanted to do was text with Brittany.

BRITTANY: I'M SORRY THINGS ARE SO BAD. ONE OF THESE DAYS YOU'RE GOING TO HAVE TO PUT AN END TO THINGS. YOU CAN'T KEEP THIS UP.

MICHAEL: I THINK YOU'RE RIGHT. BUT NO CHURCH WILL HIRE A PREACHER WHO'S BEEN DIVORCED, AND THIS IS THE ONLY THING I'M GOOD AT.

BRITTANY: I WOULDN'T SAY IT'S THE ONLY THING. LOL

Her double entendre doesn't lift his spirits. I'M SERIOUS. IF I DIVORCE HER, THEN WHAT WILL I DO?

There's such a long pause before she replies he wonders if she got interrupted or lost her connection. He checks his phone to be certain he's still connected to the Internet. Just then, he gets a response.

BRITTANY: DIVORCE IS NOT THE ONLY WAY TO PUT AN END TO THINGS.

CHAPTER TWENTY-ONE

"No, Ms. Rodriguez," Ezra Marshall says, "I did not see any tattoos on your daughter when I was preparing her for the funeral."

"Are you sure? It might have been really small. It would have been of a magnifying glass with a beam of light shining through it."

"I'm certain I would have noticed something like that. I'm sorry I couldn't be more helpful. Suicide leaves the survivors with so many unanswered questions; it's just one of the things that makes it such a painful experience."

Hope ends the phone call and exits the restroom stall at work where she's been sitting. She pulls the tattoo business card she found in Lisa's things out of her pocket and decides she'll go there after work. In her search for clues about Lisa's suicide, she's developed a feeling there are answers connected to the figure sketched on the back of the card.

She washes her hands and looks at her reflection in the mirror. The bags under her eyes still hang heavy, so she massages them again.

Whitney walks into the restroom. "What are you doing?"

"Trying to get rid of these bags under my eyes. They make me look twenty years older."

"Well, you're doing the worst thing possible for that. I was taught by a makeup lady never to massage or rub the under-eye area—only pat-pat-pat it with moisturizer or makeup. She said, 'Treat the skin around your eyes like the most expensive silk, very gently.'" She looks around. "Is anyone else in here?"

"No."

"What do you think about Carol Ann's story about Mr. Biddle?"

"It creeps me out. I mean, I've read about that kind of stuff happening, but I've never known someone it happened to."

"Me either. Maybe that explains why she's asexual."

"She's what?"

"Asexual, you know, she doesn't have sex. Didn't you know that about her?"

"No. I knew she never talked about dating, but I figured she just wanted to keep that part of her life private." Shaking her head, she says, "Dang—no sex. Most of the time I can take it or leave it, but sometimes I've got to have it. It makes me feel alive."

Whitney heads into a stall and shuts the door. "Not me, girl. I've got to have it regular and often. Horny is my middle name."

They burst into laughter, and the restroom fills with the echoes.

One of the things Hope likes about Whitney is the sound of her laugh. It's an easy, full-throated laugh that seems to start at her toes and engages every part of her as it works its way up.

She also likes how open Whitney is about herself. *I know so much more about her than she knows about me. But if they knew everything about me...* She shakes her head. *No, it's safer to keep some things to myself.*

Once work is over, she drives to the tattoo shop located in a tiny, rundown strip mall. On one side of it is a pawn shop, advertising chainsaws, rifles, and stereos. On the other side is a vape shop, offering "the latest flavors" and hemp products. Two empty spots round out the mall.

The windows of the tattoo shop are opaque, so the only way of knowing it's open is the red, pulsing digital sign on the outside. Hope opens the door and is surprised at how bright the interior is. Track lighting focuses on sketches of tattoos that adorn the walls, ranging from the simple drawing of a heart to detailed, full-color scenes so elaborate, they remind Hope of paintings she saw as a child when she went on school field trips to museums. Rows of glass cases, containing knives and swords, create an aisle.

"Can I help you?" A young-sounding voice comes from the back corner of the room, and Hope sees an open doorway to the speaker's right that probably leads to the area where the work is done.

Hope's first thought, when she gets closer, is that this person's body is a mirror image of hers. The tattoo artist is so thin, and the well-worn black T-shirt fits so loosely, it's impossible to guess if they're male or female. The dramatic haircut gives no clues either, as one side of the head is clipped close to the scalp and the remaining hair sticks out in the opposite direction, as if it was trying to run from whoever cut the other side so short.

The most obvious difference between Hope and this person is the result of Hope letting a plastic surgeon she was living with years ago do a boob job on her. He'd convinced her it would help her feel better about herself, but he was wrong. He was the one who wanted her to have larger breasts—not Hope herself.

"It's been a while since I've been in a tattoo parlor," Hope says.

"I'm just really getting started. I've got lots bigger plans than this."

Doesn't look much older than Lisa. She notices them staring at her neck where the edges of one of her tattoos is always exposed. She touches it self-consciously.

"I'd be interested in seeing what the rest of that looks like."

It's a line Hope has heard many times since having the tattoo done, but it was always delivered by a hormone-driven male who hoped she'd let him in her pants. This request has nothing to do with that; it's simple curiosity. Instead of taking off her shirt to reveal it, she decides she'll play that card only if necessary.

"I'm wondering if you can do a particular design?"

"If you can draw it, lady, I can do it."

Whether that's true or not, Hope admires the young person's confidence. Taking the pen and paper offered her, she draws Lisa's tattoo. When she finishes, she turns it around to be seen.

Immediately, the confident air disappears, and the person seems shaken, unnerved. They look at Hope, then back at the sketch. Their hands tremble as they hold the sketch.

"Lisa." They say it as if it's a prayer.

Excitement fills Hope. Perhaps here is someone who can tell her about Lisa. "Did you know her?" Like the blow of a sledgehammer, it hits her that she spoke of Lisa in the past tense. How is it possible you can be fully aware of a thing and at the same time act as though it never happened?

"You're her mom, aren't you?"

Hope tries to answer, but her throat is closed off by emotions. Instead, she nods her head.

"I heard what happened. I graduated last year and knew Lisa; we were friends at one time. My name's Greg."

Being this close to a thread that might help her unravel the truth of her daughter's life suddenly scares Hope. Does she really want to know? Will the truth make it worse? Standing on that continental divide between truth and ignorance, she hesitates.

"I...I don't know what to ask you."

Nodding his head, Greg says, "Yeah, I get it. And I don't know what to say to you. I could say I'm sorry, but you've probably already heard that, like, a thousand times from people. I mean, I am sorry for you, but I'm mostly sorry for Lisa. She could never see what a special person she was, never thought she was good enough. She listened too much to what people said."

"Why was everyone so mean to her?"

"You see, that's the thing—it wasn't everybody. There was just this one group of popular girls who didn't like her. My opinion is, they didn't like her because they felt threatened by her. They had to work hard at being pretty, you know, the hair, makeup, and tanning bed. But Lisa was beautiful without working at it."

Hope is touched by his words because they're delivered with such honesty, not just saying it to make her feel better. "Is that what this picture, this doodle, is about? That she felt like she was always under a microscope or something?"

"Yeah. That's why I wouldn't do it for her. I just didn't think it was true. You know, just because you think a thing or feel a thing, doesn't mean it's true."

She considers her own life of living with depression and all the bad choices she's made. "I know that all too well."

A moment of silence passes between them, then Hope asks, "Why do you think she did it?"

Without hesitation, he replies, "Because she couldn't take it anymore."

"Take what?"

"Life!" He spits out the word. "You parents and adults have no idea what it's like for us. This world you've given us is messed up, it makes no sense. My friends and I talk all the time about doing what Lisa did." The brief fire in him burns out, and he adds, "I just didn't think she would do it."

"You said you used to be friends. What happened?"

"I don't know. It was fine until we started getting close." He shrugs his shoulders. "I think it scared her."

This stings Hope. *What more would I expect from her when that's all she's ever seen in me? The fault lands in my lap again.*

"Can I ask you one more thing?"

"Sure."

"Did you know she was pregnant?"

The question knocks Greg off his stool, and he stumbles backward.

His reaction and look of shock give her the answer. "I'm ashamed to admit I didn't know either. They discovered it when they did her autopsy. I'm beginning to wonder if anyone knew about it."

When Greg doesn't reply, she has another thought. "Could you be the father?"

Holding up his hands as if Hope had a gun aimed at him, he says, "Impossible. We never did it, if you know what I mean. I'll admit I wanted to, but she said she was afraid it would mess things up between us. Turns out it didn't matter anyway."

Hope returns to her car outside the shop, feeling deflated. She feels no closer to figuring out why Lisa took her life than before she talked with Greg. All her questions remain. His simple-sounding reason for why she did it is too simplistic and gives her no one to hang the blame on—no one but herself.

CHAPTER TWENTY-TWO

AFTER HER MORNING RUN, LIZ steps into the shower to wash off. This hour or so before she starts her day has become her favorite time of the day. Jed is at the gym, working out, or so he says. It wouldn't surprise her if there are mornings he doesn't make it, but rather meets some of his friends for a big breakfast of eggs, sausage, bacon, and biscuits. Ever since he had a mild heart attack a couple years ago, they promised each other to commit to a healthier lifestyle, and while she's embraced the idea wholeheartedly and come to enjoy it, she's certain he misses his carb-laden, artery-choking comfort food. At first she tried to monitor and control his food, but she soon found that made her miserable.

"It's up to you," she told him. "I'm just going to focus on me."

It was more or less the same thing she had to do after his affair. The hardest thing the marriage counselor told her was, if Jed was going to be unfaithful, there was nothing she could do to stop it. "You're going to have to focus on yourself," he'd said. "Be kind to yourself, do things that bring joy and contentment to your life." That piece of advice had led her down the path of overcoming her own co-dependency, a journey that wasn't easy but resulted in bringing peace in the midst of the chaos being married to Jed sometimes brought.

Stepping out of the shower, she dries off and wraps the towel around herself. She checks on Mark, who's still sleeping soundly. She smiles at how relaxed his face looks, unlike the stressed scowl he carries most of the time when he's awake. Jed and his obsession with having a son who plays major league baseball is the source of that stress. It bothers her that Mark is caught between a tug-of-war between her and Jed, where Jed is always pushing him in a specific direction and she's wanting him to enjoy being a teenager and letting him find what he's passionate about.

Back in her bathroom, she's about to turn on the hair dryer when she hears the back door open and close and the jangle of Jed's keys as he drops them on the kitchen counter.

Wonder whether he'll smell like bacon and sausage, or like sweat.

She turns on the hair dryer so she won't have to hear him fussing at Mark for sleeping in and not going for a workout.

In a few minutes, Jed joins her in the bathroom and starts talking to her. His face tells her he's fuming, but she catches only a few of the words over the scream of the hair dryer. Switching it off, she says, "I really don't want us to get into it this morning. I know you're not happy with Mark, and you know I'm going to defend him, so let's just leave it alone."

He opens his mouth to say something, then closes it. His expression softens, and he says, "Okay." His gaze drops to her towel, and he steps closer and unfastens it, letting it fall to the floor. Because she knows it's one of the things he enjoys doing, she stands still as his eyes travel the length of her body.

Putting one arm around her waist, he pulls her into him. "I must be the luckiest man in the world."

She smiles and kisses him. *Bacon and sausage.*

"Not this morning. I've got to get to work."

"Can I have a rain check?"

"Yes, you may, sir." Winking at him, she goes into the bedroom to get dressed, and he gets in the shower.

He calls out to her. "I didn't ask you what you thought about Pastor Trent's sermon on Sunday?"

She immediately remembers the feeling of exultation that surged through her during the service. "It was inspiring. I've never experienced a feeling like that. The choir outdid themselves and provided a perfect complement to Michael's sermon. I really felt the Spirit moving through both of us."

"So, it's 'Michael,' and not 'Pastor Trent' or 'Brother Michael?'"

She senses the jealousy and suspicion coloring the edges of his question. Although she's never been unfaithful, she learned it's his guilty conscience that fuels those emotions in him. And so, she tolerates it without getting defensive. "He told me since we'll be working so closely together, he preferred I call him Michael. Are you okay with that?"

Rather than be honest with her, he ignores her question. "You're right, the music was amazing. You always do a good job with it, but for some reason this time was the best."

"Thank you."

She hears him turn off the shower and the shower door opening and banging shut.

He says, "I think we may have struck gold this time with our choice of pastors. If we can just get people in the area to come hear him, they'll want to join the church. I'm going to start introducing him around town, take him with me to the diner to eat lunch with all the guys. Honestly, I could see us having to expand the auditorium in a year or so. It's exciting, isn't it?" He walks into the bedroom wearing nothing but his wet towel over his shoulder.

Liz finds it odd that whereas women are the ones known for working in strip joints, based on Jed and what her girlfriends tell her about their husbands, it's men who tend to be the exhibitionists. For her, though, a sharp dressed man is sexier than a naked man.

She ignores his overt attempt to entice her into having sex and walks past him. Bending down to pick up her shoes, she says, "Don't you think we need to pay off the church building we have before we consider adding more space?"

"Yeah, yeah, you're right. I know I get ahead of myself sometimes. It's just exciting to think about the possibilities. Changing the topic a little bit, what's your read on Brother Michael's wife, Sarah? I've tried talking to her a couple times, but she's hard to draw out."

"I agree. Actually, she's been a bit cold toward me."

"Probably because she's jealous."

Liz sighs. "You know, I didn't ask to look the way I do. I can't help it that I'm tall and have a fast metabolism. Sure, I work out and try to take care of myself, but I inherited my looks from my mother. People think it's only people who aren't nice looking who struggle with being accepted by others, but it's been like this for me ever since high school. Girls didn't want to be my friend because they were afraid I'd steal their boyfriend. I kept thinking it would get better once I grew up, but it's still that way. It's frustrating." She stands in front of her full-length mirror for one last look at herself.

Jed joins her, half-dressed, and kisses her cheek. "I'm sorry, honey. If people would just take the time to get to know you, they'd learn how beautiful you are in the inside."

She appreciates him not making some kind of a snide, smart aleck remark and returns his kiss. "Michael and I working closely together isn't going to help things between me and Sarah."

"Why don't you drop by her house for an innocent chat? Let her see how genuine and down-to-earth you are."

"I guess I could. Of course, that could end up going really nicely, or it could blow up in my face. I have a gut feeling there's something else going on with her besides simple jealousy."

Sitting in her recliner that same afternoon, Sarah looks up from the Words With Friends game she's playing on her phone and glances at the clock on the wall.

Oh my gosh! I can't believe I've been sitting here this long. Michael will be home soon and is going to be furious. I've hardly gotten anything done he wanted me to do. And I haven't even started making supper.

She jumps out of the recliner and scurries to the bedroom, where cardboard boxes line the wall and stare at her like jurors who've just returned a guilty verdict against the defendant. Some of them she still hasn't opened, others are only partially empty.

I'm so stupid and lazy! What is wrong with me?

She picks up a couple boxes she's managed to empty and carries them out the front door. Just as she steps off the porch, an unfamiliar car pulls into the driveway.

These better not be Jehovah's Witnesses. I don't have time to talk to them.

When the car door opens and Liz Rochelle steps out, emotions fill Sarah's chest like passengers boarding a plane. Shock, panic, jealousy, anger, and shame crowd their way in, making it hard for her to breathe.

How does she always look so perfect? What's she doing here? Her face begins to burn.

Liz smiles, flashing those flawless teeth of hers. "Hi, Sarah. Looks like you've been busy today."

Which is just another way of saying I look like a wreck.

She resists looking down at the breakfast stains on her T-shirt. She tries to return Liz's smile but is certain it looks fake.

She says, "It seems like the moving boxes fill themselves up overnight, because I can't ever seem to finish emptying them."

"I know exactly what you mean. My dad was in the military, and every two or three years we had to move. I lost count of the number of schools I attended. Starting over in a new place is never easy; at least it wasn't for me."

Sarah is surprised "Miss Perfect" didn't have a perfect life. She knows she should invite her in but doesn't want her to see how little progress she's made putting the house together.

"I would ask you to come in, but everything is still such a mess."

Liz gives a small laugh. "Listen, I grew up living out of cardboard boxes. My mother got so fed up with moving all the time that she quit unpacking the boxes our clothes were in. So, my dresser and chest-of-drawers were boxes. What I learned as an adult, though, was that my mother was depressed back then and just couldn't force herself to take care of the house."

This revelation stuns Sarah, and she marvels that Liz talks about it so easily. "I'm sorry you had to live like that."

Liz waves her hand nonchalantly. "That was a long time ago. I just wish Mom had gone to get some help for her depression."

An awkward pause steps between them as they consider which direction their conversation should take.

Simultaneously, they take a stab at it and say, "Why don't—" stop, nervous laugh, "You go first—" another laugh.

Liz holds up her hand to stop Sarah. "Why don't you let me help you unpack some things?"

Sarah replies, "I was going to ask you in. Some help would be nice."

She hears Michael's voice cautioning her. *Be careful what you share about us with others. People expect their pastor's life to be perfect, and that includes you.*

With that leash and chain around her heart, she escorts Liz into the house.

CHAPTER TWENTY-THREE

DRIVING HOME FROM HIS OFFICE, Michael is so lost in thought, he barely notices any of his stops and turns. *What did Brittany mean? Was her comment an offhand one, or was there something more sinister behind it?* Before he'd been able to ask her meaning, she'd ended the phone call.

There have been moments in the past when he was so exhausted from dealing with Sarah, he thought of murdering her. He even went so far as to fantasize how he'd do it and get away with it. Because of her history of depression, he'd stage it like a suicide. No one who knew her struggles would be surprised.

But I could never actually do it, he always told himself, and he always asked God to forgive him for even thinking it.

Would Brittany do something to Sarah?

Even though he's known Brittany for a year, he really doesn't know her, just that she's sexually aggressive and risqué and has an amazing body—qualities that arouse him and he finds irresistible.

But would she murder somebody? He shakes his

head to try and sling these ominous thoughts away.

Turning into his driveway, he slams on his brakes, stopping within inches of ramming the rear-end of a car. "What the—?" Immediately, he's on guard.

Who's here? Is it someone from church? Is the house still a wreck? What kind of mood is Sarah in, and what kind of impression is she making?

He looks in his rearview mirror to make sure his hair isn't messed up, then exits the car.

There's something familiar about the visitor's car, and as he walks past it, he peers inside. What he sees gives him a jolt; it's pieces of church music.

Oh my God, it's Liz!

All he can imagine is Sarah assaulting Liz the way she's attacked him in the past, full of insecurity and rage.

Why is Liz even here? Is she looking for me?

He quick-steps to the front door, pauses to take a breath, puts on his best 'it's-a-great-day-I-hope-it's-a-great-day-for-you' smile, and walks in. The living room is empty, but the scent of Liz's perfume hangs in the air and teases him to follow it.

He's about to call out to Sarah that he's home when he hears the all-too-familiar sound of her crying. For him, her cries can be classified: the 'whimper' – meant to elicit pity; the 'wail' – meant to arouse the neighbors and embarrass him; the 'sob-can't-catch-my-breath' – from which hyperventilating and passing out often result; the 'monster' – it's full of sound and fury and the one that scares him because of the unearthly sounds she makes and demonic look she has. This one sounds like she's sobbing.

My God, what must Liz be thinking?

He finds the two of them sitting in the floor of the bedroom. Sarah is cross-legged and swaying back and forth, and Liz is on her knees, embracing Sarah. Liz looks up at him with a mixture of relief and 'what the hell is happening?'

Michael is both mortified and furious. *If she causes me to lose this church, I'll—*

He forces himself to stop thinking about long-term solutions and focus on immediate damage control. Kneeling down next to Liz so their knees barely touch, he uses his most soothing voice and says, "Sarah, it's Michael. What's the matter, darling? Have you taken your medicine today?"

She stops swaying and looks at him. "'Just take a pill, and everything will be all right,' that's always your answer. Have you ever considered what's wrong with me can't be fixed by a pill?" Turning to Liz, she asks, "Is this how Jed treats you when you've had a bad day?"

Liz blushes. "It's never a good idea to try and compare problems, Sarah. Your and Michael's situation may be very different from mine and Jed's." She looks at Michael. "I stopped by just to visit, and we started emptying boxes and putting things away. Then Sarah opened up about her struggles with depression, and I shared that I've had issues with depression in the past." She releases Sarah and takes her hand. "I just want to be a friend, Sarah; just a friend."

Sarah looks at her, then at Michael. He doesn't believe in telepathy but still tries to send her a message.

Get ahold of yourself. Don't say anything that might jeopardize my job. Don't ruin things for us.

All the air seems to come out of her, and she sags forward like a tired bean-bag chair. "You just don't understand, Liz. I'm sorry for acting this way. Michael will take care of me."

Michael reaches for a pill bottle sitting on Sarah's bedside table. He checks the label: XANAX 2mg. Shaking one out, he hands it to her. "Here, why don't you go in the bathroom and take this and splash a little water on your face? Everything's going to be okay."

Moving listlessly, she gets to her feet and heads toward the bathroom.

"I'll see Liz out," he says. Standing up, he offers his hand to Liz, who takes it and pulls herself up. He tries to keep himself in check with her, but he finds everything about her attractive – her hair, eyes, lips, neck. Stopping his gaze from traveling further down her body, he says, "I'm sorry you had to see this. I hope it won't change your view of me."

She frowns. "Of you?"

"Did I say 'me?' Oh my gosh, what a terrible faux pas. I meant Sarah." His face burns, and he swears at his stupidity.

For an instant, Liz doesn't look like she believes him. "Of course you did."

He feels exposed and panics a little. When they get to the front door, he says, "Moving to a new place and getting settled in is really stressful. I appreciate you trying to make Sarah feel welcome."

Liz gives him a steady look for a moment, a look he cannot interpret. Sweat pops out on his forehead.

She says, "Come out to the car. I want to give you something."

He follows her, and he chases questions, wondering what's on her mind.

Opening her car door, she leans in and retrieves her purse. Her hand plunges in as she peers inside. In a moment, she pulls out a business card. "Take this. It's the name of a counselor I think might help Sarah. He's really good. Tell Sarah to tell him I referred her."

Uncertainty crowds into him. "Uh...thank you. I'll...I'll be sure and give it to Sarah."

As he stares at the card, Liz gets in her car and backs out of the driveway. When he looks up, she's already driving down the street.

Tearing the business card into pieces, he shoves them in his pocket.

CHAPTER TWENTY-FOUR

AT THE OUTSIDE EDGE OF awareness, Hope hears her alarm going off as if it's an ocean buoy ringing, rocking back and forth on undulating waves and guiding sailors through a thick fog. She tries to reach for the alarm, but her arm is impossibly heavy.

This is going to be a bad day.

Depression has seeped into her bones overnight, and even though her body shape didn't change, she feels as if she's four times her normal size. Getting out of bed seems impossible.

But I've got to go to work, or I'm going to lose my job.

Only a small part of her wants to get up. The rest of her wants to give in to the depression and stay in bed, with the covers pulled over her head.

Last night, her dreams were filled with Lisa—some were pleasant ones that left her pillow damp with tears, and others were nightmares jampacked with ghouls and zombies from which she'd awake terrified and in the midst of a panic attack.

With a Herculean effort, she pushes down her covers, sits up on the edge of the bed, and turns off her alarm. *One foot in front of the other, that's the way to do it.*

Standing up, she heads to the bathroom to take a shower. She starts the water and pulls off her T-shirt. She catches sight of herself in the mirror, something she tries to avoid, and notices her ribs are showing.

Gotta make myself eat.

After her shower, she moves to the kitchen, intending to fix herself a bowl of cereal, but as she passes by the table where the pieces of the torn-up letter lie scattered, she pauses. Following the dead end she ran into at the pawn shop, she threw herself into working on the letter until after midnight last night. So far, she's scotch-taped together these random words or phrases: IT WASN'T; I CAN'T; YOU KNOW IT; LOVE; SORRY.

She slides a few of the pieces around and suddenly sees: IMPOSSIBLE, then YOUR MOM comes together. Excited that she sees these so quickly, she starts to sit down to try and find more but realizes if she does, she'll find it impossible to tear herself away and make it to work. So, she goes to the cabinet and pours herself a bowl of cereal.

Sitting at the table, spooning cereal into her mouth, she looks out the window and is thankful to see a clear sky and brilliant sun. *It's about time.* Based on her own research, she's concluded she has Seasonal Affective Disorder and refers to herself as 'solar powered.' She enjoys this spot in Luther's house because of the east-facing window, so if there's going to be any sunshine in a day, she'll catch the first rays.

Suddenly, a small herd of deer are silhouetted as they cross a soybean field. Relieved that hunting season is over, they move casually. "You're lucky Luther's not here," she says out loud, "or one of you would be hanging from a tree, being field dressed."

She's never understood the obsession men around here have for killing animals. Rabbits, squirrels, ducks, geese, deer, doves, and practically anything else that moves are fair game, as far as they are concerned. Luther has attempted to explain it as a sport.

"Well, then, it's the only sport I know of where something has to be killed," she'd retorted. "And it's awfully one-sided, because the animal never kills the human." The only reaction he'd had to that was to stare at her like she had two heads.

Leaving her half-eaten bowl of cereal on the table, she rises and heads to the bedroom to get dressed. The letter pulls at her as she passes by, but she refuses to look.

Get to work. Get to work.

Justin is standing in the parking lot when she arrives. She really doesn't want to deal with him.

All he's going to want to know is when we can get together again, which means when will I let him have sex with me.

He walks to her car, and as she gets out, he asks, "When can we get together again?"

Two points for me for getting it right.

"I don't like the idea of you being by yourself right now, you know, with Luther being gone and what happened to Lisa."

"And with you being horny and all," she replies as she quick steps past him and heads to the work entrance.

The ring of work-related keys attached to his belt jingles as he attempts to keep up with her.

Hope is certain if she turned and looked at him, he'd be panting like a dog pursuing a female in heat. The big difference, though, is that he, the male, is the one "in heat," and he believes she wants him as badly as he wants her.

She stops and whirls around so quickly, Justin can't stop, and he bowls her over. She lands hard on her hip, causing her teeth to bang shut.

Justin flails his arms in an attempt to avoid landing on top of her, and to catch himself, but being physically agile isn't one of his strengths, and he faceplants on the blacktop just as she jerks her legs to her chest to avoid him landing on them.

The sound he makes reminds her of recordings she's heard of whales, although there's nothing soothing or mystical about his sound; it's sort of like the sound of a dying animal.

She's surprised at how quickly he bounds to his feet in spite of his bulk. A large raspberry has already appeared on his left cheek, and he looks a little dazed.

"Are you okay?" he asks.

She wants to be angry about what happened, but she can't keep from imagining what the whole scene might have looked like to someone watching, so she laughs.

"I think I'm fine, but you're going to have an awfully big bruise on your face."

He gingerly touches his cheek and winces. Looking at his fingers, he says, "No blood, no foul." He reaches down and stands her up as if she were a doll. "I'm sorry I'm so clumsy. I'm just glad you weren't hurt."

Brushing herself off, she checks to see if she's dirty or has any tears in her clothes. Satisfied that everything's in order, she says, "Look, Justin, I've got lots more on my mind than spending the night with you somewhere. Just let me get to work without being late again."

He holds up his hands. "I get it, you're right, I'm sorry. That's not even the reason I was out here, waiting for you to get to work."

She pauses. "Then what?"

"My buddy, Ron, the resource officer at the school?"

"Yes, what about him?"

"He told me Lisa was being bullied by some of the girls at school."

"That's not news, Justin. I know that was going on."

"Yeah, but do you know the names of any of the girls who were doing it?"

"No. Neither Ms. Brown nor Mr. Biddle were willing to share that with me."

"About that, Ron says there's something not right about the relationship between the two of them."

"What does that mean?"

"I'm not sure, but that's still not what I'm trying to tell you. I'm trying to tell you Ron has some names, names of the girls who were bullying Lisa."

Just then, the employee door opens, and Whitney steps outside. Looking at Hope, she says, "There you are! You've got to get in here right now. Hurry!"

CHAPTER TWENTY-FIVE

Hope stands frozen between the desire to hear more from Justin about who was bullying Lisa and being pulled by Whitney's panicky plea. Finally, she says to Justin, "We'll talk later, maybe at lunch." She then hurries toward Whitney. When she gets close enough, she doesn't have to yell, she says, "What's wrong?"

Whitney waves her closer as she whispers loudly, "Just hurry up." She looks around to see if anyone else is close by. Spotting Justin lumbering toward them, she holds up her palm at him. "Stop right there, big boy. You go on about your business, and quit being so nosey."

He stops in his tracks and looks as hurt as a seven-year-old who gets a sweater for his birthday.

Ignoring him, Whitney grabs Hope by the arm and pushes her through the door. With her face inches from hers, she whispers, "Where the hell have you been? I've been trying to call you! She closes her eyes and slowly shakes her head. "Don't tell me—you had your phone turned off again, didn't you?" She fixes her with a stare. "When are you going to start operating like you're in the year 2020 with the rest of us? What's the point in you even having a phone if you don't use it?"

Hope retrieves her phone from her purse and stares at it. "Sorry, I thought it was turned on."

Whitney rolls her eyes. "Please, Hope, darling, you are the worst liar in the world, so don't even try telling me that. You don't even know when was the last time you—" She stops abruptly and expels a breath of exasperation. "See? You got me sidetracked." She looks around. "First of all, you need to get clocked in so you won't lose your job. 'You-know-who' is already on the warpath this morning. Go clock in, and meet me in the bathroom."

Hope stands there for a moment, trying to process everything, until Whitney takes her by the shoulders and turns her around. Nudging her forward, she says, "Go clock in."

Hope winds her way through the back hallways to the time clock and punches in, all the while wondering what Whitney wants to tell her. She reminds herself that her friend can be quite overreactive, so what she has to tell might not be nearly as dramatic as she portrays it.

When she opens the bathroom door, Whitney pulls her inside. Her eyes are wider than normal, and she looks like she's about to bust. "You remember Carol Ann telling us what happened with Mr. Biddle?"

"Yeah, sure I do."

"Well, you won't believe what she's done."

Whitney pauses for dramatic effect, and Hope says, "Will you just tell me?"

"She's hired a lawyer, and they are going to file a lawsuit against Biddle."

"How does something like that work? I mean, it was a long time ago, and the way Carol Ann told us it wasn't like he raped her; it was consensual sex."

She thinks about the series of older men she lived with when she first arrived in western Kentucky as a teenager. In her mind, she'd always thought of herself as being the one who took advantage of them, giving them sex, sure, but they gave her a place to live, bought her clothes, took care of her.

"What are you saying?" Whitney's question pulls her away from her musings. "It's against the law for an adult to have sex with a minor, especially a person in a position of power using that as leverage to coerce them or make them think it's about love and they're so special. It's disgusting! They're depraved predators and deserve to be castrated with a dull knife. Haven't you heard of the MeToo Movement?"

Hope is taken aback by the forcefulness of Whitney's ire, which causes her to wonder about her history. In a quiet voice, she asks, "Did anything like that ever happen to you?"

Whitney looks away. "That's not important."

Hope steps into her field of vision. "Yes, it is, if it did." She waits a moment. "Do you want to talk about it?"

Swiping tears off her cheeks, Whitney says,

"It was my mother's uncle. The man was more like a daddy to me than an uncle. I looked up to him, loved him, would have done anything for him. And ultimately, I did." She shakes her head. "But he's been dead for over ten years, so it don't matter."

"I'm sorry. To be honest with you, this is a really confusing subject for me."

"What do you mean?"

Just then, Faye Harris walks into the bathroom and almost bumps into them. In a clipped tongue, she says, "Good morning. If you've both clocked in, why aren't you at your desks working? And if you aren't clocked in, well..."

Whitney says, "We are clocked in, but my period started on my way to work, and I forgot to bring any tampons with me. Hope was just letting me have one of hers."

Faye looks from one of them to the other. "Very well." She then steps into a stall and shuts the door.

Whitney holds open the bathroom door and nods at Hope to leave.

As soon as Hope enters the office, she senses something is off with Carol Ann, who doesn't look up or speak. Instead of sitting with shoulders squared, like she usually does, they're slumped, and she looks smaller, like she's folded in on herself.

I know that feeling. I just figured she'd be excited, or something, about going after Mr. Biddle. She looks scared.

Taking a seat at her desk, she turns on her

computer and waits for it to boot up. She scrolls through work emails with one eye and tries to peek at Carol Ann with the other.

Whitney walks in and assumes her position at her workstation. After a moment, she says, "Will somebody say something? Jesus—we're acting like strangers."

"I'm not sure I want to do it," Carol Ann says. "My lawyer says I'll have to testify on the stand about all the intimate details of what Mr. Biddle and I did. My reputation will be ruined, because I'll sound like I was a little slut. And we know he'll deny it all, or he'll say I pursued him." She shakes her head. "And maybe I did. I was such a different person back then."

Faye sticks her head in the door. "Good to see the Three Musketeers are hard at it this morning. Thank you for all you do to help the company." Just as quickly, she's gone.

Whitney gives a mock salute. "And thank you to the company for helping me pay for my Mustang."

Carol Ann and Hope look at each other and grin. Hope says, "Looks like we're going to have to have one of those three-drink lunches today. We can sort through everything then. Okay?"

Carol Ann nods.

Whitney stands and salutes Hope. "Aye, aye, Captain."

Huddled in a corner booth, the three women stare at their drinks in silence.

Feeling emotionally spent, Hope speaks. "See why this is so confusing for me? I mean, I landed here with nothing but a baby. What else was I supposed to do?"

"I had no idea," Whitney says. "Man, you've had a hard life, Hope."

"Why haven't you ever told us about any of this?" Carol Ann asks.

"Because it wouldn't change anything that's happened." She pauses, then adds, "But it might have changed the present."

"What's that supposed to mean?" Whitney asks.

"Look, I've never really had any friends since I left New York. Sure, I've known people, but I've never had people in my life like you two, like the friends you are. I don't want to lose that, to lose you." She's surprised at the catch in her voice.

"Girl, what makes you think you're going to lose us?" Whitney exclaims.

Hope's throat feels closed off, but she manages to squeak out what she wants to say. "Now that you've heard the truth about me and the kind of person I used to be, doesn't that change how you feel about me?"

"None of this changes anything for me," Whitney says.

"Well, it does for me," Carol Ann replies.

They look at her, and Hope's heart stops.

"It makes me admire you and look up to you. To have been through all you've been through, and you're still working at life, still trying—

that's more than just amazing. It makes me love you more."

Hope's chest feels as if it's going to break. She folds her arms on the table and lays her head on them, cradling her face, and begins to cry. It's not a cry interspersed with wails and gasps for breaths, no, it's purely a torrent of tears, so much so that they create a puddle that leaks past her arms and begins to dribble off the table.

Whitney puts her arms around Hope's waist and pulls her tight against her.

Carol Ann lays her face on her back and gently pats her, as if coaxing a whimpering baby back to sleep.

A warmth spreads through Hope she's never felt before. *Am I dreaming? Will I wake to find myself all alone?*

For several moments, no one moves.

Eventually, Whitney releases her grip on Hope and sniffs back tears. "Do you all have any idea what time it is? It's nearly two o'clock. Faye is going to have a cow, if she hasn't already."

Carol Ann sits up and wipes her tears.

Taking a deep breath, Hope raises her head and leans back against the booth. "Whew. I feel like I've run a marathon, not that I would really know how that feels." She smiles. "You guys are too much, you know that?"

They smile, take hold of each other's hand, and squeeze.

"The Three Musketeers," Whitney says.

"The Three Musketeers," Hope repeats.

"What are we going to tell Faye?" Carol Ann

asks.

Whitney answers, "We'll tell her we had a flat tire and had to change the tire ourselves. We'll make us sound really helpless and girly-girly. She don't have to know I can change a tire as good as any man, better than most." She raises one arm and flexes her bicep.

"Before we leave, I want to say something," Hope begins. "Carol Ann, my situation when I was a teenager wasn't the same as your situation when you were in high school. The men I was with were all sleazeballs and had no morals. Mr. Biddle, though, was a teacher, a coach, a man who was supposed to seek the best for his students. I'll guarantee you, he knew better. He completely took advantage of you. But I can't imagine what it would be like to tell the story for everyone to hear. So, whatever you decide to do, I'm behind you one hundred percent."

"And that goes double for me," Whitney says.

"Thank you," Carol Ann replies. "That means a lot."

CHAPTER TWENTY-SIX

After work, Hope sits in her car in the parking lot.

What a day this has been.

She still can't believe she told her whole story to Carol Ann and Whitney. It dawns on her that they're the only people who know everything, and that it's the first time she's ever said it aloud, even to herself.

Conjuring up all the images and feelings from her past had the unintended result of feeding her depression. She feels the darkness closing in on her, and her heart has difficulty beating. The thought of going home, where all the memories of Lisa are, and seeing the closed door to her bedroom, is too much for her.

She pulls out her phone and powers it on. After a moment, she dials Justin.

He answers on the first ring, "Hey, I've been trying to call you all day. What happened?"

She ignores his question. "Why have you been calling me?"

"Have you forgotten? We were going to get the names of the bullies from my buddy, Ron, and see if we could get any closer to figuring out why Lisa...you know."

Hope closes her eyes and nods slowly. "Killed herself."

"I'm sorry. There's just no easy way to say that. Are you okay?"

Okay? What does that mean? What am I supposed to say? She gives a one-word answer, "Sure." *That's what everyone wants to hear me say.* "I just don't feel like spending the night in my house. Can I spend the night with you?"

There's a pause on the other end. "You know I'd be fine with it, but I don't know what Mama would say. She's really old-fashioned, you know."

Hope sighs. *A grown man still living with his mother—what does that say about him? Why am I even talking to him?*

He speaks up, "We could stay in a motel somewhere, like we usually do."

She hates sleeping in motels, especially the cheap kind—the tiny bars of soap, the one-dose bottles of shampoo and conditioner, showers without enough pressure to wash off soap, and pillows that go flat as soon as you lay your head on them. But it sounds like her only option, if she doesn't want to go home.

"Okay," she answers unenthusiastically.

In the motel room, Hope, Justin, and Ron sit around the small circular table that threatens to turn over every time one of them rests their elbows on it.

"Y'all know I shouldn't be doing this," Ron says. "It's not supposed to be any of my business, but Justin here says you're in a world of hurt not knowing why your daughter done herself in. That really sucks."

Hope says nothing.

Justin glances at her, then says, "Yeah, we understand, and we appreciate you doing anything that can help us understand what was going on at school."

"Let me tell you," Ron says, "kids aren't like they used to be. These kids nowadays are mean, really mean. It's like they don't have a conscience anymore. The deeper they can cut you, the bigger the thrill it gives them. Maybe not all of them are that way, but a lot of them are. And the names of the four girls I'm going to give you are the worst of the worst. All of the girls in school are afraid of them, but they suck up to them just the same, like they want to be one of them. Acceptance, that's what I think they're looking for."

Hope tries to remember what it was like when she was in school, but those memories are so faint, she finds nothing to use for comparison. She says, "And you've seen these girls pick on Lisa and be mean to her?"

He reaches inside his shirt pocket and produces a folded piece of paper. Unfolding it, he presses out the creases and slides it toward Hope and Justin.

Their eyes fall on the names: Shelly Weathers, Karen Tubbs, Darlene Mason, Lacey Thornbird.

Ron taps the paper with his index finger. "These here, they're the ones that gave Lisa trouble."

Hope touches each of the names and tries to imagine what Lisa must have been going through. Looking up at Ron, she asks, "Why didn't you do anything about it? Why didn't you let me know? Let someone know?"

Ron chews on his lip. "I tried talking to the principal about it one time, but he made it clear that school business is school business. My job was to protect the students from somebody coming in from the outside intent on causing them harm. He said he'd take care of behavior problems in the school."

"You talking about Biddle?" Justin asks.

"Yep."

"I've only met him once, but I don't have a very high opinion of him."

"You and me both."

Hope thinks about Carol Ann and wonders what she'll do because now Hope wants her to sue Biddle, and sue the school system, too. "Somebody needs to pay," she says emphatically. "Pay for all they've done, and everything they've allowed to be done."

"Just don't mention my name," Ron says. "My wife's pregnant with our first kid, and I really need the extra money this job gives me."

Hope fixes him with a stare. "I'll respect your wish, but I won't respect the fact that you were unwilling to step up and do something to protect my daughter. I hope when your child is in school, there will be someone with more backbone than you to look out for kids' safety."

Justin speaks up. "There's no need to attack Ron."

Hope stabs him with her eyes.

"That's okay," Ron says, "she's right. And there hasn't been a moment since Lisa died that I haven't thought about that." He stands up. "I hope these names help you get some closure, because I don't think I ever will." He stands and walks quietly out of the room.

Hope picks up the list of names. "I'm calling in sick tomorrow and going to the school."

"Aren't you afraid of getting fired?"

"This is more important than my job."

He looks down at his hands.

"What?" she asks.

"I've got to have a job, or Mama will kick me out. I can't go with you tomorrow."

"You know what, Justin? One of these days, you're going to realize you're a grown-ass man and don't have to be under your mother's thumb your entire life. If and when that day comes, get back in touch with me. Until then, this is the last time we're spending the night together. If you want sex tonight, I'll let you have it, because I guess I owe you that much for the room. But after that, we're done. I'll go to the school by myself."

At eight-thirty the next morning, after calling Faye to tell her she was sick and not coming to work, then calling Whitney and Carol Ann to tell them the truth, Hope walks into the school. Her knees feel weak, and her heart thunders against her chest.

I'm doing this for you, Lisa, is what she's told herself all morning, especially when fear threatened to make her back out on her mission.

At the front desk, she asks, "I'd like to speak to Mr. Biddle."

"Do you have an appointment with him?"

"No, but I need to see him. It's about my daughter, Lisa Rodriguez."

"Yes, of course, I thought I recognized you. I'm sorry, but he hasn't come in to work yet."

Hope hadn't considered this possibility. She just figured principals were always at school when the kids were.

"Do you know when he's going to be here?"

"I really don't. Usually, if he's running late, he'll call me and let me know, but I haven't heard from him this morning."

About that time, the guidance counselor walks through the office.

"Ms. Brown," the secretary hails her, "Ms. Rodriguez is here to see Mr. Biddle, but he's not in."

She turns and looks at Hope. "Oh, hi there, it's Hope, isn't it?"

Hope nods.

"Can I help you with something?"

Hope is uncertain what to do. She had only one plan, and now that's not going to happen.

"I...I just wanted to talk to him about

something involving Lisa."

Ms. Brown gives her a kindly smile. "Why don't you come in my office, and we'll see if maybe I can help you."

With nothing better to do, Hope agrees and follows her to her office. The walls have posters of various colleges enticing prospective students with pictures of happy boys and girls, with perfect teeth and perfect smiles, looking like they don't have a care in the world. On Ms. Brown's desk sit various stacks of papers and envelopes, some open, some still sealed. In the window sill, a small bonsai tree strikes a pose.

Ms. Brown points to a loveseat. "Why don't you have a seat?" She then sits in an armchair across from the loveseat.

Hope follows her direction and takes a seat.

"If you don't mind me asking, how have you been doing?"

Hope doesn't want to get into that subject with her. "Okay, I guess. I'm here because I have some information that might help explain why Lisa took her life."

Ms. Brown's expression becomes guarded, and she turns a little pale. "Really? That's...that's very interesting. Trying to find the answer to the why question often plagues the survivors of suicide. Do you want to share with me what you've learned?"

"I was wanting to talk to Mr. Biddle about it."

"I realize that, but...he's not here...and I am. Maybe I can help."

Hope reaches in her back pocket and pulls

out the list Ron gave her last night. "I have the names of some girls who were bullying her. I want to know why something wasn't done about this. Why didn't someone intervene and try to help my daughter?" She hears her voice trembling with emotion but doesn't want to lose control and start crying. She swallows and takes a couple breaths to calm herself.

"We have a very strong anti-bullying campaign here at the school, at all the schools in our district. It's something we take very seriously."

"So, you're saying you all have it under control and nobody is getting bullied?"

Ms. Brown's face pinkens. "Well, I wouldn't go so far as to say that. Kids are so mean nowadays."

"So I've heard."

"Can I see the names you have?"

Hope hands her the list and watches her expression change from uncertainty and defensiveness to worry and something else—maybe fear.

She looks up from the list and asks, "Can you tell me why you think these specific girls were the ones bullying Lisa?"

"Someone from here at the school told me."

"A student? Because if a student told you, then you have to admit they might just be giving random names to get someone else in trouble. I really don't think these girls—"

Hope cuts her off. "I got the names from someone who works here, an adult, not from a student."

A long pause ensues, and Hope watches Ms.

Brown filtering through responses. Finally, she gives Hope her full attention and says, "I don't know what to say."

A knock sounds on her door, but before she can get up to answer it, Mr. Biddle strides in while asking, "What's going on here?"

Both women are startled. Hope is uncertain what to do or say, but Ms. Brown stands up, her face more red than pink now. "Mr. Biddle, Ms. Rodriguez and I are having a private conversation. You know the rule about coming in my office if the door is shut. I do not appreciate you barging in here like this."

Hope is shocked and sees Mr. Biddle is, too, which amuses her. He quickly recovers, though, and says, "Ms. Brown, I think you're forgetting about our agreement."

It looks as if he punctured a tire with a screwdriver. Ms. Brown sits down and turns pale, so pale that even her lips are white. For a second, Hope thinks she's going to faint, but she doesn't.

In a tiny voice, Ms. Brown says, "I'm just trying to help Ms. Rodriguez get some answers, that's all. She has some names of girls she was told were bullying Lisa."

Biddle turns on Hope, with anger touching the edges of his eyes. "I demand to know who they are."

She replies, "I don't know what you're holding over Ms. Brown's head, but you have no such power over me. You don't scare me or intimidate me, and you certainly can't bully me."

He blinks several times, and the muscles in his jaws flex. "Now look here," he begins, but Hope stands up and faces him.

"I'm keeping the names of the people to myself. I'll do my own investigation. And if I find my daughter was being bullied and nothing was being done about it, I'm going to sue your ass." She walks past him to leave but stops at the door and turns around. "Another thing, Mr. Biddle. You need to be getting yourself ready, because the sky is fixing to open up on you and every dirty thing you've ever done is about to be exposed. People say the truth will set you free, but for you, the truth is going to send you to hell."

She takes a satisfied moment to watch the blood drain from his face, then leaves.

As she steps into the hallway, students are bustling to class, so she waits until the congestion thins out. Just then, she detects a familiar smell.

What is that? It takes her a moment, then it hits her—*It's the fragrance that was on the denim shirt I found in Lisa's locker.*

She looks around, but by then the hallway is deserted, and classroom doors are closing.

CHAPTER TWENTY-SEVEN

SITTING ON THE STAGE AT church, Michael puts on his most benevolent smile as he scans the Sunday morning crowd. He can barely contain his excitement.

There's got to be at least fifty or sixty more people here than last Sunday! Thank you, Lord, for the increase.

Even though Sarah is always quick to say numbers aren't the most important thing, he trusts more in his father's wisdom when he told Michael, "As long as you put butts in the pews, your job is secure."

He just hopes today's sermon will be on par with his first one. Helen's comment to him this past Monday has been worse than an earworm: "The problem with a new player hitting a home run his first time up to bat is, fans expect him to hit a home run every time he bats and certainly don't anticipate him striking out."

The thought of "striking out" this morning makes sweat beads pop out on his forehead.

Damn you, Helen. Forgive me, Lord.

Just then, the music starts, and he shifts his

attention to the praise-band and choir. It's immediately evident Liz has them primed for a performance that'll at least equal last week's. He marvels at how much talent she has. She's passionate about her music ministry—passionate and equally good at it.

His mind wanders from the music and zeroes in on Liz's lithe body as she directs. She doesn't just use her hands, like other choir directors he's seen. She uses every part of her—her hands, arms, head, feet, and legs all move as if choreographed. Her hips sway in rhythm to the beat. He wishes he could sit with the choir, just so he could see what her face looks like.

He feels himself getting aroused and quickly crosses his legs and looks back at the audience. The first face he sees is Sarah's. Her eyes are like hot coals, glaring at him. He smiles at her, but her expression doesn't change.

He looks down at the Bible in his lap. It used to be his father's, one of many. It was a gift from father to son when Michael left for seminary school. The older man told his son, "It's the most important book you'll use. Study it, live it, share it."

Studying it and sharing it is easy. It's living it that's hard.

Suddenly, he's aware of silence—no music. Looking toward Liz, he sees her facing him with an expectant expression. A tiny wrinkle of a frown shows as she gives him the briefest of nods. He's missed his cue to start preaching.

He jumps to his feet and strides to the podium.

"I don't know about you all, but I was so captivated by the music, I forgot where I was. Let's give them all another hand." He leads the audience in applause. When the applause dies down, he says, "We're so blessed to have Liz as part of the ministry team. Thank you, Liz."

He looks to her, and they exchange a smile. He then begins his sermon.

It doesn't flow like he thought it would, not like he'd practiced it. He has difficulty reciting a couple passages from memory, passages he knew as well as he knew his own name. And he leaves out one of the main points of his lesson. But apparently none of that matters, because as people shake his hand while leaving the service, they heap words of praise on him for how moving his sermon was, some with tears in their eyes.

He spots Helen coming his way, and he braces himself to be drawn up short by her. She offers him her hand, and he shakes it.

She says, "At least you didn't strike out. But you still didn't have enough Bible in it to suit me."

Before he can think of a reply, she releases his hand and heads out the door. While watching her, someone claps him hard on the back.

"Brother Michael! What an outstanding sermon!"

He recognizes Jed's voice before looking.

They engage in the same power-handshake they did the first time they met. Michael squeezes for all he's worth.

"Thank you, Jed."

"Did you see that crowd? I'm telling you, we're going to be busting at the seams if this keeps up."

Michael taps the brakes on his own enthusiasm lest he sound boastful. "It is exciting. As long as we seek to do His will, He will bless our efforts."

Jed nods. "Well said, Brother Michael, well said. Hey, Liz and I were talking this morning and would like for you and Sarah to come to our house for dinner today. You can follow us home."

"You mean for lunch?"

Jed laughs. "Around here, dinner is lunch, and supper is the evening meal."

Anxiety and tension slither in-between Michael's shoulder blades. It's the pressure to perform, instilled in him as a child when he and his mother would accompany his father on revivals and eat meals in church member's homes. "Remember," his father would say, "how you behave is a reflection on me. Mind your manners, be polite, and eat whatever they offer you. This is how I make a living, so make a good impression on them."

This "pressure to perform" is what Sarah hates most about being a pastor's wife. He wonders how she'll respond to Jed and Liz's invitation. He then thinks about being in Liz's house, a more intimate look at who and how she is.

Smiling, he says to Jed, "We'd be delighted to break bread with you. Thank you for asking."

Michael squeezes the steering wheel and grits his teeth as he follows Jed's car.

"I don't want to go," Sarah says. "I hate doing this. Why don't you drop me off at the house? Tell them I got sick. Then you can go by yourself, which is what you'd rather do anyway. You can really chum it up with Liz."

His anger boils over. "Look, we're going together, and you're going to behave yourself. I'm sick of this attitude of yours. Do you know how many women would love to be in the position you're in? Be thankful, and quit your whining!"

Sarah pulls away as if she's been struck. "You really are an evil man, you know that?" She tries to sniff back her tears.

Just then, Jed turns on his blinker and pulls into the driveway of a massive house.

Michael stares in awe as he follows. "Wow, what a huge house. There's no telling what something like that cost."

Flipping down the sun visor on her side, Sarah checks her makeup. She pulls a tissue out of her purse and wipes off the mascara that tried to run from her tears. "I'll do as you ask, but I can't say how much longer I can do this."

They exit their car, smiling and hold hands as they follow Jed, Liz, and their son, Mark, inside the house.

During the meal, Michael feels like a juggler as he tries to manage his end of the conversation and Sarah's, too, at times answering for her without sounding dismissive, and other times trying to draw her into the conversation without making her mad and obstinate. The hardest thing for him is not staring at Liz. "Radiant" is the only word that fits her. Her self-confidence draws him in and turns him on.

After dessert, Jed says, "Let's go in the living room, where it's more comfortable."

"If you all will excuse me," Mark says, "I'll let you adults have your alone time."

"Why don't you go lift some weights?" Jed asks. "Or maybe go for a run?"

"Sure, Dad," Mark answers, without enthusiasm.

"I'll clear these dishes," Liz says. "You guys go ahead."

"Can I help?" Sarah asks.

"Sure, that'd be nice."

Michael hadn't calculated this happening. Sarah on her own, without him being able to monitor her? How many ways could that go wrong?

In the living room, he half-listens to Jed talking about Mark and his prospects for college and the major leagues. It's impossible not to think about the ticking timebomb in the kitchen. Suddenly, he notices Jed has stopped talking.

"Are you listening?" Jed asks him.

"Sure, sure. I know you're awfully proud of Mark. Wouldn't that be something if somebody from a small town like Bardwell made it to the major leagues?"

"Yes, it would, but I was talking about our church and if we need to start thinking about expanding the auditorium."

Michael winces over losing track of the conversation. "I'm sorry, I guess my mind was drifting a bit. I'm always pretty exhausted after I preach. I read one time that speaking in public for forty-five minutes is as exhausting as working an eight-hour day. It certainly feels that way."

"I just don't want us to go to two services like some churches do when their numbers expand," Jed says. "A church family needs to meet together, everyone, to build closeness and relationships."

"I couldn't agree more. But I've only been here a few weeks. Let's give it time to see how many of our visitors are just curiosity seekers, checking out the new guy in town. My father used to say when a new preacher is hired, a third of the members are excited, a third are unhappy about it, and the other third really don't care; the same is true when a preacher leaves."

"That's a pretty dismal picture. I'm a pretty good judge of the pulse of our church and community, and I think there's a large majority who are excited about you. These two sermons you've presented have been excellent."

He's about to add something else when Sarah walks briskly into the room. Liz trails her, with a concerned look on her face. Michael reads Sarah's body language and is alarmed.

The bomb exploded.

"We need to go," she says curtly. She looks

at Jed and says, "Thank you for having us." Without another word, she walks out of the house and to the car.

Michael's face burns red. "I...I apologize...she gets upset sometimes...I—"

Liz interjects, "I think you should go to her." Her lips are a firm, thin line, and a hardness tinges her tone.

"Uh...sure. Thank you both for having us."

As he approaches the car, part of him feels like he's walking on eggshells, dreading to hear what in the world happened in the kitchen. But another part of him is so furious, he fears what he might do once the two of them are alone together. As he opens the car door, he decides he'll let her fire the first volley.

The clicking of his seatbelt sounds unnaturally loud. Driving out the driveway, he turns toward home, practically holding his breath in anticipation.

But Sarah is as silent as a tomb and still as the occupant of one.

It's an unnerving silence, and it puts Michael further on edge, because he knows the pressure is building in her and will most certainly erupt. And just like a volcano, the longer the pressure builds, the more damaging the explosion will be.

When the car comes to a stop in their driveway, she unbuckles herself and heads inside. He quickly unbuckles and follows her.

In the living room, she's facing him when he enters, so he pushes the door shut behind him with his foot. She's trembling, but from which emotion, he isn't certain. He waits.

"Do you love me?" she asks.

"How many times do I have to say I love you? A million? Over and over I've told you, yet you continue to ask me. Frankly, I get tired of being asked."

Her face contorts so that one side of her mouth goes up and her eye on that side closes to a slit. Through clinched teeth, she asks, "Do you wish I was dead?"

He hesitates for a split second, long enough to debate whether to give her an honest answer.

"I know you do," she says. "But you're not going to kill me, not physically anyway. You're going to make me so miserable that I'll kill myself. Then you'll be free, free to have all the women you want."

He takes a step toward her, but she holds up her hand to stop. So, he says, "What's brought all this on, Sarah? What happened when you and Liz were in the kitchen?"

An odd-sounding cackle comes out of her mouth. "She asked me a question, that's all. A simple question. She asked if I'd gotten in touch with the counselor she'd told you about."

Michael hears the blade of a guillotine as it plunges toward him. He closes his eyes in search of an explanation.

Into the silence, Sarah says, "I don't think you want me to get better, that you want my depression to devour me and bring my life to an end. And I think that's the most heinous and diabolical thing I've ever heard of a husband doing—hiding what could be a cure for his wife's fatal disease."

Michael forces himself to cry. "It's not like that at all, Sarah. I have no better excuse than I lost the contact information for the therapist and kept forgetting to ask Liz to give it to me again. I know that sounds lame and probably unbelievable, but it's the truth." He takes a step toward her, then another, until eventually they're only a foot apart. "Please forgive me, darling. I'm a horrible husband and man, but I'm not cruel. I would never want anything to happen to you." Kneeling in front of her, he goes on, "I love you, Sarah, I really do."

Her expression changes, and she begins to cry. "Do you really?"

"Absolutely, one hundred percent."

She puts her hands on his face and tugs until he's standing.

"We'll get that info from Liz, and we'll make you an appointment. It's going to get better. I'll even go with you, if you want me to."

A small smile creases her face. "Would you really?"

"For certain."

She reaches up to kiss him, and he obliges her unspoken request by kissing and embracing her.

CHAPTER TWENTY-EIGHT

AS JED WALKS THROUGH THE abandoned factory, he speaks to the two men and woman, all dressed in business suits, who accompany him.

"As a life-long member of this community, and a member of the Industrial Development Board, I can assure you we would be thrilled to have Osaka International come in and reopen this paper mill plant. We have the skilled workers you need, because most of the people who worked here have stuck around, hoping someone would buy the plant and restart it."

The older of the two men speaks to the woman in Japanese. She nods in reply and says to Jed, "We are looking for a setting that has strong family values, a quiet place where we can carve out a niche in the market and then begin to grow."

Jed smiles broadly. "Then Bardwell is the place for you. We are steeped in family values. Why, some families have lived here for four or more generations. There's hardly any crime, other than the occasional drunk driver or someone breaking the speed limit, which I have to admit, I'm guilty of at times."

The older man frowns and says something.

The woman gives Jed a concerned look. "So, you sometimes drive when you are drunk?"

"Oh my gosh, no! That's not what I was saying." He laughs nervously. "I was saying I break the speed limit sometimes, not the drunk driving thing. Language is a funny thing, easy to misinterpret."

The woman speaks to the older man, who nods at Jed and laughs.

The four of them continue walking, with the younger man making notes on an iPad and taking photos with his phone.

The woman moves closer to Jed so only he can hear her. "I hope this is not inappropriate, but Mr. Osaka has a teenage grandson he is raising who is a big fan of Kentucky basketball. I am certain it would please Mr. Osaka if some season tickets that are very close to the floor could be part of the agreement to reopen this facility."

Jed looks at her to see if she is joking, but her facial expression is blank.

His mind spins. *Geez! Floor seats can cost six thousand dollars, IF they're available.*

"How many do you think he would like?"

"I think four would be a good number."

That's nearly twenty-five thousand dollars!

The old man gives a general wave of his hand at the factory and says, "Very nice, very nice."

Jed bows to him. "Thank you, sir. Thank you very much."

The woman leans in and says, "Will you be able to manage the request?"

Without any way of knowing exactly how the industrial board can make that kind of arrangement work without raising the ire of auditors and the public, he smiles and says, "Absolutely. That will not be a problem."

They exit the building, and the three visitors huddle for a few moments, while Jed holds his breath, hoping for good news.

When they turn and face him, the young lady says, "Mr. Osaka has some concerns about coming here. We understand that one of the students in your high school recently committed suicide. Is that a common occurrence around here? Mr. Osaka does not want to bring his grandson to a school that has these kinds of problems."

Another surprise that catches Jed off guard. His "salesman-mind" starts moving as fast as a tap dancer. "I can see why he would be concerned, but the truth is, this girl was an outsider; that is, she wasn't from here. She was different from the other kids and had difficulty fitting in. I think all the kids were nice to her and tried to include her in their groups, but she had some mental problems, too. There was no father in the picture, and her mother, I believe, wasn't the best example. It's just hard for people who aren't from here to understand our ways." As soon as he hears the words coming out of his mouth, he would have given a year's salary to reel them back in. Before he can backtrack on his comment, Mr. Osaka motions for the woman.

When she faces Jed again, she says, "Unfortunately for you, Mr. Osaka understood what you said. He said that his son will be in the same situation as this young girl—an outsider, unfamiliar with the ways of the people here, no father in the picture. He said, 'This is not the place for my family.'"

"Wait, wait, let me explain. My mouth sometimes overruns my brain. I…"

He watches in despair as the three of them get inside their car. The woman rolls down her window.

Jed says, "Please satisfy my curiosity. If he understands English, why did everything have to be relayed through you?"

"It is just our way. Mr. Osaka thanks you for your time and wishes you success in finding a buyer." She puts on sunglasses, and her face disappears as the window rolls up.

Jed kicks the door of his car and cries out in pain as he grabs his foot. He sends a stream of cuss words ricocheting off the vacant parking lot.

When the pain subsides, he leans back against his car, thinking of how he's going to explain this to the members of the industrial board without making himself sound like the reason the deal fell through. The only reason they hadn't hired an outside recruiter was that he'd convinced them he could clinch the deal himself and save that money. The only good thing is, he isn't going to have to figure out a way to pay for season basketball tickets.

Limping and feeling glum, he gets in his car and drives home.

Liz greets him at the door and reaches for his arm. "What have you done to yourself? I saw you limping."

"I stubbed my toe."

"Stubbed your toe? Doing what?"

"I'll explain after I've had a drink. Things didn't go well with Osaka."

"Oh, Jed, I'm sorry. Go sit in your chair, and I'll bring you a drink."

He collapses onto his leather chair and rests his feet on the footstool. Bending over, he takes the shoe off his injured foot and gingerly touches his toes. He grits his teeth to keep from crying out. "I think there's something broken," he says as Liz walks in and hands him his drink.

The back door opens and closes, and Liz calls, "Hey, Mark, bring an ice pack to the living room, please. And hurry."

Jed starts to protest, not wanting to make this a bigger deal than it is, but knows the ice pack will help.

Liz sits on the footstool. "I'm going to take your sock off so we can get a look."

Jed downs his drink in one gulp and grips the arm of the chair. "Jesus, that hurts!"

"Jed, please," Liz scolds, "don't use the Lord's name that way."

"Wow," Mark says as he enters with the icepack, "those toes look broken to me. Let me hold it on there. I know a thing or two about icing injuries down."

Jed appreciates the attention from his son in spite of how much it hurts for his toes to be touched.

"How'd it happen, Mom?"

"I haven't heard the story yet either. Tell us, Jed."

He relates the events at the factory, including the Osakas' questions about the suicide, but leaves out his ill-fated comments related to it. "I was so upset about losing the deal, I kicked the car. Not my smartest move. It's just, if it hadn't been for that stupid girl killing herself..."

"Don't call her stupid, Dad," Mark says. "You didn't even know her."

Liz looks at him in surprise and says, "That's true, but you weren't talking so nice about her the other day either."

He looks away. "Yeah, well, I guess maybe I was just repeating what other kids were saying. Plus, I thought about what you said about my attitude."

Jed sees an opportunity to align himself with his son, something he's rarely been able to do lately. "You're right, Mark. I had no call to say that."

"I'm going to fix me a sandwich," Mark says. "I'm hungry." He heads to the kitchen.

"What do you think that was about?" Liz asks.

"You heard him."

"I did, but I think there's more to it than that. Do you think he's lost some weight lately?"

"Lost weight? I haven't noticed. I'm sure the

coach would have said something to me about it if that was happening. Maybe it's just the clothes he's wearing that makes it look that way to you."

"Mmm-hmm, I'm not so sure." She opens her mouth to say something else but doesn't.

"What? What were you going to say?"

"Now's not a good time."

"Not a good time for what?"

"More bad news. Plus, it's just a rumor. What we need to do now is go to the emergency room and get this foot X-rayed."

"I am *not* going to the E.R. because I kicked my car. How stupid is that going to sound?"

"Not as stupid as being more concerned about what people say about you than you are about having broken bones. Honestly, Jed, sometimes you're worse than a teenager."

That night, as Jed is settling into bed with Liz's help, he says, "By the way, what was that bad news you didn't want to tell me about?"

"I was hoping you'd forgotten about that. I don't like spreading gossip. But with all you're doing in trying to recruit businesses to Bardwell, I don't want you to get blindsided."

"Well, now you have my complete attention. What's about to happen?"

"Someone's filed a lawsuit against Lloyd Biddle."

"Biddle?! What in the world about?"

"A woman says when she was a student in school and he was her basketball coach, they had a sexual relationship."

Jed's stomach turns as if he's eaten something rancid, and a feeling of nausea washes over him. "You have got to be kidding me."

"I wouldn't kid about something this serious."

"So, is this someone who's trying to cash in on this MeToo movement every woman in America seems to be doing lately? They're coming out of the woodwork."

In an even tone, Liz says, "Maybe that's because they finally feel brave enough to come forward."

"I'm going to keep my mouth shut. Seems like lately everything that comes out of it gets me in trouble. But if this is true and the word gets out, then Bardwell should just roll up the sidewalks and go out of business, because nobody's going to want to move here."

Liz stands. "You're right, you should have kept your mouth shut. I love our town as much as you do, but when that's all you can think about, when that's how you measure every interaction, when what happens to our town is more important than a young girl losing her innocence to a man who's trusted to look out for her best interests, then you and I are on opposite sides. It makes me feel like I don't know you anymore."

CHAPTER TWENTY-NINE

DESPITE HOPE'S THREAT TO MR. Biddle that she'd investigate the girls who bullied Lisa, she really doesn't know what to do next. Like all the details of Lisa's life, the list of names means nothing to her, not a clue who they are or how to find out about them.

If I hadn't been living the life of a turtle in its shell for the past sixteen years, I could ask other parents if they know the girls, or I could even be a friend of one of their parents.

Ron is the only source she's connected to the girls, and he made it clear he wouldn't be divulging any details about them.

Then there was that whiff of cologne in the school hallway. *Can you catch a suspect by their smell? If I had a bloodhound, I could.* She laughs to herself at how ridiculous it would look for her to be walking a bloodhound in the school building.

The shirt has to have belonged to a close friend. A boyfriend? *Do they even call it boyfriend/girlfriend nowadays?* And could this boy be the father of the baby Lisa was carrying? Did he know she was pregnant? Did she know she was pregnant?

Hope sighs. *Questions, questions, and more questions.*

She feels the tendrils of depression rising from the darkness where her heart now lives. They begin wrapping around her like kudzu vines. She finds it hard to breathe, and all her joints begin to ache.

Please leave me alone, don't do this to me.

"Are you okay, Hope?"

Whitney's voice jars her, and she looks over at her.

"You've been doing nothing but staring at your computer screen for the last hour," Whitney tells her.

Looking up at the clock on the wall, Hope says, "Thank goodness it's almost time to leave, and that today is Friday."

Carol Ann says, "I don't know how you're making it, holding up as well as you are. It's got to be so hard."

Hope nods absentmindedly, still not completely engaged in the moment with them. She's doing everything she can to keep depression from pulling her onto the floor and suffocating the life out of her.

Whitney switches off her computer. "Let's call it quits. You two want to go get a drink somewhere?"

"Sorry, I've got to go meet with my lawyer," Carol Ann says.

Hope grabs hold of Carol Ann's trouble, trouble that's separate from hers, and focuses solely on it. "How's all that going? You really don't talk about it."

"My lawyer says I'm not supposed to talk about it to anyone. But I can tell you pretty soon I will be able to. I think he wants to put together a press release about the lawsuit and maybe have me do a press conference with local media."

Whitney swears. "Things are going to hit the proverbial fan when that happens."

"I know. It scares me to death. I keep asking myself if I'm doing the right thing and if I can really go through it all."

"You can do it," Hope says. "You're strong, Carol Ann, not weak like me. You've got what it takes to see this thing through and hold people accountable for what they've done."

"How can you say you're weak?" Carol Ann asks. "A weak person would never have come back to work after losing her daughter. A weak person wouldn't be trying to be here for me and my stuff. No, you're strong, Hope."

"She speaks the truth," Whitney agrees.

The words of praise and encouragement have no impact on Hope, because they're sucked in and destroyed by the black hole of her depression. She switches off her computer. "I'm going home. See you guys Monday, I guess." Moving like a person twice her age, she stands up and heads toward the parking lot.

On the drive home, she searches her mind for something to get angry about, a technique she's learned will at least give her some energy.

She alights upon Luther and starts a checklist

of things about him that irritate her: his scraggly excuse for a beard, his infernal family that always wants to do 'family' things together, the fact that he never picks up after himself, his obsession with hunting, his job that takes him away from home for nearly a month at a time.

Just like right now, I have to be in that house all alone—ALL ALONE. It makes me furious!

She presses down on the gas pedal until the fence posts in the fields beside the road look like a picket fence. The speedometer moves past seventy-five.

A car coming in the opposite direction flashes its headlights at her. Figuring it's a warning of a speed-trap up ahead, she toys with the idea of pushing the gas pedal to the floor, just to see how fast she can go before reaching the radar. But instead, she lets off the gas and touches the brakes. Half a mile later, she spots the state trooper car nestled underneath some pine trees.

Sadly, though, all the adrenalin she'd generated begins ebbing away.

At the house, she doesn't bother turning on any lights but goes straight to the bed, crawls in with her clothes and shoes on, and pulls the covers over her head.

———◆———

When Hope wakes up inside her cocoon of covers, she has no idea what time it is or if it's day or night. She fishes for her phone, powers it on, and waits until it shows her it's Saturday, 9:47 a.m.

You've got to do something. Either kill yourself and be done with it, or do something about it. Once again, she curses her Catholic upbringing and its prohibition on suicide. *Yeah, but if you'd raised your daughter Catholic, she'd probably still be here.*

That's the trouble with having a conscience that's also a smart aleck. It never misses an opportunity to slice and dice you.

She decides to see if a shower will help and finds it does. After putting on a pot of coffee, she studies the letter puzzle and moves some pieces around. Light a bolt out of the blue, she sees: DEAR LISA. In the next instant, she sees: I LOVED YOU.

'LOVED' — is there anything more painful to a teenager than unrequited love?

"Oh, my sweet, sweet Lisa..."

The beeper on the coffee maker goes off, indicating the brew is finished. She looks at it for a few seconds, then walks to a cabinet, takes out a Yeti cup, and fills it.

Stepping outside, she looks into the bright sun and says, "I'm coming to see you, Lisa."

◆

Hope often had heard people talk about going to the grave of a loved one and talking to them. It all sounded rather morbid and crazy to her. *How are you going to have a conversation with a dead person?* But she finds herself staring at the rounded mound of bare dirt she and that preacher fella shoveled onto Lisa's coffin. A small, three-by-five inch metal plate attached to a metal spike sticks out of the ground where Lisa's feet would be. It has Lisa's name, date of birth, and date of death on it. Until a headstone is put in place, this is the only means for visitors to identify where the remains of their loved ones are.

Hope unfolds the quilt she found in the trunk of her car, lays it beside the grave, and sits down on it cross-legged. She sips from her coffee mug and watches a granddaddy long-legs spider traverse the grave and disappear underneath the scattered leaves on the other side.

"I don't know what to say," she begins. "I miss you. I know that sounds strange, because it probably looked to you like I ignored you most of the time. But I wasn't ignoring you, I just didn't know what to say to you once you became a teenager. I didn't feel like I knew you anymore. And now I'm learning things about you I never knew. I know you had a boyfriend. I don't know his name yet, but I will. I know he broke up with you, and I'm really sad for you about that. It must have hurt you really bad." A surge of emotion pushes into her throat, cutting off her voice.

After a few moments, she continues. "I'm just really, really..." Again, her voice betrays her and cuts off. For several moments, all she can do is cry.

Eventually, she's able to get a clear breath. "I'm sorry about lots of things, Lisa. The main one is, I'm sorry I wasn't a better mother to you. You deserved better. There's no telling what you could have become if you'd lived with someone else. I should have let Social Services take you and place you with a family when you were a baby. But I was a kid having a kid, scared and alone. You were all I had, and I didn't want to let you go."

Hope hears feet rustling through leaves behind her. She jumps up and turns around.

"Ms. Rodriguez, I didn't expect to see you here."

She stares at him as her heart gallops inside her chest.

"Remember? I'm Greg—"

"Yeah, from the tattoo parlor, right?"

"Yes, ma'am." He smiles. "I've never seen you here, I hope you don't mind me coming. If you want me to leave, I will."

He starts to make a move to turn around, and Hope says, "No, don't go."

Greg steps closer.

"You've been here before?" Hope asks.

"Sure. I come every morning about this time. I know it's weird and everything, but I just like talking to Lisa, seeing how she's doing, and letting her know how everything here is going. I told her about you coming by the shop and that you seemed real nice."

Hope gapes at him.

"I can tell you're upset with me," Greg says. "I'm sorry, and I'll not come here anymore, if that's what you want."

Hope swallows to clear her throat. "I don't mind you coming. I just had no idea...Lisa meant so much to you. I never knew you...she never mentioned you to me...but that doesn't mean anything, because..." Realizing she's rambling and only talking to herself, she shuts up.

An awkward silence ensues, and they gaze at Lisa's grave.

"I'm not very good at this," Hope says, "this 'talking to people' thing. And I've for sure never talked to someone who's dead, but just this morning, something told me I needed to come here and talk to Lisa."

"I get it," Greg says. "But the way I see it is, Lisa died, which only means she's not here anymore. But that doesn't mean she's not alive somewhere and can't hear or see us. We just can't see or hear her. That's why it feels real when I talk to her here. Sounds crazy, doesn't it?"

"Actually, I kind of like the way it sounds. It means I can get some things off my chest I've been holding inside because I didn't know what to do with them. There's lots I need to tell her. I just wish she could talk to me or give me a sign or something. I have so many questions only she can answer." She pauses, then says, "Or maybe you can answer a couple of questions."

"I'll help if I can."

Hope fishes in her pocket and pulls out the paper with the names of the girls who were supposedly bullying Lisa. Handing it to Greg, she asks, "Do you know any of these girls?"

It takes him only a second. "Sure, I know who all of them are. These are the popular girls I was telling you about who were so jealous of Lisa and felt threatened by her. Their parents are rich compared to most people around here, which makes teachers let them get away with stuff others get in trouble for. It really made me mad that Mr. Biddle knew they were mean to her but never did anything about it."

Hope's anger awakens. "Yeah, well he's fixing to get what's coming to him."

Greg raises his eyebrows. "What do you mean?"

"I'm not supposed to say. Just stay tuned, and you'll hear all about it."

He hands her back the list, and she stuffs it in her pocket.

"Another question?" she asks.

"Sure."

"She and a boy were seeing each other. I wish I could find out who it was."

"If she was, I'll bet it was completely hush-hush, because that's just the way Lisa was. If it's true, it kind of hurts—like I wasn't good enough for her."

"I don't believe that's what she would think. She didn't want to lose your friendship, that was more important to her, that's how special you were to her."

He hangs his head. "But not special enough to live for."

Like a sharply honed knife, the truth slices through all the superficial and extraneous matters, leaving it as the only thing that matters.

Hope's shoulders sag. "Yeah, and then there's that."

CHAPTER THIRTY

SITTING IN THE FLOOR OF the bathroom in his office, a smile of satisfaction spreads across Michael's face as he tries to catch his breath. His hands are shaking as he looks at his phone and types.

MICHAEL: OMG, THAT WAS GOOD! YOU ARE UNBELIEVABLE.

BRITTANY: I'M GLAD YOU ENJOYED IT.

MICHAEL: NEVER DREAMED THIS VIRTUAL STUFF COULD FEEL ALMOST AS GOOD AS THE REAL THING.

BRITTANY: I MISS THE REAL THING. WHEN CAN I COME AND MEET YOU SOMEWHERE?

Fear and anxiety jump in and sweep away all Michael's post-orgasmic feelings.

MICHAEL: I MISS THE REAL THING, TOO. WOULD LOVE TO SEE YOU, BUT THINGS AROUND HERE ARE STILL TOUCH AND GO. I DON'T KNOW ENOUGH ABOUT THIS AREA TO FIND A PLACE WHERE WE CAN MEET AND

NOT GET CAUGHT.

He imagines the scowl on her face at his text and knows she's not going to like it. Holding his breath, he waits for an angry reply.

BRITTANY: FOR ALL I KNOW YOU'RE DOING THIS SEXTING THING WITH SIX OTHER WOMEN. APPARENTLY I'M NOT GOOD ENOUGH FOR YOU. I'M GETTING TIRED OF BEING AVAILABLE ONLY WHEN YOU WANT TO GET YOUR ROCKS OFF. SURE, THIS IS FUN, BUT I WANT MORE. YOU NEED TO DECIDE WHO YOU WANT, ME OR THAT FAT COW YOU'RE MARRIED TO.

Michael cringes in the face of her implied threat, but he also feels like he should defend Sarah.

MICHAEL: DON'T TALK ABOUT SARAH LIKE THAT. SHE'S A GOOD PERSON.

BRITTANY: LOL! SO, YOU CAN WHINE AND COMPLAIN TO ME ABOUT HER, BUT I'M NOT ALLOWED TO GIVE MY OPINION? GIVE ME A BREAK!!! AND DON'T EVER TELL ME WHAT TO DO OR WHAT NOT TO DO!!!!!

Michael looks at the clock on his phone and knows he's been in the bathroom an extraordinary amount of time. But how to extricate himself rather quickly while also mollifying Brittany?

MICHAEL: YOU'RE RIGHT. I SHOULDN'T HAVE SAID IT THAT WAY. I WOULD NEVER TRY TO CONTROL

YOU OR TELL YOU WHAT TO DO. PLEASE BE PATIENT WITH ME. I DON'T KNOW WHAT I WOULD DO WITHOUT YOU. YOU HAVE NO IDEA HOW INSANE MY LIFE IS. YOU'RE THE ONLY THING THAT KEEPS ME SANE. I REALLY NEED YOU.

There is a long pause, long enough that Michael wonders if she's already ended the conversation on her end.

BRITTANY: I'M SORRY I GOT SO MAD. YOU KNOW I'LL ALWAYS BE HERE FOR YOU. I'M CRAZY ABOUT YOU. BUT YOU GOTTA KNOW I CAN'T HANG AROUND FOREVER. THERE ARE WAYS TO MAKE SOME CHANGES IN THIS SITUATION.

Michael is relieved she bought his cry for help but also hears a warning bell ringing somewhere. *What would she do?*

They end their conversation, and he rises from the floor and looks in the mirror. Immediately, an arrow of guilt shoots through his heart, and tears well up in his eyes. Brushing his hair out of his eyes, he utters a silent prayer, *Be merciful to me, a sinner.*

Powering off the phone, he steps out of the bathroom and steps over to his desk. He's about to open the bottom desk drawer when he hears the metallic sound of Helen's walker approaching his office door. Quickly, he drops the phone into his pants pocket.

"You okay in here?" she asks. "I kept buzzing

the intercom, or at least I thought I was doing it correctly."

Michael feels his cheeks burn. "I was...uh...in the bathroom. Something I ate didn't set very well with my stomach."

"I hope it's not the stomach flu, it's going around, you know. Stay away from me if you do. Old women like me would probably keel over from it. I heard Sister Qualls lost fifteen pounds from having it, not that that wasn't a good thing for her. Bless her heart, she just blew up after her husband, Herbert, died suddenly."

He thought about saying something about the sin of spreading gossip but decided it wasn't worth the effort. "I don't believe it's the flu. I don't have any fever or aches, just some—"

"Loose bowels?" she finishes his sentence. "That's a problem that can get you in trouble in a heartbeat. Cough or sneeze, and oops, you got a problem in your caboose."

He still can't figure out when she's being dead serious or trying to make a light-hearted, funny comment, so instead he shifts the direction of the conversation. "Were you needing me for something? Is that why you were paging me over the intercom?"

"Well, of course I was, you think I was doing it just to pass the time? Your wife, Sarah, called and said to remind you of you all's appointment. She said she tried calling and texting you on your phone, but you didn't answer."

She gazes at him as if she's waiting for a reply and explanation. *You nosey old lady, it's none of your business.*

"Is there anything else?" he asks.

"I suppose not," she answers and begins the process of turning herself around.

"Did Sarah mention what our appointment was for?"

"No. Why? Don't you know?"

"Thank you, Helen." He watches her make her way to her desk.

At least Sarah didn't mention the counseling to her. That's all I need, is for people in the church to hear their new pastor and his wife are having marital problems or his wife is mentally ill and seeing a counselor.

He checks the time and sees he's running late. Turning off his computer and closing the books he'd been studying, he pauses.

What am I forgetting?

He stands there for a few seconds, but nothing registers, so he starts to exit his office.

Suddenly, he feels the weight of the phone in his pants pocket. Panicked, he spins around, returns to his desk, and puts it back in its hiding place.

Whew, that was close!

When he pulls in the driveway at home, Sarah immediately heads out of the house to meet him. The scowl on her face tells him everything, and he braces himself for a tongue lashing.

Jerking open the passenger door, she says, "Where have you been? We're going to be late!" The words are thrown at him like stones.

"I'm sorry, I got so involved in studying, I lost track of the time." He puts the car in reverse and backs out of the driveway.

"I tried calling and texting you. Why didn't you answer me?"

"My irritable bowel has been acting up. I must have been in the bathroom when you tried to reach me." It sometimes amazes him how quickly he can come up with a lie.

"You don't know him like I do," Sarah says to Dr. Elliot. "His mind is like a sewer, constantly thinking about women and sex and pornography."

"But when you tell me you know what he's thinking," Dr. Elliot comments, "you realize you're saying you're a mind reader, and I really don't think that's possible. I think it would be more accurate to say you *think* you know what's in his head."

"So, you're taking his side? I knew this was a waste of time."

"I don't mean to be taking sides, if that's what it sounds like. I'm just trying to understand where you're coming from."

Michael feels a little sorry for Sarah and how the focus is on her, but he's pleased the counselor seems to have believed his explanation of things.

An uncomfortable silence makes the room feel smaller, and Michael and Sarah look at Dr. Elliot, waiting for him to say something. But he sits quietly and returns their gaze, looking from one to the other.

Sarah crosses her legs and flexes her foot back

and forth. "Aren't you going to say something?" she finally asks.

"Is there anything either of you would like to say?"

Michael looks at her and says, "I think you should mention your struggles with depression."

She whirls and glares at him. "There it is. Throw me under the bus, why don't you." In a mocking tone, she says, "'The problem, dear Doctor, is my crazy wife.'" She looks at the doctor. "He is so predictable, it disgusts me. Look, he's an actor, an Academy Award-winning actor. All preachers are. They know how to play the part to make people believe whatever they want them to believe. The whole lot are charlatans."

"That's a pretty broad statement, Sarah. I think we'd call that generalization, simply because you don't know every preacher in the world. Surely, there are sincere ones somewhere." He leans forward. "Why don't you tell me about your depression?"

She mimics his movement and says, "I'll tell you what, I'll tell you about my depression if you'll tell me about that bad-fitting toupee you wear."

Without thinking, Michael says in a sharp tone, "Sarah! There's no call for that."

"Why not? He's asking us to be honest about ourselves, and yet he can't be honest with the world about the fact that he's going bald or is bald. Which is it, Dr. Elliot?"

Elliot reaches up and pulls off his hairpiece,

revealing a hairless scalp. "It's okay, Michael, because to some degree Sarah is right. I've had a hard time getting used to being this way ever since I underwent chemotherapy a month ago. Maybe it's time for me to get over myself," and he tosses the toupee into the trash can.

Sarah bursts into tears. "I'm so sorry. I had no idea you'd had cancer, or I would never have said something so cruel. I'm really not a mean person, at least when I'm not around him." She nods toward Michael.

"It's true," Michael agrees with her. "It's like when she found an unfamiliar cell phone in my pocket. I told her I found it on the church parking lot and meant to put it in the church's lost-and-found box, thinking someone from church had dropped it. But she said it was mine and I was using it clandestinely for talking to and meeting women. I hate myself that I seem to bring out the worst in her. Maybe you can help me with that, help me figure out how I do that."

"That is certainly a goal we can work on," Dr. Elliot answers.

Sarah sighs. "And maybe you can help me with my depression."

Dr. Elliot smiles. "Finally, you both have defined goals that are worthy of our time. I think I should see you separately for a time to work on these issues before I see you together again. Is that okay with both of you?"

They both give a nod of assent.

On the way out of the office, Michael breathes a mental sigh of relief that all his feverish dancing around Sarah's accusations kept Dr. Elliot distracted from the real problem, which is Michael himself.

CHAPTER THIRTY-ONE

HOPE STARES AT THE IMAGE on TV of Carol Ann flanked by her lawyer, a studious-looking man with wire-rimmed glasses, wearing a red tie and dark suit. Carol Ann's face looks drawn and tense, and she looks heavier than she actually is.

I guess it's true the camera adds fifteen pounds to a person.

The paper gripped in Carol Ann's hand betrays her nervous tremors. Looking at it, she begins reading.

Hope holds her breath as Carol Ann does the bravest thing she's ever witnessed, unveiling herself and her darkest secret for all the world to see. It's a testimony of truth, filled with admissions of her own mistakes and descriptions of her and Biddle's affair.

When Carol Ann finishes, Hope releases her pent-up breath in a rush and inhales sharply. *She's really done it...really done it.* Her heart swells with admiration for Carol Ann, but then feelings of shame and regret about herself show up like an unwelcome guest. Memory can be a curse, because we can't choose what we forget or remember. Images of the different men she's lived with stroll through her memory. She shudders to think what kind of negative impact her life had on Lisa and fears it played a major role in her demise.

Back on the TV, reporters are shouting questions at Carol Ann, but her lawyer deflects them all.

This is going to be like an atom bomb going off around here. It's going to keep getting bigger.

Both Hope and Whitney have told Carol Ann they don't believe she was the only one Biddle took advantage of. "Girl, they're going to start coming out of the woodwork," Whitney said. "You wait and see. These women around here have just been waiting for a brave woman to step up and speak out. It's going to be just like the MeToo Movement—Bill Cosby, Harvey Weinstein, Jeffrey Epstein—once a little light gets shown on evil, the windows and doors will burst open, and truth will step out looking like a superhero."

Hope fiddles with the idea of Lisa being involved with Biddle and him being the father of her baby. On the one hand it doesn't seem plausible, but on the other it makes perfect sense.

How could Lisa not have daddy issues and desire to be with an older man?

Hope feels nauseated at the thought of Lisa having sex with such a despicable man.

She turns off the TV and goes into the kitchen to fix herself a cup of coffee. On the way there, she catches her reflection in a wall mirror—hair askew, dark circles around her eyes, and still dressed in the clothes she slept in. This is what her weekends have become, silent hours spent doing nothing more than succumbing to the quicksand of her depression and its accusations of her contributions to Lisa's demise.

Once again, she stares at Luther's gun cabinet and the rifles, shotguns, and pistols arrayed behind the unlocked glass door. Walking over to it, she opens the door and slides her index finger down the slick, oiled barrel of a rifle.

Despite her protests, Luther made certain she knew how to use his guns. "You've got a right to protect yourself if somebody breaks in the house when I'm not here," he told her.

Reaching to her right, she picks up the double-barreled, 12-gauge shotgun, with its barrels shortened to nineteen inches, thanks to Luther and a hacksaw. "It won't kill nothing far off," Luther told her, "but up close, it's deadly."

She pushes the opening lever to the left, and the gun breaks open in the middle, its empty barrels staring up at her. In the bottom of the gun cabinet are boxes of various types of ammunition for each of the guns. The box of shotgun shells sits with its lid open, begging her to notice.

Bending over, Hope pulls out two shells, slips them into the barrels, and snaps the gun shut.

A sense of calm comes over her as relief from all her troubles lies within reach. She upends the gun and tucks the barrel under her chin. The metal is cool against her skin. Holding the barrel in place with one hand, she stretches her other arm in search of the safety. When she finds it, she pushes it off.

Her thumb touches the trigger guard, and she's just about to touch the trigger when she hears a knock at her door, followed by the sound of Whitney's voice. "Listen here, you little scarecrow, come open this door, and let us in 'cause we know you're in there."

Hope remembers finding her Mama T with blood and guts splattered all over the room and decides she's not going to subject her friends to the same grisly sight of herself. She lowers the gun and calls, "Come in, it's not locked."

Whitney bursts through the door, with Carol Ann close behind. When they see Hope standing with the gun in her hands, they halt.

"What's going on here?" Whitney asks.

"Hope?" Concern cuts deep lines in Carol Ann's forehead.

Hope looks at them, uncertain of what to say. "I was just..."

Whitney takes quick steps to Hope and pulls the gun away from her. "I know what you were just about to do. It's as plain as that blue streak in your hair." She fumbles clumsily with the gun. "How do you turn this thing off?"

Hope fears she's going to accidentally pull the trigger and it'll wound one or both of her friends. "Let me have it." She removes the shells and returns the gun to the cabinet.

Carol Ann moves in front of Hope. Taking her

hands, she says, "This has gone too far, Hope. You've got to get some help."

Hope shakes her head in confusion. "I was just watching you on TV. How did you get here so quickly?"

"It was all taped. My lawyer was afraid of doing it live, so he invited the news people with the understanding they couldn't broadcast it live and if I completely broke down, they'd pause the recording until I could pull myself together."

Ignoring this side issue, Whitney says, "Carol Ann's right, we're going to find you a therapist who'll help you get through this rough patch. We can't stand by and watch you sit and stare at our computer at work like you're a zombie. And you're not eating either. Girl, I could miss a week's worth of eating, and you wouldn't be able to see any difference. But you? Uh-uh, you got no margin for error when it comes to that topic."

"Don't get me wrong," Hope replies, "I really appreciate you all being concerned enough about me to drive out here and check on me, but I've tried the counseling thing when my parents died. It was a joke. The woman was crazier than my Mama T."

"Who you going to talk to, then?" Whitney asks. "'Cause you for sure going to talk to somebody."

"Don't you have anybody you trust, that you could lean on?" Carol Ann asks.

Suddenly, Hope remembers the pastor who preached Lisa's funeral and how he helped bury her. "There might be a person...I really don't know him, though. He took care of Lisa's funeral. I don't even know his name or where he is."

Carol Ann begins tapping on the screen of her phone. In a matter of seconds, she says, "Michael Trent is his name. He's the pastor of the Grace Community Church, in Bardwell. He's married, his wife's name is Sarah, and they don't have any kids."

Whitney says to Hope, "That's what a phone can do for you if you actually use it," and she adds an exaggerated eyeroll to go with her comment.

"He seemed like an honest man," Hope says, "and like he genuinely cared, not fake, if you know what I mean." The more she turns the idea over in her mind, the more she warms up to it, and her mood lifts a bit. "But I'm not a member of his church. You think he'll still talk to me?"

"Of course he will," Carol Ann says. "Pastors are supposed to be servants to everyone, no matter if they go to church or not. And you might enjoy going to church, getting out and being around more people."

That step seems huge to Hope, so she shifts the conversation. "Tell me how you're doing since you've gone public with the whole Biddle thing."

"I'm scared, and I have doubts that I did the right thing. When I told my mom about it, she told me her next-door neighbor molested her when she was young, and when she told her mother about it, her mother said those things just happen to girls sometimes and she'd get over it."

The group falls silent as the weight of Carol Ann's story presses down on them.

"I don't even know what to say," Whitney comments, "except that's just messed up. And you did the right thing, Carol Ann. I've told you once, and I'm telling you again, people like Biddle don't do that kind of stuff only one time. They're perverts who leave a string of victims in their wake. You wait and see."

CHAPTER THIRTY-TWO

SUNDAY MORNING, MICHAEL SITS IN his office at church, eyes closed and head bowed. Tears slip down his cheeks as he says, "Holy God and Father, Creator of the universe, I come to You on hands and knees, an unworthy servant, begging for forgiveness. I am a vile, unfaithful, and revolting human, who willfully sins daily. I know You are angry with me, but please don't turn Your face away from me. I want to be different, but my obsession, perhaps addiction, with sex turns my flesh away from you. I hate myself because of it and wish it could be exorcised out of me, but that's never going to happen. It is my curse, my cross that I must bear. Help me, please help me...help me to be stronger...to keep my focus on you—"

A light tap sounds on his office door, the signal from the deacon in charge that it's time for him to enter the sanctuary.

Taking out his handkerchief, he dries his tears and blows his nose. He inhales deeply and looks toward the ceiling. "Be with me, Lord, I cannot live without Thee."

As soon as he enters the auditorium, electricity fills the air. Smiling broadly, he scans the crowd as he walks down the aisle, waving at some, nodding at others, while everyone smiles back at him.

There are hardly any seats left. Jed may be right. We may need to think about expansion.

He takes a seat in one of the large chairs on the stage as Liz gives a downbeat to the praise band and choir. As music fills the building and people in the audience raise their hands to God, Michael blinks back tears.

Turning his attention to the crowd, he practices an old habit and looks for faces of attractive women. Several return his gaze, with eyes filled with admiration and desire. He pauses on one face, a new one, that gives him a sense of familiarity.

Do I know her?

To keep from staring, he turns back toward Liz and marvels at her ability to get so much out of the praise team and in selecting songs that seamlessly build an air of intensity.

Suddenly, a bell goes off in his head, and he looks back at the visitor. *The funeral! That's the mother of the girl who committed suicide. Her name is...* He racks his brain but finds nothing more than the last name, *Rodriguez*.

When the time comes for him to deliver his sermon, he walks up to the pulpit and says, "What a wonderful day to be in the house of the Lord. Amen?"

A chorus of "Amen"s erupts from the audience,

and he smiles.

"This morning, I want to talk to you about one of the most important things in the world—" He pauses for effect, then says, "Hope. Hope is our anchor in stormy seas." Immediately, something clicks in his head, and he looks at Hope Rodriguez, whose eyes are wide.

Throughout his sermon, Michael looks at Hope, and his brain splits; one part manages his sermon notes and speaking, and another part focuses on Hope.

What is it about her? She's not all that attractive, but something about her fascinates me.

He remembers the moment in her house when he took her home, a moment that felt like she wanted him to stay, as in spend the night in bed with her. He'd teetered on the edge then and managed to rein in his impulses.

Why is she here this morning?

He looks at the people sitting around her, none of whom looks like she belongs with them. He notices Jed entering the auditorium halfway through the sermon, looking haggard and in a hurry.

Hmmm, wonder what's up with Jed? Maybe the hoopla over Mr. Biddle has him upset.

After he finishes preaching, he hurries to the vestibule before dismissal to get to speak to Hope Rodriguez.

Not that she's more important than any other visitor, but I want to make certain she knows she's welcome.

He pretends to himself he has no ulterior motives. Denial is the pencil people use to draw a mirage.

Hope is the first person to exit the auditorium; she heads toward the exit, where he's standing. She keeps her head down, hardly glancing up, until she gets close to the door when she looks up and sees him.

Michael smiles at her and takes a step toward her. Extending his hand, he says, "It's Hope Rodriguez, isn't it?"

She folds her arms across her chest and says something inaudible while furtively looking toward the door.

Michael lowers his arm to his side. "How have you been doing?"

She shifts back and forth on her feet and answers, "Okay, I guess."

"I'm glad to hear it. I'm also glad you visited us today. If there's ever anything I can do to help, please come see me."

She looks him steadily in the eye. "You mean that?"

"Certainly." Reaching in the inside pocket of his jacket, he pulls out a business card and hands it to her. "These are the numbers you can reach me at, or you can simply drop by my office."

Without another word, she snatches the card out of his hand and exits the building.

Michael quickly transitions into his role of greeter, glad-hander, and dutifully-thankful-pastor as the church members file past him and heap praise on him. He notices Jed's hanging back from everyone, no back slapping and smiles, which is very atypical behavior.

When the last member leaves, Jed approaches him. "Another great sermon, Brother Michael." The words are familiar, but there's no energy underneath them. And Michael notices bags under his eyes.

"What's wrong, Jed?"

Wringing his hands, Jed says, "It's this thing involving our high school principal, Mr. Biddle. This kind of news is devastating when we're trying to attract new business and industry. Even if it turns out not to be true, it's the initial story that gets the most play." His face reddens, and his voice takes on more of an edge. "I went straight to him as soon as I heard about this and confronted him. He flatly denies it, says he doesn't even remember this woman who claims she was on his ball team."

Michael had tried to watch a replay of Carole Ann's statement but found himself feeling so uncomfortable about his own foibles that he turned it off. "What would be her motivation, if it's not true?" Michael asks.

"The same thing that makes the world go 'round—money. She's hoping she'll get some kind of financial settlement before it ever goes to trial, you know, a mediated settlement. What kind of man takes advantage of girls like that? I mean, I admit, I've made some mistakes in the past, but to seduce a young girl to satisfy your sexual urges? How sick do you have to be to be a slave to those kinds of sexual desires? Best thing to do to someone like that is throw them in prison and let the inmates take care of them."

Michael hopes his burning face doesn't betray him and instead looks like he shares Jed's righteous indignation. "Does Biddle strike you as that kind of person?"

"Not in the least. But I've read sexual predators all look very normal on the outside, like your friendly next-door neighbor. She says for all we know, you could be one. That's how normal they look."

Michael's knees nearly buckle, and the world spins around him. For a moment, he's afraid he's going to faint. Grabbing at his throat, he loosens his tie and unbuttons the top button of his shirt. "I can't catch my breath," he gasps.

Jed throws his arm around him and holds him tight. "Come sit down," he says as he leads him to a chair. "Sit down, and put your head between your knees. It looks like you're trying to have a panic attack. I know what that's like, feels like you're having a heart attack."

Michael obeys Jed's directions and begins to regain his breath and wits. Jed's innocuous accusation had felt like a hunting knife being driven into his chest.

Get ahold of yourself and calm down, or you're going to ruin everything.

He sits upright and gives Jed a sheepish grin. "I didn't take time to eat breakfast this morning. I think my blood sugar dropped suddenly. I'm sorry to give you a scare."

Jed laughed. "Well, you did! You'll give me a heart attack. We can't lose the best pastor we ever had just when you're getting started. You saw that crowd today, didn't you? You are packing the pews, Brother, I mean packing those pews!"

CHAPTER THIRTY-THREE

AS THE SUN RELEASES ITS hold on the day and nighttime takes over, Hope drives her car into the church parking lot and parks across from the only other car there, which she assumes belongs to Michael. When she'd called him to make this appointment, he'd insisted she drop any formal ways of addressing him and simply call him "Michael." It felt odd to do so, because of her childhood experience as a Catholic. "Men of the cloth," as her mother used to refer to the priests, were to be revered and addressed as "Father."

Michael's easygoing, unassuming manner, and *that smile of his*, helped her feel at ease. *I've never been around anyone like him—a man brimming with self-confidence, but with humility, too.* However, there was another element to him, *or is it just me?*, that intrigued and attracted her to him. It was what she felt when he took her home from Lisa's funeral, a hesitation in leaving that felt like he was drawn to her and wanted to stay with her.

Don't be so stupid! He's a pastor, you idiot, quit fantasizing.

Yet it was how he looked at her when she

visited his church, once again a brief moment together, still it was filled with tension, like they were playing tug-of-war with each other.

She shook her head to clear her thoughts.

You're here because you need help. Stay focused on that.

Getting out of her car, Hope walks to the side entrance that's lit up where Michael told her he'd be waiting to let her in. A window down the side of the building reveals a glowing light from inside. Other than these two, there are no other lights on.

She squints against the light and peers through the glass doors. Almost immediately, Michael appears through a semi-dark entrance inside and approaches the doors.

Twisting open the door lock, he pushes open the door and smiles at her. "Come in, Hope. I'm pleased to see you."

She slips past him and watches nervously as he locks the door behind her. The tiniest of warnings sounds in her brain, but she quickly sweeps it aside.

"We have to keep the building locked," he explains, "even though this is a rural area. We just can't take any chances."

"Yeah, I know," she agrees. "Idiots are everywhere."

They stand looking at each other for a second, then he says, "Why don't you follow me to my office?"

As she follows behind him, she can't help noticing he has a nice looking butt. She hears

Carol Ann chastising her for noticing and Whitney giving her a thumbs up.

Entering his office, she takes in the shelves loaded with books, his desk with an open Bible on it, and a sitting area with armchairs and loveseat. "Have you read all those books?"

He laughs. "Not all of them yet, but eventually I intend to. A lot of them were my dad's. He was a preacher, too." He points to the loveseat, and she sits down as he sits across from her.

"Is that how somebody gets to be a pastor?" she asks. "It's like a family thing?"

He laughs again. "No, no, it's not like that at all. How long have you been going to church?"

She knew this visit was to be about her, but his quick shift makes her feel defensive. "Since I've lived here, I haven't been to church."

He raises his eyebrows. "Really? So, how old were you the last time you went to church?"

She thinks for a moment and says, "Probably fourteen." *And ten lifetimes ago.*

Leaning forward, he says, "That's interesting. What kind of church was it?"

She pulls her legs up underneath her and looks at her hands. "Catholic."

"I see. So, you were raised Catholic?"

She nods without looking.

He sits back in his chair. "I'm sorry, Hope, I don't mean to be nosey. None of that is my business, and it isn't why you came to see me. I'm just a curious person by nature. Please, accept my apology."

This prompts her to look up. "It's okay. It's my

fault. I'm just not the kind of person who talks about themselves. I don't open up very easily. You didn't do anything wrong."

"Would you like some bottled water?'"

"That'd be nice."

He walks behind his desk, bends over, and stands up with a bottle in each hand. "Public speakers have to keep hydrated," he says, with a smile.

She eyes him as they both take a drink. She can think of no reason why she should feel nervous or hesitant with him. "If you can't trust a priest, who can you trust?" her mother used to say.

But how many walls should I let down? What do I trust him with?

She takes a drink, then says, "I feel like I'm walking in quicksand."

Michael scoots to the edge of his chair and leans toward her, with his forearms on his knees. His eyes draw her in. She feels like she's in an innertube, going over a waterfall. Fear and excitement race through her veins, and she clenches her fists.

"I've never heard anyone use that description before," Michael says, "but it makes me think I know how you feel, like putting one foot in front of the other takes all the strength you can muster, and yet you sink deeper and deeper, barely able to breathe."

Hope sits there, spellbound. Fear evaporates, and excitement turns into wonder. "That's exactly it. How is it possible that someone like you could experience that feeling? You're a man of God and a healer of souls. Your life is the life everyone envies."

Michael's eyes redden. In a voice barely more than a whisper, he says, "Maybe I shouldn't have told you that." He looks away.

Something shifts in Hope, and she feels the need to comfort him. She starts to reach out and touch him but quickly changes her mind. "I'm glad you told me, and I'm sorry you've been to the place I find myself. So, if you've been there, maybe you can help me find my way out."

When he raises his face, silver streaks are where tears have traced their way down his cheeks. "Maybe we can find our way out of the quicksand together."

Hope is stunned by his unspoken admission. "I went to see a counselor once when I was in high school. But she acted like my problems weren't important. It was a real turnoff, which is why I've never gone to a counselor since then. You're...you're different. I'm not sure what I expected when I came here tonight, but it certainly wasn't this. You've lived in dark places, too, haven't you?"

He nods and crosses his legs. "This isn't supposed to be about me, Hope. You came here for help, not to help me. I'll be honest, I haven't had a lot of experience doing counseling. There was a class on it I took when I was in seminary, but actually doing it is...it's a lot different. It's just that—" He stops and looks away.

"It's just what?" she asks.

He looks back at her. "You're just so easy to

talk to. I don't know why. I mean, I barely know you, and yet I feel like I've known you forever. It makes me feel a little crazy, and I don't know what to do about it."

Three hours later, Hope follows Michael to the door leading to the parking lot. Rather than having sat through a counseling session, she feels like she's been on a date. She told him her entire story and cried so much, he ran out of Kleenex and let her use his handkerchief, the same handkerchief she now clutches in her fist. And he told her about growing up in the shadow of his severe, exacting father.

He unlocks the door and looks at her. "How do you feel?"

Giving him a weak smile, she says, "Exhausted, but lighter. You know a lot about me, and that scares me a little."

He takes her hand (not for the first time this evening). "I will never betray the trust you placed in me tonight. I feel honored that you felt safe enough to share your story with me. And I appreciate you letting me unburden myself a bit by telling you about me and Dad. If that was something I shouldn't have done, I apologize. It's just I felt God spoke to me and told me to share with you. And so, I hope you'll reciprocate the confidentiality I give you."

If I don't leave this second, I am going to kiss this man. And if I do that, I won't be able to stop whatever happens next.

"You can trust me," she says quickly.

Taking her hand from his, she dashes out the door and toward her car.

CHAPTER THIRTY-FOUR

MICHAEL WATCHES HOPE DRIVE AWAY. *What in the world just happened?*

Like an angry mob, a chorus of condemning voices (professors at seminary, classmates, his father, even his own) chastise him for how he completely mishandled the counseling session with Hope. He'd never met anyone he was so completely comfortable with right from the start.

It just felt natural to open up to her about myself, which is why it didn't feel like a counseling session. He almost feels like they had a first date, so much so that he had an overwhelming urge to give her a kiss before she left. *Thank God I had enough self-control to stop myself.*

Walking slowly back to his office, he thinks about how intrigued he is by Hope. *What a story she has!* Repeatedly knocked down by life, yet she survives. There's a depth to her he's rarely encountered.

Sitting down at his desk, his eyes travel down to the lower right-hand drawer. He glances at the clock on his desk to see if he has time to text

Brittany and is shocked to see how late it is.

Sarah's going to be furious. So, if she's going to be furious anyway...

Reaching down, he opens the drawer, takes out Strong's Concordance, and opens it to remove his secret phone. After powering it on, he sends a text.

MICHAEL: HEY, IT'S ME. GOT TIME TO CHAT?

Five minutes pass with no reply, then ten minutes.

She must be busy.

He opens the browser and types in a few letters. Instantly, one of his favorite porn sites appears. His heart starts pounding, and his face burns.

Michael awakes with a jerk.

Jed stands on the other side of his desk, hair askew, obviously dressed in haste, with a look of concern on his face. "Brother Michael, are you okay?"

Michael looks around, wide-eyed, trying to orient himself. He's in his office. The side of his face feels damp, and he reaches up and touches it.

I must have fallen asleep and drooled on myself.

Looking down, he sees a circle of moisture on his desk, but he also sees his secret phone lying on his lap and the concordance open on the floor. Panic seizes him.

"What time is it?"

"Man, it's one o'clock in the morning! Sarah

called me, frantic that she couldn't get you on the phone. She said you were coming here to do a counseling session with someone." Agitation gives his words an extra punch Michael feels deep in his chest.

His mind spins, trying to make sense of what's happened and figure out a way to cover himself.

Last thing I remember is looking at porn and pleasuring myself. Could I have passed out, or simply laid my head on the desk to catch my breath and fell asleep?

"I'm sorry to have worried everybody," he says, "and specifically to drag you out of bed in the middle of the night. I did have a counseling session with someone. I turned my phone off so we wouldn't be interrupted, and I forgot to turn it back on. After the session, I decided to study some, and I guess I fell asleep. I feel so stupid right now."

Jed's face relaxes. "And I'm sorry for yelling at you. I tend to be a bear when I get roused up in the middle of the night. Who was your counseling session with?" Michael opens his mouth to reply, but Jed stops him. "No, don't tell me. That's none of my business. I don't know why I even asked. Did the session go well?"

Palming the phone, Michael bends down and drops it into the concordance as he answers, "Yes, it did. I need to get these books cleaned up and get home to Sarah." He closes the book, places it on his desk, and stands up.

"The old Strong's Concordance," Jed says with a smile as he picks it up. "I've got one of these.

It's been around a long time, hasn't it?"

Fear nearly knocks Michael's legs out from under him, and he grabs the edge of the desk to keep from collapsing.

Jed drops the book on the desk and reaches across to grab Michael's arm. "Are you sure you're all right?"

Michael puts his Bible on top of the concordance and keeps his hand there. "I think I stood up too quickly. I'm fine, though." He tries to smile, but his strained face doesn't cooperate fully. "You're correct about Strong's. It's been a staple in serious Bible student libraries for decades."

His attempt at lessening Jed's concern fails miserably. Jed folds his arms across his chest. "Somethings not right here, I can feel it. Tell me what's going on."

Alarms clang in Michael's head, and the quote "Ask not for whom the bell tolls; it tolls for thee" blazes like a neon sign. For a millisecond, he considers coming clean with Jed, but he quickly banishes the thought.

It would be tantamount to committing suicide.

Instead, he feigns ignorance and paints it with an accusation. "What do you mean? Do you think I'm lying?"

Jed drops his hands to his sides. "No, no, that didn't come out right. Please don't be offended. I just want to know if you have a health issue you've not told us about. Maybe you're afraid to let anyone know. I know plenty of really good doctors and specialists I can get you in to see, if that's the problem. I just want to be helpful to you, Brother Michael."

Michael breathes easier. "And I apologize to you. I shouldn't be so defensive. I promise I'm fine and don't have any health problems I'm aware of." He takes out his phone and powers it on. "I'm going to let Sarah know everything is okay and head home. Again, I'm sorry you had your sleep disturbed." He dials her number, and she answers on the first ring. "It's me, sweetheart." He jerks the phone away from his ear as she screams at him. When her voice dies down, he holds the phone closer and says, "I know. I'm so sorry I worried you. Jed is here at the office with me. I accidently fell asleep. I'll tell you all about it when I get home. I'm headed there now." The other end of the line goes dead as she hangs up without further comment.

He gives Jed a sheepish grin. "Looks like I'm headed for the doghouse for a few days."

"I've been there more than a few times," Jed amiably replies. "Buy her some flowers; that's what I always do."

Michael moves from behind his desk and heads toward the door. "That's a good idea. Let's both head home. And again, let me apologize for —"

Jed cuts him off. "You've apologized once, no need to repeat it. Apology accepted. Let's go home."

Shame and remorse ball up in Michael's stomach as he drives home, and for a moment he thinks he may throw up.

Lord God in heaven, I wish You would strike me dead so I could be delivered from my cursed body that enslaves me. I hate myself and deserve nothing but damnation from You. Whatever Sarah hurls at me, I deserve ten times more. It's my behavior that depresses her and makes her act crazy. I want to do right, I really do, but I don't think I will ever escape from the chains of my fleshly appetite.

The streetlights blur as tears fill his eyes. He stops at a traffic light and pounds the steering wheel with his fists as he screams. It's a cry of desperation, of a tormented soul, of a wild animal with its leg caught in the jaws of a trap. Suddenly, he jerks open his door and vomits on the pavement.

CHAPTER THIRTY-FIVE

LIKE BREAD DOUGH RISING IN a warm room, dread swells in Michael's chest the closer he gets to his house, where he expects to find a wrath-filled Sarah; so, it surprises him to see no lights on when he pulls in the driveway.

That's either a really good sign or a really bad one. Either she's gone to bed, or she's done something to herself.

He imagines himself walking in and finding her dead by her own hand.

The outpouring of grief and support from this community would be huge. It would probably create another surge in attendance at church, which might trigger a serious discussion about expanding the size of the sanctuary.

He sees himself standing on the stage, preaching to a sea of faces with expressions of adoration and sympathy on them.

Shaking his head, he says to himself, *You really are a hopelessly sick, narcissistic SOB.*

Inserting his key into the back door lock, he quietly steps inside, trying not to wake Sarah, if indeed she is asleep.

As soon as the door clicks shut behind him, an unearthly shriek, much like the cry of a banshee, pierces his ears, small fists pummel his body, and sharp fingernails tear at his shirt and face.

"I'm going to kill you!" Sarah screams.

Michael throws up his arms to protect his face and stumbles backward into the door.

"You're driving me insane!" Sarah yells. Buttons fly off as she gets a grip on his shirt and jerks it open.

It's the shock of her attack more so than the pain from her fists that pushes Michael backward, but now, as her fingernails rake across his exposed chest, searing pain causes him to cry out. He starts to strike her in self-defense but stops himself just in time and wraps his arms around her in a bear hug.

"Sarah, get ahold of yourself."

A stream of swear words like he's never heard from her shoots out her mouth. Unable to move her arms, she kicks at his shins and headbutts his mouth.

He flings her to the floor and grabs his leg as the taste of warm blood touches his tongue. He hears her scuffling on the floor but can't see her.

"You've cheated on me for the last time," she says, but instead of it being a loud cry, it's the deep growl of a tortured beast intent on devouring its tormentor.

Michael braces himself for another onslaught. Instead, he hears a kitchen drawer opening to his right and the sound of Sarah rifling through it.

She's looking for a knife!

He fumbles around and finds the light switch. Bright light sweeps away the darkness in a flash and reveals the two combatants squinting at each other. Parallel bloody trails run down his chest, and his face is blotchy. Across the room, Sarah holds a butcher knife over her head. Her chest heaves as she tries to catch her breath.

"Sarah, please listen to me. I haven't done anything. I had my counseling session, which did last longer than I expected, but then I decided to study some, and I accidently fell asleep. Jed found me asleep at my desk. I hadn't gone anywhere."

"You know I don't believe you, don't you? I have no reason to."

"I know, and that's my fault. But Jed can verify part of my story. Will you put the knife down, please?"

She looks at the knife as if she's never seen it and immediately drops it on the floor. "Who were you counseling? No, wait, I know your answer, 'I can't tell you, it's confidential.' And it's just that kind of situation that makes it difficult for pastors' wives to trust their husbands. People look at you almost as if you're a god. But we wives know differently. You've got feet of clay."

Michael understands the verse she's referencing from the book of Daniel. Nodding in agreement with her, he says, "You're right. We're just as human as everyone else, especially me. You know full well I'm weak, but I'm working on being a changed man. That man who hurt you so badly has grown up and matured. I no longer chase after childish things. Where I messed up tonight is not calling as soon as the counseling session was over, and for that I apologize, sincerely." He takes a tentative step toward her to measure her reaction.

Her expression transforms from one of anger to one of fear. "You scare me," she says.

He takes another step. "Why? You know I would never do anything to hurt you."

"But you have hurt me. And if I make the choice to hold you close to me, then I'm giving you an incredible amount of power over me. You can hurt me so badly, Michael, you can hurt me like nobody else, and that terrifies me."

"For the rest of my life, I'll regret hurting you. But you have got to believe I'm a changed man." He moves to within six feet of her, kneels down, bows his head, and waits.

Several moments pass in the silent room. Eventually, Sarah says, "I went hiking with my Pawpaw when I was a kid. We came to a creek that had a log across it, and Pawpaw told me to walk across. I asked him, 'How will I know it'll hold me up and not break?' He answered, 'You won't know until you try it.' That's exactly how I feel right now. For me, the creek is trust, and the log is your promise. I want to cross to the other side with you, but I'm afraid to trust your promise."

Michael tries to make himself cry, because he knows it'll make Sarah cave in to his wishes, but for whatever reason, no tears come. He looks at his savaged chest and rises just enough so she can see it.

"Jesus didn't deserve a scourging, but I deserve mine. I will bare these marks as a witness against me and the pain I've put you through."

Sarah winces as she looks at his chest and tears well up in her eyes. "I can't believe I did that to you. I never meant to hurt you. I'm so sorry." She reaches for a washcloth and wets it in the sink. "Come sit in a chair, and let me tend to you."

He acquiesces to her and sits in the chair.

Setting a first-aid kit on the table, she gently dabs at his wounds. Her face is inches from his, and he smells a faint hint of her perfume.

She really is a good woman. I should be more grateful for her. No other woman would have put up with me as long as she has.

She kisses his chest. "I'm so, so sorry, Michael. Please forgive me."

He takes her chin in his hand, bends down, and kisses her on the lips, not just a perfunctory touching of lips, but a kiss he hopes conveys to her how much he appreciates her. She responds by teasing his mouth open with her tongue, and he feels his inner fire ignite. "I've never known anyone who kisses like you do," he's told her many times, and he's meant it each time. Her kisses take him from zero to sixty in a matter of seconds.

His excitement rises, and Sarah breaks away and takes a deep breath. Looking toward the bulge in his pants, she says coyly, "I think somebody needs to let off some pressure."

Michael stands and pulls her to her feet. "You're right."

Leading her by the hand, they head down the hallway to their bedroom.

CHAPTER THIRTY-SIX

PUTTING IN HER EARRINGS, LIZ walks over to the bed, where Jed lies sleeping under the covers. The background noise of the morning news on WPSD-TV is the only sound in the room.

She shakes him by the shoulder and says, "Jed, are you going to get up? I've called you four times. You're not sick, are you?"

He slowly rises to a sitting position and scratches the top of his head. "Gee, I can't get awake. That late-night escapade with Brother Michael cost me several hours of good sleep." Rubbing his eyes, he yawns, then gets out of bed and disappears into the bathroom.

"I barely remember you coming back home. What was that all about anyway?"

"You know, I'm not really sure. I mean, I know what was said, but I'm not sure I got the whole story."

"Sarah sounded really freaked out when she called you."

"She was, because she couldn't get ahold of him and wasn't sure where he was."

Liz joins him at the double-sink vanity and large mirror for a last look at her makeup as he rubs shaving cream on his face. "I think she's very insecure and gets upset easily."

"I agree."

"I assume you found him."

"Yeah. He was in his office at the church. And get this—he was asleep."

"Asleep? Like, sleeping on the loveseat in his office?"

"No, he was asleep at his desk. He'd had a counseling session with someone and decided to do some studying afterward for his Sunday sermon and accidently fell asleep."

Rather than continuing to talk to each other's reflection in the mirror, she turns to face him. "I guess that's a little odd, but he certainly isn't the first person who ever fell asleep at their desk. It's just unfortunate it was in the middle of the night and frightened Sarah. Why didn't she just call him?"

"He had his phone turned off," Jed replies. "Didn't want the counseling session interrupted."

"Okay, I guess I can see that, too. So, what makes you uncertain about what was going on?"

"I got the feeling he was trying to hide something. He acted nervous, so nervous I thought he was going to pass out at one point. He turned pale as a sheet, then he got real defensive."

Liz mulls this over, trying to picture the scene.

He turns and looks at her. "Uh oh, I've seen that look before."

"I'm trying to figure out what he was trying to hide from you. There have been times when I've wondered if Michael is really what he acts like he is, if there's something going on behind the facade."

"I'll turn the tables, then. What makes you suspicious?"

Liz hesitates, wondering if she should say it. Taking a deep breath, she says, "I think he's attracted to me."

Jed gives a little laugh and turns back to the mirror to finish shaving. "He wouldn't be a normal man if he didn't find you attractive."

"No, it's more than that. He tends to invade my space when we're together, planning a worship service. Nothing that's blatant and easy to see and call out. It's very subtle."

"Maybe he's just being over-friendly or trying too hard. He's a very passionate man, you know, and sometimes those kinds of people aren't so aware of personal boundaries. Maybe you're hypersensitive to that kind of thing."

"Don't try to tell me I'm hypersensitive," Liz snaps.

"I'm sorry, I didn't mean it the way it sounded."

"Yes, you did. How quickly you want to defend the pastor over your wife." She spins around and walks out of the bedroom.

"Aw, Liz, come on," he calls after her, "don't be mad at me."

Suddenly, what she sees on the TV screen stops her. "Jed, get in here quick."

Joining her while wiping off his face with a

hand towel, he says, "Please forgive me."

Ignoring his comment, she points at the TV. "Look!"

The screen is filled with a mugshot of Lloyd Biddle. The voice of the news anchor says, "The original lawsuit that was brought by Carol Ann Gleason has now grown into a class action lawsuit, as seven other women and three unnamed juveniles have come forward with allegations of sexual impropriety by Biddle. We'll have more on this breaking story at noon."

Liz grabs the remote, turns off the TV, and whirls around at Jed. "You and Biddle are as thick as thieves. I swear to you, if you are involved in any of this, I will use pruning shears and make you a eunuch and enjoy doing it." By the time she finishes, she's inches from his face, but his eyes are glued to the blank TV screen.

"This can't be true," he says quietly while shaking his head. A little louder, he says, "It just can't be. This is going to ruin everything."

She narrows her eyes and slaps him hard across the face.

He jumps back. "What was that for?"

"Did you hear what I said to you?" she screams.

"About what?"

"About what I'll do to you if you're involved?"

"What do you mean by 'involved?'"

She swears at him as frustration, and anger and disgust boil up in her. She spits out her accusation one word at a time. "If. You've. Touched. A. Girl—"

Jed's eyes grow wide, and he throws up his

hand. "Liz, no! I have never...would never do anything like that. I can't believe you'd think such a thing."

"I never thought you'd cheat on me."

"Are you ever going to forgive me for that?"

"I've forgiven you long ago, but I haven't forgotten it, because I can't."

His shoulders sag. "You're right...you're right."

"Tell me what you meant when you said this situation with Biddle is going to ruin everything?"

"It gives our school and community a black eye prospective businesses won't ignore. I'm working my tail off trying to help sell our community to people who express an interest in coming here. You won't believe all the things they pay attention to when analyzing a location. And schools are a big one."

She shakes her head. "You know what's sad about this? It's that you're more concerned with money than you are with the unbelievable amount of damage that man has done to girls. How would you feel if you had a daughter and she was a victim?" Without waiting for a reply, she walks out of the room.

As she passes Mark's bedroom, she sees the door is half-open, and he's sitting on the edge of his bed with his head in his hands. She taps once on the door and goes in.

"Hey, big guy, what's going on?"

When she gets closer, she sees he's been crying. Her heart splits in two. Reaching behind with her foot, she pushes the door shut, then sits down beside him and rubs his back.

"Mark? Talk to me. I know something's been troubling you."

Without looking at her, he says, "There's nothing you can do. It's too late."

She lays her head on his shoulder. "Oh Mark, please don't shut me out. It's never too late. Give me a chance to see if I can help."

He looks at her with red-rimmed, bloodshot eyes. "Believe me, Mom, you can't fix this. I'm so stupid, stupid, stupid. I just didn't think far enough ahead...didn't realize...didn't imagine things would turn out this way. And now, what's done is done."

Every fiber of Liz's body screams at her to break her son open and dig through him until she finds the cancer she's suspected has been eating away at him and yank it out. But she knows the harder she pushes, the more likely he'll shut down. So, she bites her tongue to keep it in place. But that doesn't stop tears from cascading down her angular cheeks.

This unlocks another chamber in Mark's heart, and he falls into her arms, burying his face in her chest and sobbing.

CHAPTER THIRTY-SEVEN

"WELL, WELL, LOOK AT YOU," Whitney says as Hope walks into their office.

Carol Ann looks at her, too, and smiles. "What's happened to you?"

Hope ignores them, goes to her desk, and turns on her computer. "I don't know what you all are talking about."

"You don't know?" Whitney queries her. "Then you must not have paid attention when you looked in the mirror this morning, because what we see," she motions her finger between her and Carol Ann, "what we see is someone who has some light in her eyes, and maybe even the trace of a smile. What do you think, Carol Ann? Is that a smile I see?"

Carol Ann picks up the conversation baton and says, "Oh, that's a smile for sure. The kind that can't be hidden even if she tried."

Hope tries to keep a straight face in spite of knowing they're right, and a smile is begging to spread across her face.

"Come on," Whitney teases, "tell us what happened. Did Luther come home and you all had welcome-home sex all night last night?"

Hope responds with a very real expression of disgust on her face. "Sex is not what Luther does well, trust me. But anyway, he didn't come home."

"If she doesn't want to tell us, leave her alone," Carol Ann says. "I guess we're not that kind of friends to her." She shapes her face into her best overly-dramatic expression of hurt.

Hope laughs in spite of herself. "Okay, you two. You're impossible. The truth is, I took your advice, and it helped." Turning her back to them, she types in her username and password on her computer.

The next thing she knows, both her friends appear behind her computer screen. "If you think that's enough information," Whitney says, "then you've got another thing coming. We're here, and we want details."

"Okay, I give up. I went and talked to the man who did Lisa's funeral, Michael Trent." Just saying his name out loud gives her a feeling of excitement.

Whitney points at her and says to Carol Ann, "Look at her pupils. They're as big as nickels. I believe somebody done got the hots for a preacher man." Ripples of laughter spill out of her.

"Look, before you start getting any ideas, he's married, and he's the pastor of the church."

"That don't stop him from being good looking."

"Whitney, really!" Carol Ann retorts. "Can

you not think of anything but how a man looks? He's devoted his life to saving sinners and helping people. Let's give him some respect."

Whitney gives her a dubious look. "You're serious, aren't you? Well, whatever you say, but if he's good looking, then that's God's fault, and I'm going to thank Him for it."

Carol Ann ignores her and says to Hope, "I'm proud of you for talking to him and happy it helped you. Will you see him again?"

Instead of giving the enthusiastic "Yes" she feels, Hope answers, "I really haven't thought about that. I'm just happy not wearing that black cape of depression, even if it's just for today. Now, you all better get to your desks."

Carol Ann walks around the desk and gives Hope a hug. "It's nice to see you smile." She then heads to her desk.

Whitney walks past them and huffs, "Well, I'm going to Google me a picture of this man, just to see what I'm missing."

For lunch, the three of them decide to keep it simple and eat at Burger King.

While standing in line to order, an older man wearing faded overalls and a tired-looking ball cap walks up to Carol Ann and says, "Are you the one saying those things about Mr. Biddle?"

She turns white and stammers, "E-Excuse me?"

"Yeah, you're the one all right. So, you let him have sex with you when you were seventeen, and now you're going to complain about it? Well, you should have kept your legs together back then. Why ruin the reputation of a good man?" He ambles off, without waiting for a response.

Hope throws her arm around Carol Ann's waist, fearing she's about to faint.

But Whitney says in a loud voice, "Oh, hell no!" She stomps off after the man and catches him just as he reaches an exit door. She taps him hard on the shoulder. "Hey, you!"

The man turns around and gives her an uncertain look.

Continuing to speak loudly, Whitney says, "You have any daughters or granddaughters?"

He looks around and sees everyone in the restaurant is staring at the confrontation. "What business is that of yours?"

"Are you ashamed to answer the question?" Whitney prods.

"No. I have a twelve-year-old granddaughter."

"How would you feel if she told you her principal had sex with her?"

"I'd kill him. But that's different. She's only twelve."

"Would you feel the same way if she was thirteen?"

"Of course."

"What about if she was fourteen, or fifteen, or sixteen, or seventeen?"

The implications of any answer he might give, coupled with the weight of her unspoken accusation, settles on his face and pulls down the corners of his eyes. He mumbles, "Well...I don't know...I mean...maybe I was wrong."

Waving her finger in his face, Whitney says, "No, no, no. You're not going to come in here and insult my friend loud enough for everyone to hear and then make an apology in a whisper." She points at Carol Ann. "You're going to march over there and tell her and everyone in here you're sorry, because believe you me—you are."

He hangs his head and makes his way to Carol Ann, with the scent of shame and regret following in his wake.

Hope holds Carol Ann tightly, as much to keep herself in place as to support her friend. She feels like she's in a movie and everything's moving in slow motion.

Red lines crisscross the whites of the old man's eyes as he stops within a few feet of the two of them. Grey beard stubble lies unshaven in the deep creases of his face. He looks at Carol Ann with uncertainty, and a part of Hope feels sorry for him.

He removes his cap, wadding it up in his hands, and reveals a few threads of hair combed over his bald head. Clearing his throat, he says in a trembling voice, "I'm sorry for what I said, and I'm sorry I embarrassed you."

There's a smattering of applause as he leaves.

"I need to sit down," Carol Ann whispers to Hope.

They find a corner booth and collapse onto the seat.

Whitney joins them and says, "What kind of craziness was that?"

Carol Ann finds her voice and says, "It's the kind of craziness my lawyer said would happen. I thought he was just being extra precautious, but I guess he was right. I've noticed some people looking at me and whispering in their friend's ear, but I dismissed it as being my own paranoia. What that man just said to me is what everybody must be thinking." Tears well up in her eyes. "I should have just kept my mouth shut."

"No," Hope says, "you're doing the right thing. It's just that doing the right thing sometimes comes with a high price tag."

Whitney chimes in, "You've become a heroine for all the women around here who've suffered a similar experience, and trust me, there's plenty of them. I'll admit to you, I had a really hard time believing all the things Bill Cosby was accused of. Even though I didn't know him personally, I admired him so much. I didn't want to believe what those women were saying. But I've learned people like him, like Biddle, use my kind of admiration as a weapon in their secret, sinister life. It's like all those priests who abused little boys for years. Those boys practically worshipped them and would do anything for them." Her eyes grow sad, and she stares at the table. "And they did do anything for them."

Silence fills in the spaces between the three women.

After several moments, Hope says, "I've been thinking a lot about those older men I lived with when I first arrived in Paducah. I told you all I was taking advantage of them, but now I see they were taking advantage of my desperate situation. If they'd been the kind of person they ought to be, they would have offered to help me without expecting me to give them sex. They would have pointed me in a direction where I could get the kind of help I really needed." She sighs. "It makes me really sad now."

Whitney reaches across the table and holds open her hands. "Both of you, give me your hands."

With a pensive smile, Carol Ann complies, and Hope follows her lead.

Squeezing their hands, Whitney says, "I'm so proud to know you two strong women. Life hasn't been kind to you, but you haven't let it destroy you. And isn't that what matters?"

Hope says, "You wouldn't say that about me if you knew how many times I've wanted to call it quits."

Carol Ann looks at her. "But you haven't. You're the real hero here, Hope. I haven't told you this, but you're the one who gave me the strength to go public with my story about Mr. Biddle. I look at you and everything you've been through, and it takes my breath away."

"Yes," Whitney agrees, "what Carol Ann said."

CHAPTER THIRTY-EIGHT

Before stepping into his morning shower, Michael inspects the injuries Sarah inflicted on him the night before. His chest looks like a bear took a swipe at him, which, although it's painful to the touch, it'll be easy to keep hidden. The most troubling wound is his left eye, which is bruised and slightly swollen.

No way to hide it. And the coloring is likely to get more pronounced for the next day or so.

He considers calling Helen and telling her he's not feeling well and won't be in, but he hates setting a precedent of not being dependable. Of all the people in the church, he wants her on his side.

When he steps in the shower and the water hits his chest, a small cry of pain escapes, and he covers himself protectively with his arms.

"Are you okay, Michael?" Sarah asks through the bathroom door.

"Yeah, just stubbed my toe getting in. I'm fine."

He begins washing off the night of passion they had last night. Not since they first met has

Sarah been as aggressive and accommodating as she was last night. It was like the guilt she felt for attacking him forced her to try her best to prove herself worthy of his forgiveness.

Almost immediately, he becomes aroused but reaches for the faucet and turns off the hot water.

I haven't got time for this.

Once he's dressed, he starts through the kitchen on his way out the back door.

"I fixed you breakfast," Sarah says, pointing at the table with a plate of eggs, bacon, and toast sitting on it. "I'll pour you a cup of coffee."

"That's awfully nice, Sarah, but I'm running a little late and need to be on my way. Is that okay?"

The sting and disappointment are immediately visible on her face. "I'm sorry."

She chisels a forced smile onto her face. "Oh, it's okay. I'll just eat it myself. No worries."

Even though he knows she doesn't mean it, he appreciates her effort. Putting his hand on her shoulder, he says, "I love you, and I'll see you this evening."

Sounding like a little child, she says, "Can't I have a kiss?"

"Sure."

He leans down, kisses her forehead, then heads out the door.

As soon as he enters Helen's office, she stands up and says, "You have a visitor in your office. She said she's an old friend and wanted to surprise you. I normally wouldn't have let her in without you being here, but..." She pauses, looking for the right words. "But because of the way she's dressed, I didn't think I should have her sitting out here, waiting for you."

Michael freezes, and a chill runs up his spine.

Helen squints at him. "What happened to your eye?"

He has difficulty reining in his racing thoughts, so he mutely stares at her.

She touches the side of her eye. "Your eye. What happened to your eye?"

"Oh, that. It sounds rather cliché, but I ran into an open closet door during the night." He chuckles. "Boy, did I see stars. It looks worse than it is. No doubt I'll get some kidding over it." He looks toward his closed office door. "Did she say what her name is?"

She studies him closely, with the wisdom and experience of a lifetime educator who's heard every story and excuse in the book. She answers, "She wouldn't say, didn't want to give the surprise away. And if it turns out you don't know her and she's some kind of kook, I'll apologize and turn in my resignation. Nobody needs an old fool for a secretary, especially a church."

"I'm sure there'll be no need for that. But I can't imagine who it might be." Trying to look casual, he walks to his office door and enters the unknown.

Denial is knowing the truth but refusing to admit it, which is why finding Brittany sitting on the edge of his desk, wearing an impossibly short skirt, isn't a complete surprise, but it still gives him a shock strong enough, it pushes him backward against the closing door.

Smiling, Brittany slowly crosses her legs, deliberately revealing she's not wearing anything underneath her skirt. "It's about time you got here."

Michael feels like his head is going to explode. He charges toward her. Through clinched teeth, he whispers, "What the hell are you doing here?!"

She throws her arms around his neck, pulls him to her, and kisses him, forcing her tongue into his mouth. He returns her passion and feels warmth spreading throughout him until he opens his eyes, and instead of seeing her, he sees the visage of Kaa, the huge, powerful snake in *The Jungle Book*.

He jerks away from her, gasping. He feels like a trapped animal, because he knows his willpower is no match for hers. "Are you trying to get me in trouble? I told you you shouldn't come here. What if someone walks in? What if my secretary tells the church leaders about you? And what if word gets back to Sarah?"

Brittany slides off his desk and slithers toward him, backing him into a corner. She presses her hand on his crotch. "Haven't you missed me? Or have you already found someone here to play with?" With her last question, she squeezes him like a vise.

Michael doubles over in pain. "Let me go! Let me go!" She releases him, and he falls to his knees in agony.

She pushes him over, straddles his chest on her knees, and pins his shoulders to the floor.

He feels as powerless as a condemned convict strapped to an electric chair. "Brittany, please, there's no reason to be angry with me. I promise, there's no one else who's taken your place. I shouldn't have gotten so upset with you. It's just the unexpected shock of finding you in my office; I lost my mind for a minute."

She grinds herself on him and touches her finger to his lips. "You know what I want. Nobody does it like you do."

In spite of the chaos in his head, Michaels feels himself getting aroused.

She climbs off him and says, "Take me on your desk, like you used to in Kansas."

A quote from the Book of Proverbs comes to his mind: *With persuasive words she led him astray; she seduced him with her smooth talk. All at once he followed her like an ox going to the slaughter, like a deer stepping into a noose till an arrow pierces his liver, like a bird darting into a snare, little knowing it will cost him his life.* But the warning has no effect on him, and he consents to Brittany's bidding.

As soon as they finish, lust leaves him, and in its place shame and regret move in.

"I know what comes next," she says, "I've seen it before. You feel really bad for being such a bad boy. But you'll get over it, and you'll remember what happened and smile. I know you better than you know yourself. Wouldn't it be nice if you could have me anytime you wanted? If we were married, you could."

He knows he needs to answer her carefully, drawing a line with her that won't feel like a line. "I've never enjoyed anyone like I do you. You are incredible. And it would be a dream come true if we were together forever. I've just got to figure out a way to make it happen so I can still serve as a pastor."

She laughs at him. "You are a piece of work, you know that, don't you? Who in their right mind wants to serve God but lives the kind of secret life you do? It's like you have multiple personalities or something. You're only interested in being a pastor because of your daddy." In a mocking tone, she says, "Little boy doesn't want to disappoint Daddy." She grabs the front of his shirt and jerks him close. "I've told you, I won't keep waiting around for you to make a plan. I'll make it for you and carry it out. Then you won't have any excuses."

She straightens her clothes, checks her face in a small mirror from her purse, and prances out of his office.

CHAPTER THIRTY-NINE

Dr. Elliot leans forward and puts his elbows on his knees. He looks from Sarah to Michael and back to Sarah.

"You all have seen me several times now, so I'm going to be honest with you, Sarah, even though I suspect in doing so, it may hurt your feelings or make you mad, and you won't come back."

Sarah blinks her eyes several times but says nothing.

Michael holds his breath, sensing what the counselor says next will be critical in determining the direction his and Sarah's relationship takes in the future.

He's either going to say I'm a lying SOB or she's crazy.

"I believe," Dr. Elliot begins, "that you, Sarah, have what is called conjugal paranoia, or delusional jealousy. Some refer to it as the 'Othello Syndrome.' My basis is, you can't produce one concrete fact that Michael is being unfaithful to you; it's only what you believe and feel."

Relief floods Michael, and he relaxes but watches Sarah out the corner of his eye.

Elliot continues, "I think I understand why you feel the way you do, Sarah. Michael has admittedly been unfaithful in the past, and the scar from that filters everything you see and believe."

Cracks appear in Sarah's perfectly made-up facade—one corner of her mouth quivers, and that quiver travels down to her chin. Her lips part as her breathing becomes irregular and her eyes close.

Michael senses she's on the verge of disintegrating. He reaches over to place his hand over hers, but just before they touch, she jumps up from the loveseat. Her face turns red.

Her closed mouth twists and puckers as if she's taken a drink of something sour and can't decide whether to swallow it or spit it out. Looking at Michael, she says, "Of course you win. What should have I expected? You've got the smooth words and calm exterior, while I'm an emotional volcano and look like an insane woman." She turns on Dr. Elliot. "And you, I can't believe you charge the kind of money you charge when you're clearly inept. You believe him rather than me because you're a man, too, and men always side with men against the woman. For all I know, you're as big a philanderer as he is."

The heat behind her words pushes Elliot back in his chair. "I appreciate you being honest with me about how you feel. You know, there are medications that might can help you with..." He stops, and his eyes grow wide.

Sarah has her fist drawn back. "You sorry little—"

Michael lunges for her, and the blow meant for Dr. Elliot lands squarely on his nose. Stinging stars populate his vision, but he still manages to get his arms around Sarah. "Sarah, please!"

There's a clatter behind him. Turning his head, he sees Dr. Elliot has tumbled backward out of his chair.

Sarah wrenches herself free from his grasp. "Let me go!"

Michael is torn between helping Elliot off the floor while apologizing to him for Sarah's behavior or ushering Sarah out of the office before anything else happens. However, it's a feeling of warmth moving down his upper lip that makes him pause. Reaching up, he touches it with his fingers and sees it's blood.

Sarah sees it, too, causing her mood and demeanor to pivot on a dime. "Oh, Michael, what have I done?" She grabs a box of tissue off the lamp table, pulls out a handful, and carefully holds it against his nose. "I'm so, so sorry. I didn't mean to hit you." She looks at Elliot struggling to his feet. "I didn't mean to hit anyone. I just lost my temper. Please forgive me."

Even though she's squeezing his nose too hard, Michael holds his tongue and gives her room for words and acts of penance.

"Well," Dr. Elliot says as he rights his chair, "that's certainly a new experience for me."

Michael and Sarah turn to face him.

"Dr. Elliot," Sarah says, "I'm sorry for my behavior. I still don't agree with your diagnosis, but I shouldn't have lost control like that."

"I accept your apology, Sarah, and I would be more than happy for you to continue seeing me. Perhaps I can help you."

In a cold tone that's new to Michael's ears, she says, "That won't be necessary. I know what I need to do." She gives the handful of bloody tissues to Michael and says, "I'll be in the car."

Confused, Michael watches her retreat through the door. Instead of following her, he turns his attention to Elliot. "I regret this happened, and I apologize for Sarah's actions. Please don't think badly of her. She's really a good woman, with a good heart, who always means well."

"Sarah's already apologized. You don't have to apologize for her. I hope you'll encourage her to find another counselor, perhaps one with more experience than I. I can't help feeling like there's something in you all's situation I'm missing."

"I'll keep that in mind," Michael replies. *What you've seen is exactly what I want you to see.*

As he walks to the car to join Sarah, he's uncertain what shape she'll be in. Her statement to Dr. Elliot, "I know what I need to do," was something he's never heard her say in the calm, calculated way she said it.

After he gets in the car, he asks, "Are you okay?"

"I'm fine."

Familiar words, but without the normal either indignant sound or tender tone. It feels colder and more deliberate. A tiny warning bell sounds in the corner of his mind.

"Look, don't let what Dr. Elliot said bother you. He's young and doesn't know what he's talking about. I've never even heard of that—what did he call it?"

"Conjugal paranoia, or delusional jealousy. I'm delusional, Michael. Nothing I see or hear is real. You're officially married to a crazy woman."

He starts the car and starts driving home. "Let's find a different counselor to see. Someone who might really help us."

"There's no need to do that. What you need to understand is that your career is never going to go as far as God wants it to as long as you're married to me. It just can't."

"That's crazy, Sarah."

"See? You agree that I'm crazy."

"It's just a figure of speech. I didn't mean it like that. No matter what you say, I'm not divorcing you. We're in this together for the rest of our lives."

"I agree with you."

"Then what are you talking about?" The alarm bell rings a little louder.

"It's not important, just the babblings of a crazy woman. Just always remember this, Michael: I love you more than anything in this world."

A chill sneaks down Michael's back. "And I love you, too, Sarah—always. But you're kind of scaring me the way you're talking."

"There's nothing to be scared of. I'm going to take care of everything."

CHAPTER FORTY

For the first time in memory, Hope awakens without being prodded by her alarm. She smiles and rolls over.

Is this what 'happy' feels like?

For so many years, she's carried the curse of depression that she can't remember feeling any other way, which is why what she now feels is so foreign to her. Sure, it feels wonderful, but can she trust it? Is it safe to embrace it? Or will it disappear if she touches it, like a child trying to catch bubbles?

The reason for the change? Michael Trent. She has another meeting scheduled with him after work tonight, her third meeting in two weeks. Never has she talked with someone with so much knowledge and understanding of God and the Bible. The way he describes it makes God feel so much more real to her. She could listen to him for hours and has started attending his church regularly. Even though she can feel people talking about her, she's able to ignore it by focusing solely on Michael.

I'm there for him, not for them.

She's even begun to enjoy the music at church, which at first seemed jarring and out of place because it was so different from what she listened to at the Catholic church of her childhood. That a woman directs all the music is another impressive point.

No doubt her mother would roll over in her grave if she could see and hear the kind of worship Hope's attending. "But going somewhere is better than going nowhere," is what she would tell her mother.

Hope wonders what Lisa would think of it. Quick as a wink, regret climbs onto Hope's chest and presses down. It's a physical pain and makes Hope wince. With great effort, she flings off the bedcovers and jumps out of bed, hoping to leave regret in the tangled sheets.

She walks to the kitchen to fix a cup of coffee. What she sees there startles her so badly, she screams.

Luther is sitting at the table, looking at the puzzle pieces of the letter from Lisa's school locker. Her scream jolts him to his feet, and he knocks his knee against the tabletop.

"Ow!" Grabbing his knee, he says, "You scared the life out of me!"

"Well, you scared me to death! How long have you been here? Why didn't you come wake me and tell me you were home?"

"I rolled in about an hour ago and decided you might need your sleep more than needing to know I was home." He stops and cocks his head as he looks at her. "What's happened to you? You look different."

"I just got out of bed. Give me a break."

"No, it's not that. I've seen you when you first get up. There's something different, though, something about your eyes."

Hope feels like she did when Carol Ann and Whitney gave her the third degree. "You just haven't seen me in a few weeks. I'm still the same me."

He gives her a sideways smile, walks to her, and leans in to give her a kiss. "I know I sure have missed you."

The last thing she wants to do is kiss Luther. She turns her cheek toward him. "You better not. I think I may be coming down with something."

He looks at her like a ten-year-old who got socks for Christmas. "But I was looking forward to..."

"Yeah, well, maybe later," she attempts to soften the disappointment.

He sweeps his hand toward the table. "What's all this?"

She hesitates before walking toward it, fearing it might suck the happiness from her and replace it with the embalming fluid of despair. She takes a couple of steps toward it. "It's a letter to Lisa that Justin and I found when we went through the things in her school locker." She looks at the puzzle and is surprised to see many more pieces fitted together. Caution takes a back seat to curiosity, and she steps closer.

"I wasn't sure what it was," Luther says, "but

I found several pieces that fit together. Is that okay?"

Barely conscious of what he's saying, she says, "Yeah, sure." Her eyes scan what she can read.

"Sounds to me like it was some kind of a love letter from a boyfriend, or something like that. It appears his name is..."

Hope's eyes alight upon the name just as he pronounces it. "Mark."

As if in a trance, she slides back the chair, sits down at the table, and begins sliding pieces into place Luther hadn't yet done.

He pulls up a chair next to hers and starts to help, but she stays his hand and says, "No, let me finish it."

Silently, the words fall into place, speaking the aching words of teenage love:

Dear Lisa, this is the hardest thing I believe I have ever done. It's so hard I don't have the courage to do it to your face. I've told you many times that I love you and I meant it every time. That's what I don't want you to ever forget. You're the coolest person I've ever known. You're the only person who really gets me and I can just be myself around you, not the super cool athlete everyone expects me to be.

I've been lost in my head ever since you told me you were pregnant. You know it freaked me out. It wasn't something I ever thought about that happening. It's made everything seem impossible. If my parents find out, they will disown me, at least my dad will. You and your mom are different from the people around here. They won't understand why I was seeing somebody like you when I can have my choice of any girl in school.

You told me you want to keep the baby. I'm sorry, but I can't deal with something like that. I have big plans for myself, Lisa. I want to go to college and make something of myself. No school is going to give me a scholarship if they learn about us. It'll ruin my reputation.

So, here's the hard thing. We can't be together anymore.

I will never forget you, and I will always love you.
Mark

Like a passenger on a hot-air balloon ride who's leaned too far over the rail and fallen out, Hope plummets through the air toward the quicksand of depression she only recently escaped.

Unexpectedly, Luther throws her a rescue rope. He slams his fist on the table. "If that's not the most selfish bunch of B.S. I've ever heard. Wait till I get hold of that pissant. All he was worried about was himself, not Lisa."

Hope tries to kindle a flame of anger in herself that could give her the strength to stop her fall, but the weight of sadness is like a wet blanket and snuffs it out. She feels as if her heart has quit beating, and everything around her grows dark.

When Hope comes to, she opens her eyes and sees Luther's face looking down at hers. His arms embrace her as he holds her in his lap while sitting in one of the recliners.

"Hey," he says softly, "glad to see you back."

Lying limply in his arms, she asks, "What happened?"

"It was that letter from that Mark boy. You fainted and nearly hit the floor, but I caught you just in time. How do you feel?"

"How could I have been so blind, Luther? How could I have not known what was going on with my daughter? What kind of mother have I been?" Just when she thought her heart had begun healing, she feels it tearing in two again.

"You've got to quit beating yourself up about it, Hope. The only thing a parent knows about their teenager is what that teenager wants them to know. It's just the way it is. Every parent is in the same boat as you, it's just they don't know it." He folds her into his chest and squeezes gently. "It's going to be okay," he whispers.

Despite her recent ambivalent feelings about Luther, Hope enjoys the feeling of being held and comforted by him, and she kisses the bottom of his neck, the small indentation just above the collar of his T-shirt.

"Thank you for being good to me, and trying to be helpful. I just don't know if I'll ever be completely whole again."

She suddenly remembers her appointment with Michael and is disappointed it doesn't lift her mood.

If I can't get excited about that, there's no hope for me.

She toys with calling and cancelling the

appointment but decides to take a nap in Luther's arms and see how she feels upon waking.

CHAPTER FORTY-ONE

LLOYD BIDDLE STARES INTO THE TV camera, poised and resolute.

Carol Ann, watching from her home, holds her breath.

Biddle nods at someone offscreen, then begins. "My name is Lloyd Biddle. For the past thirty years, I've devoted my life to helping mold the lives of young people across western Kentucky, assisting them in any way I can to achieve their full potential. I've done this as a basketball coach – a very successful one, I might add – and as a principal, which is my present position.

"Everyone is aware that I've been accused of one of the most heinous crimes a man can make, that is, taking advantage of young girls and engaging in sexual activities with them." He pauses and stares, unblinking. "Let me make this unequivocally clear—that accusation is a lie."

Carol Ann's hands and feet grow cold.

Biddle looks down and picks up a few pages of paper. Moving the top one to the back, he looks at the next page for a second, then looks back to the camera.

"I have never and would never be guilty of doing such a thing. My record of conduct is impeccable and unblemished. I've been involved with hundreds, perhaps thousands, of young people and have never been accused by a single one of them of treating them in any but a fair and honorable way. That is, until Carol Ann Harper brought her allegation." He turns another page. "I've been asked if I remember Carol Ann, and I've answered that I do. She was an excellent player and team member. But she went through a very emotional situation while she was a student, something she confided in me, and something I'll never share, because she trusted me to keep it confidential."

Carol Ann's jaw drops open, and her eyes bug out in disbelief. "What in the world—?!"

Biddle continues. "I think perhaps she's become confused over the years over what happened to her, and instead of pointing her finger at the real perpetrator, she's pointing at me. I feel very sorry for Carol Ann and am praying for her, because she needs help.

"What she never expected was how her single accusation would trigger a small avalanche of similar accusations by people who didn't like me when I coached them, possibly because I had to bench them or cut them from the team, and now they've found a way to get revenge, something they've been wanting to do ever since they were a kid."

He folds another page over and drinks a sip of water. "To all of you, I say I'm sorry for any pain I caused you when you were young, but I'm sure if you're honest with yourself, you'll admit I did the right thing, the thing that was fairest to the team as a whole. Please, don't let your desire for vengeance cloud your judgement. Be honest with yourself, and withdraw your complaint. There will be no hard feelings on my part if you do so. That is all I have to say."

The camera swings over to a reporter who begins a recap of what Biddle said.

Carol Ann sits in stunned silence. *I cannot believe what I just heard.* She gets up and starts pacing in her bedroom. *Or maybe I can believe it. He always knew just the right thing to say to make you doubt your own truth and trust in him.*

Her cell phone rings, and she answers. Whitney's voice comes blaring through. "Get yourself ready, girl, because we are going to hurt that man! Have you ever heard so much B.S. coming from one man's mouth? Seriously, how are you? You're not letting him rattle you, are you?"

Finally, her friend takes a breath, and Carol Ann replies, "At first, I couldn't believe what I was hearing, but then I remembered how easily he manipulated me by twisting reality to suit himself. He's good at it, which is what makes him so dangerous. The huge majority of people who've known him through the years idolize him because they were never touched by the sick side of him, and those people are going to believe him, not me." Her shoulders sag with a feeling of defeat. "So what's the point of doing this?"

"Whoa, whoa, whoa, whoa, whoa. You can't back down and let him win without a fight. He's a monster that needs to pay for what he's done and be put away to keep him from finding more victims."

"But what if the other victims drop out of the lawsuit?"

"I've got your back all the way on this. And Hope will, too. We'll stand beside you every step of the way."

"I really appreciate that, Whitney, but I don't know anymore..." Her phone buzzes with another call, and she sees it's her lawyer. "Hey Whitney, I've got to take another call. It's my lawyer."

"You go ahead, honey. Just don't forget—I'm here for you to the bitter end."

Carol Ann ends the call and answers her lawyer.

"Carol Ann," he says in an authoritative voice, "this is the sort of thing we talked about would probably happen. It's his attempt to win in the court of public opinion. But none of that will matter when we get him in the courtroom."

She listens without replying, weighing what he's saying.

When she doesn't answer, his voice softens. "Hey, are you all right?"

"To be honest, I'm feeling kind of rattled and overwhelmed. I mean, I knew he'd probably pull this kind of stunt, but to see it and hear it...I don't know if I'm strong enough..."

"I understand, but that was his biggest blow, his best shot. He's got nothing left in his arsenal, whereas we've got your detailed story, and the detailed stories of the other women who are coming forward. All of your stories combined will be nothing short of a landslide when we present the case to a jury. They'll have no other choice but to convict his ass."

His words buoy her a bit. "But what if the others start dropping out after seeing his rebuttal?"

"That's very unlikely to happen. What it should do is fuel everyone's fire a little more."

"But what if?"

"Let's just cross that bridge when and if it materializes."

CHAPTER FORTY-TWO

MICHAEL NERVOUSLY CHECKS THE TIME, then looks out the church doors at the parking lot. Hope was supposed to meet him at 7:00, and it's fifteen after.

She's never been late, I hope she hasn't forgotten.

As for him, he nearly forgot. Ever since Brittany's visit and Sarah's solemn pronouncement, he's been on high alert for anything unusual and practically hovered over Sarah. He's been taking more breaks at the office, going home to check on her, texting her during the day, even fixing supper a few nights. He's been so attentive, Sarah's become even more suspicious—if that's possible.

"What's gotten into you?" she asked the other night. "You've never been like this before. Is there something going on you need to tell me about?"

"I'm just trying to be a better husband," he told her. "I know I've failed you miserably, and I want to make up for it."

With a blank expression, she nodded her head. "Whatever you say."

Nothing he did seemed to bring her out of the place of numbness she seemed to be in. There weren't the tears he was used to seeing when she was depressed. It's as if she has no feelings at all.

Maybe she's made up her mind to kill herself. If she has, I'm okay with it, God forgive me. It'll release her from her misery. I just don't want Brittany to do something to harm her. It needs to be Sarah's choice.

There are moments when he fantasizes what life would be like as a single man. And those fantasies always involve women and the freedom of movement he would have to be with them.

However, there's one woman presently he can't quit obsessing about, and that's Hope Rodriguez. Something about her makes him feel completely at ease. The give and take and flow of their conversations is unlike anything he's ever experienced. He trusts her, which he knows makes him sound crazy, but it's still true. He's even gone so far as to talk to her about his unhappiness with Sarah.

The time I have with Hope keeps me from going completely mad.

He's about to check the time again when Hope pulls into the parking lot. He breathes a sigh of relief.

Smiling, he holds the door open for her but immediately is set on edge. Something's wrong. He doesn't yet know what, but something's definitely wrong.

Has Sarah found out about her and said something to her? Has someone at church upset her? Have I made her uncomfortable by sharing too much about myself?

Does she doubt my motives?

All these questions and more swirl in his mind as he follows her into his office and shuts the door. Hope takes her usual place on the loveseat and pulls her feet up underneath her. She stares at the floor and tugs absently on the section of hair that has the blue dye in it.

Michael senses a heaviness in her. He takes a seat in one of the wingback chairs and waits. He's learned Hope can't be prodded into talking. Mostly, she sits quietly at first, then begins slowly.

Minutes pass.

"Why?" Hope finally says. "That's what you're going to help me figure out tonight. Why did Lisa take her life? Why did God let it happen?" She looks at him with those deep eyes of hers. "Answer those questions for me, and I can keep on living. If not, what's the point of being here anymore?"

Michael is taken aback. Other than the first time they met when she related her tragic life story, she's been increasingly happy each time they've met. "What's happened, Hope? Because I know something has."

"Nothing new has happened. It's just, I've come to the realization I've been kidding myself, pretending I can be happy and enjoy living. Because when I have to stare in the face of losing Lisa, it crushes me. I can't make any sense of it." She wraps her arms around her legs and pulls her knees to her chest. "You've got to help me."

The heaviness in the room settles on Michael's shoulders, making his chest feel tight. Hope's second question is the same question he's struggled with forever—Why does God let bad things happen to good people? She expects him to answer it for her when he can't answer it for himself.

God, if I've ever needed wisdom, it's now.

"Tell me this, why do you think Lisa killed herself?"

Tiny tears cling to Hope's eyelashes and splash onto her cheeks as she blinks. "I keep chasing that around. She was definitely bullied and never felt like she fit in here. She was pregnant, and her boyfriend dumped her when he learned about it. And she suffered from depression." Hope begins to hyperventilate. Between gasps, she says, "And she had a mother who never showed her she loved her, like she should have. Which reason is it?"

Michael reaches his hands toward her. "Oh, Hope…"

She surprises him when she unfolds herself and comes, sits on the arm of the chair, and lays her head against his shoulder. The warmth of her body against his gives him a chill.

Don't let yourself go down that path, not now, not with her hurting so badly.

Turning his body toward her, he puts his hands on her shoulders and squares her so they face each other. "Maybe it's all those things, Hope, not just one thing. My father used to tell me people didn't seek counseling from him because of one thing, rather it was multiple things, even though they may have thought it was one thing.

So, perhaps you have the answer, or answers, to why Lisa did what she did."

"So, you agree I was an awful mother?"

"I can't say that, because I didn't know you two. But there's no doubt you were a flawed mother, because you are a human, and we're all flawed." He pauses for a second as she searches his face. Emotions fill his chest, and he fights back tears as he says, "You might be looking at the most flawed person on the face of the Earth."

She frowns and puts her palm on the side of his face. "That can't be true. You're the purest person I've ever met. The only time I feel complete is when I'm talking to you."

Her gesture pushes him over the edge, and tears roll down his cheeks.

Tipping their heads toward each other, they rest the crowns of their heads against each other and weep together.

A corner of Michael's mind clings desperately to logic and rational thinking. He hears it faintly calling him to pull back quickly, or disaster will surely follow. With great effort, he sits back up and wipes his tears with the backs of his hands.

Hope mirrors his movements.

They sit and stare for a few moments, their minds jumbled up with confusing thoughts and feelings.

When he's finally able to take a deep breath, Michael says, "Here's the thing—finding the answer to why Lisa took her life won't change the fact that she's no longer here and will never come back. I know that's painful to hear, but it's nothing you didn't already know. 'Why' keeps you looking backward, and anyone who's looking backward will have difficulty walking forward."

Hope sits with this a few seconds before saying, "That makes sense. Okay, but can you answer my question about God?"

"To try and explain God...I mean, who am I that I should be able to understand the un-understandable? One of Job's friends in the Old Testament said God's ways are beyond understanding. There are untold numbers of books written on the subject, with each author giving his opinion on what the answer is. But who knows which, if any, of them is right?"

Hope's look of disappointment in his answer is obvious.

He looks down at his hands. "I know you want a better answer than that. People expect their pastor to have all the answers. Maybe other pastors do, but I clearly don't. However, let me share this thought, and it comes from Job's answer to his wife when she's upset about all that's happened to him. He basically says to her that we eagerly embrace all the good God gives us in our lives, supplying us with our every need, so why shouldn't we be willing to embrace the bad?"

"Why should we embrace it?"

"Because there must be a purpose to it, a purpose we may or may not ever understand."

Hope rests back against the loveseat. "I don't know...I'll have to spend some time thinking about that."

Feeling exhausted, Michael rests his head on the back of the chair, stretches his legs on the floor, and looks up at the ceiling. He sighs, "I understand. It's a lot to wrap your head around."

"This was a pretty heavy conversation, wasn't it?"

"The heaviest," he agrees.

Several seconds pass before she says, "But the funny thing is, even though I may not have gotten the answers I was looking for, I still feel better after talking with you about it." She reaches down and takes his hand in hers. "Thank you for being you."

In that split second, all the evil in Michael comes rushing forward, shoving to the side any rational thought. He envisions himself turning to her, embracing her, and making love to her on the loveseat.

CHAPTER FORTY-THREE

"HOW COULD YOU BE SO stupid?!" Jed yells as he charges toward Mark.

Liz quickly steps in front of their son. Her makeup has tear tracks traced through it. "That's not helpful. He knows he made a mistake and doesn't need you to point it out to him."

Jed pulls up short, his eyes bulging. "So, you're going to take up for him?"

"Not for what he did, no. But he was brave enough to come to me and tell me the truth about Lisa and the baby. He deserves respect for that."

Jed looks over her shoulder at Mark. "Quit hiding behind your mother's skirts. Be a man, and face me."

Hesitantly, Mark steps out from behind Liz, positions himself beside her, and focuses on the floor.

"Do you realize what you've done?" Jed yells. "If this story gets out, if any colleges hear about it, you're completely screwed. All our work and plans will go up in smoke. You realize that? Everything is lost. I can't believe you were so stupid."

Mark mumbles a reply.

"Speak up if you have something to say," Jed scolds him. "And look at me when you speak."

Mark raises his head and says, "You mean all *your* plans will go up in smoke."

Jed looks confused. "What does that mean?"

"It's always been about what you wanted me to do, not what I wanted to do."

Jed backs up a half-step. "That's not true. Everything I've ever done has been for you."

"That's a lie," Liz says firmly as she turns to face him.

Her words couldn't have stunned him any more if they'd been a slap in the face. His crimson complexion fades to pale. He looks uncertainly at Mark, then at Liz.

"This is not the time or place for that, I don't think," he says, and he looks back at Mark.

"He knows," Liz says calmly.

"I've always known," Mark adds.

The crimson color returns, starting at Jed's neck and pushing through his face, like an old-fashioned thermometer. He turns on Liz.

"Why did you tell him?!"

"She didn't," Mark explains. "I just figured it out. Parents think kids are so dumb and don't pay attention to what's going on in the house. But it's the parents who are dumb. You create some sort of alternate reality in your head and convince yourself it's real and everyone sees it the same way. So, let me give you a dose of my reality, the reality you won't want to see. I loved

Lisa Rodriguez. She was special to me, and she made me feel special. I saw things in her no one else took the time to see—" His emotions choke off his voice.

Liz reaches over and takes ahold of his hand.

"I'm not ashamed of loving Lisa. I hate that she got pregnant, because that for sure wasn't planned. But you know what I hate the most?" Anger begins to scorch the edge of his words, and he moves forward until he's in Jed's face. "It's that I let my fear of letting you down and you being disappointed in me make me turn my back on her and desert her." He begins to yell. "I was the only person she had in this world, and I let her down because of you!" He punches his father's chest with his index finger. "And that's why she killed herself. She killed herself because of me! Aren't you proud of me now?!" Spinning around, he punches his fist through the sheetrock of his parents' bedroom wall.

Liz cries out, and Jed grabs his arm and pulls it back. "Don't! You're going to injure yourself."

Mark shoves him away. "I hope it broke every bone in my hand!"

Jed loses his balance, and Liz lets go of Mark to try and catch him. But he stumbles onto the floor.

Liz kneels beside him. "The world won't fit into your frame, Jed. It never has and never will." She helps him to his feet.

Running his fingers through his hair, he says, "Okay, I'm sorry I reacted the way I did, and I'm sorry I've pushed you so hard. But there's been no real harm done yet. We just have to keep this quiet. The three of us, it's our secret. No one will ever know, and it won't have any impact on your chances for college." He pauses, then adds, "If college is something you want to do."

Liz says, "I don't know what you mean, 'keep it quiet.'"

"I mean, no one knows about the baby except you and me and Mark, right? So, as long as we don't tell—"

Liz looks at Mark but speaks to Jed. "Mark wants to go talk to Lisa's mother and tell her how sorry he is. And I'm on board with his decision."

"No, no, no, guys," Jed says quickly. "We can't let this get out. It's been hard enough to keep the suicide quiet, and then this silly lawsuit against Biddle has come up. If the high school's most popular student and star ballplayer turns out to have gotten a girl pregnant, our town's going to have more black eyes than a prize fighter."

"It is *not* a silly lawsuit!" The words come out of Liz's mouth like a flamethrower. "I hope it sets this town on fire and burns it to the ground!"

"Liz, you can't mean that. Not after all the years we've spent together, trying to make this a better place to live."

"The problem is, what you think makes a place better and what I think are very different. With you, it's always about the money. With me, it's being a decent person, trying to live my life the way Christ would have me to." She hesitates and looks at Mark. Turning back to Jed, she says, "I might as well say it. You're part of what's wrong with our town, Jed. I'm sorry to say that, because I love you, love you deeply. But I don't know that I can live with you anymore."

This time, her words hit him in the chest with the force of a sledgehammer. He looks at Mark with the eyes of man sentenced to die.

Tears course down Mark's face. "Dad, we love you, but you've got to change."

CHAPTER FORTY-FOUR

LATE THAT AFTERNOON, HOPE HEARS a knock on her front door. She starts to tell Luther to answer it, until she remembers he's run to town for some groceries.

She pads barefoot to the door and opens it. A woman and man, *no, he's a teenager*, stand there. Something about the woman looks familiar, but Hope can't place her. It certainly isn't anyone she knows, because she doesn't know anyone who looks as well-put-together as this woman.

The woman gives her a curious look—a similar look of recognition maybe? "Hi, my name is Liz Rochelle, and this is my son, Mark."

Whatever the woman says after "Mark," Hope doesn't hear because all the blood rushes to her head, and her heartbeat *thrumms* in her ears. She knows for certain this is *the* Mark. But she's uncertain why he and his mother—*how do I know her?*—are at her door.

The woman's mouth keeps moving, and slowly Hope's hearing returns. "You are Hope Rodriguez, aren't you? I feel like I've either met or seen you before."

Mark shuffles his feet and keeps his head down. "Yeah, I'm Hope."

"May we come in?" Liz asks.

Hope grips the doorknob and stiffens her back. "Why should I?"

Glancing at Mark, Liz says, "There's something we want to talk to you about, something you should know. We should have called first, and I apologize for that. It's just that this has just come up and..." Her voice trails off.

To Hope, the woman's eyes say more than her words. Her eyes speak of hurt, anguish, and fatigue. "Okay, come on in." She steps back out of the way and lets them in.

Liz looks around the meagerly furnished living room, with its two recliners.

"It's not much," Hope says, "but it suits me. You two sit in the recliners. I'll sit on the floor." When Liz walks away from her, it dawns on her where she's seen her. "You're the music director at church, aren't you?"

A look of surprise softens the worry lines in Liz's face. "That's where I've seen you, isn't it? We've never met, but I've seen you in the audience."

Hope nods. "Michael preached Hope's funeral. Not that you'd know, because you weren't there. Nobody was."

Mark raises his head to look at her. His cheeks are red, and his eyes look tired. When their eyes meet, Hope feels something shift in her heart.

He looks to Liz, then back at Hope. "I need to tell you who I am."

"I know who you are. I found the letter."

He bends over, elbows on knees, and looks at the floor. "Oh, yeah, I forgot about that."

Hope waits on him to say what's on his mind.

Liz gently rubs his back and quietly says, "You can do this."

It pains Hope to think about the countless number of times she should have done something like that to Lisa, and that she'll never have the chance again.

Even though he's as big as a grown man, Mark looks like a child to Hope, and she can't help feeling sorry for him.

When he finally looks at her, his hands are trembling. "I will never forgive myself for what I did to Lisa. It's all my fault that she...did what she did. My fault, and nobody else's. I loved her, but I freaked out and got scared. What I did was selfish." He rubs his eyes with his fists. "All I know to say is, I'm sorry, sorrier than you'll ever know." Taking a deep breath, he concludes, "I just had to come say that to you."

Quiet rules the room for several moments.

Liz speaks first. "We, Mark and I both, want to do anything and everything we can to help you. I don't know what that might look like, and we can figure that out as we go forward. I just want you to know this doesn't end here, not by a long shot."

Hope feels a window open in her heart and breeze blowing through, bringing her something she's never felt. "You all didn't have to come here and do this. I want you to know it really means something to me. Mark, I can see why Lisa loved you. But you've got something wrong, and you need to get it fixed now, or you'll be tormented the rest of your life. First thing is, I forgive you."

"Don't say that," Mark cries. "Please don't say that. I don't deserve your forgiveness."

"You don't know me, Mark, but I bet I can say for certain you've never met anyone who's made as many mistakes in their life as I have. Not little mistakes—I'm talking major, life-changing mistakes. Here's the thing, though, that I've learned recently from meeting and talking with Michael. I guess you all call him pastor or something, but I just call him Michael. Here's what he told me: 'God doesn't forgive us because we deserve it. He forgives us because we need it.'"

Mark's tears dry as he listens.

"I'm forgiving you, Mark, because God has forgiven me."

Although her words are meant for Mark, they also slice open Liz's heart, and she begins to sob. Getting out of the recliner, she crawls on her knees to Hope and embraces her. "I've never met anyone like you," she says through her tears. "You've touched me to my core. I love you."

Hope is unsure of what to do with such a sudden expression of emotion and love from someone she doesn't know. A warm sensation fills her, and she returns Liz's embrace. Without expecting it or sensing it coming, her cheeks are wet.

Liz releases one of her arms from Hope and

extends her hand toward Mark, who joins them on the floor. It's a trio of love and grace and mercy.

Minutes pass before, one-by-one, their tears dry, and they sit back and look at each other.

Hope looks at Mark. "There's one more thing I need you to know: Lisa didn't commit suicide because of one thing; it wasn't just because of you. It's not that simple. She did what she did because of me, because of you, because of the girls at school who were bullying her, because of this town that refused to accept her because of how she looked, because of her depression, because she decided to quit trying. So, you see? There's plenty of blame to go around. But at the end of the day, what does that change? She's still gone, and never coming back."

"But it has changed me," he replies. "And I'm going to make things change at school, make other kids see how small and judgmental they've been, because this can never happen again."

Liz smiles at him. "And I'm going to try to change our community, starting at our church. We're judgmental and prejudiced sometimes without even knowing it, and I'm including myself in that. 'For God so loved the *world*,' not just certain people."

"And if you all do that," Hope says, "then Lisa's suicide will mean something. Michael says sometimes a bad thing has to happen to make a good thing."

CHAPTER FORTY-FIVE

ON A BRIGHT, SUNNY SATURDAY in early April, the kind of day that promises winter's grip has loosened for good, Hope winds her way through the cemetery and stops in front of the section where Lisa's grave lies. For the first time since she started making these trips, her heart doesn't feel like a stone, nor does she dread seeing the grave.

She looks approvingly at the headstone Liz paid for. It's her first time seeing the finished product, and she runs her hand over the slick, polished granite, then traces her finger through the deeply carved letters of Lisa's name and years of her life. Overhead, a mourning dove coos its plaintive song.

Kneeling down at the foot of the grave, Hope says, "It's me again, but you know that, don't you? I hope you don't mind me coming here and bothering you. It just helps to talk to you.

"I want you to know I'm not mad at you anymore for killing yourself. Have I mentioned that before? That I was mad at you? Well, I was—really mad. But I figured out that was about me being mad at myself.

"I think I understand why you did it, and I kinda don't blame you. Life's not easy, no matter how old you are.

"I've got big things to tell you. First of all, I met Mark. Yeah, that Mark. He's really something else, like you need me to tell you that. He came to apologize to me for breaking up with you. His mom came, too. They paid for this nice headstone.

"I don't know how it works where you are, but I don't want you to be worrying about me, not anymore. I had it rough for a while, but I'm lots better now. I'm going to be okay.

She turns the inside of her forearm toward the grave. "See what I had done? Your friend Greg tattooed it for me. It's a semicolon, like the punctuation thing. I thought when you died that my life was over, too, as in a period at the end of a sentence, with nothing to follow. A period tells you when a thought is finished. But a semicolon is like a long pause, longer than a comma, and it says what follows is connected to what was before. That's what this period of time has been for me, a semicolon. Now, though, I'm going forward and taking my memory of you with me. We'll always be connected." She pauses briefly.

"I bet you're surprised to hear all this, aren't you? Doesn't sound possible, does it? And for sure, it sounds different for me. So, you want to know how it happened? That's the biggest news I've been wanting to tell you. I met a man. I know, I know, you're thinking, 'My God, Mom, not another one.' But this is completely different, completely. He is the most incredible, humble, Godly, pure man I've ever met. He makes me feel whole and complete." A bright smile fills her face. "I don't know what's going to happen between us, but I have a feeling it's going to be something very special."

~ THE END ~

AUTHOR'S NOTES:

[*Hope's Way* deals with the difficult subject of suicide. If you, or someone you know, are thinking about suicide, please, before you do anything else, stop right now and call the National Suicide Prevention Hotline at 1-800-273-8255. Suicide is a permanent answer to a temporary problem.]

[If you are someone who struggles with sex addiction, I urge you to go online to the website of Sex Addicts Anonymous (SAA). You don't have to struggle alone. There are others who can help you.]

Thank you so much for reading *Hope's Way*. There are so many of you who are loyal fans of all my books, and I can't thank you enough for spreading the word about them to others. If you're new to my books, you'll want to start reading the others. My books have been described as "Books With Heart," stories that touch readers' hearts and move them.

One of the best things you can do to help an author is post a review of their book on Amazon and Goodreads. So, please take a moment to do that for me.

Hope's Way wasn't an easy story to write.

Portraying characters that have terrible flaws in such a way that readers still have empathy for them is quite a challenge. It's easy to demonize people like Hope and Michael, who make terribly selfish choices that hurt both themselves and those around them. But they're still human beings worthy of compassion and understanding. We all act the way we do for a reason. Not that the reason is an excuse for bad behavior, but the reason can at least explain things and offer a starting place for change.

At first, *Hope's Way* was going to be a solitary book, but the further I got into the story, I realized I couldn't resolve all the issues raised without expanding the storyline. That's why there are three books in the series, rather than one 200,000-word book. :-)

Be sure and read the next book in the series, *Hope Lost*, as Hope Rodriguez's story continues. Hope's life becomes more complicated, and there are dramatic developments in Michael's life. What will happen with their relationship? Also, you'll learn what happens with Carol Ann's lawsuit against Lloyd Biddle.

As a special treat for you, here's the first chapter from

Hope Lost:

CHAPTER ONE

TENSION SQUEEZES THE MUSCLES IN Michael's neck and shoulders as he makes his way home. It's Friday afternoon, and he still doesn't know what he's going to preach about this Sunday, which means he'll be back in the office tomorrow, continuing to pray God will give him a sign.

As if that's not enough weighing on him, Sarah hasn't responded to any of his texts this afternoon. It wouldn't be the first time she hasn't responded to him. It's become a passive-aggressive game she plays, pretending she didn't get a text just so it'll put him on edge. Ever since her veiled threat to hurt herself, he's continued to try and keep a watchful eye on her, even though there have been no outward signs she's about to do something.

Pulling into the driveway, he shuts off the engine and gets out of the car.

A light breeze, warmed by the lengthening days of late April, carries with it the scent of wisteria blooming in the top of the maple tree in their front yard. The smell takes him to childhood and images of his grandmother, who used to wear a perfume that smelled of wisteria. He smiles at the memory.

Opening the back door of the house and stepping into the kitchen, it doesn't surprise him that there are no aromas of supper cooking. He's essentially taken over that chore since Sarah has gotten into this mood of hers in which she does hardly anything around the house except watch the Discovery ID channel. He makes his way to the den, where the image of Detective Joe Kenda fills the TV screen as he relates the details of the murder case this particular episode will dramatize.

Michael tried joking with Sarah about her obsession with these kinds of shows: "Should I be sleeping with one eye open? Are you planning to do me in?"

Sarah reacted to the questions with a stony expression, which did nothing to settle Michael's unease.

He continues toward the bedroom, assuming she's taking a nap—another daily ritual for her.

The bedroom door is almost shut but not latched. Not wanting to wake her, he slowly pushes open the door.

As he suspected, she's lying on her back in the middle of their bed in the dim room, but she's on top of the covers, rather than under them, and there are no wrinkles that indicate she's tossed and turned. Another oddity is, she's dressed like she's going to church, even wearing a pair of dress shoes.

He considers backing out of the room and going to start supper so she can finish her nap, but something draws him closer to the bed. Each step he takes feels heavier than the first, as if he's wearing shoes with lead soles.

He frowns and whispers, "Sarah?"

It's not until he stands beside the bed that he realizes her eyes are open. "Sarah?" he says clearly. When there's no reply or movement from her, he moans, "Oh, Sarah."

He crawls onto the bed beside her and lays his hand on her chest, hoping against hope he'll feel her heart beating—but there's nothing. He puts two fingers on the side of her neck, like he learned in a life-saving CPR class. It confirms what he already knows.

"Oh, Sarah, Sarah," he says to her, "why did you have to do this? We could have worked things out. I'm sorry I—"

He stops in mid-sentence as he spies something lying on the bed on the other side of her. It's a piece of paper.

He switches on her bedside lamp and, reaching across her, picks up the paper. It's folded in half. As he unfolds it, several odd-looking pills fall onto the bed. He picks up one. It's a small, purple rectangle that's segmented.

What in the world is this?

When he turns his attention to the message on the paper, he sees it's made up of letters cut from magazines, giving it an almost comical look. He then reads the message: YOU'RE WELCOME.

Michael stares in disbelief and shock. He

suddenly feels as if he's having an out-of-body experience and looking down at himself and Sarah. It's a quiet, unfeeling place. He floats there, waiting to see what the man will do. Then, just as quickly, he's thrown back into reality, and every emotion imaginable rushes in from every region of his body with the force of a runaway train.

He tries to make his mind work but is unable to string together any coherent thoughts. He jumps off the bed, leaving the paper to find its own resting place, and begins pacing back and forth.

Think, think, think, Michael! What are you going to do?

The pills? He can't figure out where the pills came from, assuming that's what killed her, and he's certain it is. He's never seen any pills like them, nor has he seen any pill bottles from a pharmacy recently.

He stops pacing and looks at Sarah. When he does, a new thought hits him so strongly, he staggers backward.

Brittany! Did Brittany do this and make it look like Sarah did it to herself?

He grabs his chest as a knifing pain shoots through him. Sweat covers his face, and he can't catch his breath. He drops to his knees, falls on his side, and curls into a fetal position. The light in the room dims.

Please, Lord, please go ahead and take me, too. Let this be the end of my miserable life. My only hope is that Your grace will cover me.

He closes his eyes and waits for death to come. Instead, the pain in his chest slowly subsides, and his breathing returns to normal. At first, Michael interprets it as he's died, which brings tremendous relief to him. But when he opens his eyes and sees he's still in the bedroom, disappointment chases away relief. But disappointment barely makes an appearance before an avalanche of emotions tumbles in: regret, sadness, guilt, confusion, suspicion, and fear.

He gets to his feet and spots the letter lying on the floor. Picking it up, he looks again at the message.

If the police see this and word gets out about it, everyone's going to think I'm somehow to blame, that I drove her to suicide. It'll be the end of my ministry here. Or if they find Jenny's fingerprints, that'll open up an even messier situation.

Taking the letter with him, he goes to the kitchen, where he tears the letter into pieces and drops them in the trash can.

DISCUSSION QUESTIONS FOR BOOKCLUBS

1. Have you ever known anyone who committed suicide?
How did it make you feel?
How did it affect the family?
Were any of those effects long-lasting?

2. Were you bullied in school?
How did you deal with it?
Is bullying different nowadays than it was when you were growing up?
What would you say to someone who is being bullied?

3. Which character in *Hope's Way* did you have the most empathy for? Why?

4. Did your opinion of any of the characters change as you went further in the book?

5. Choose three of the characters, and describe each of them with three adjectives.

6. Had you ever heard of Conjugal Paranoia before reading *Hope's Way*?

7. What did you enjoy most about *Hope's Way*?

8. What did you least enjoy about the book?

9. Of all the characters in the book, which one did you most identify with?

10. What do you think will happen in *Hope Lost*?

About the Author

You can follow David Johnson on Facebook
www.facebook.com/DavidJohnsonbookpage

He would also like to hear from you with any questions or comments. You may contact him at *davidjohnsonbooks@gmail.com*

Made in the USA
Middletown, DE
08 January 2022

58078874R00210